Thin Ice

(A Miranda's Rights Mystery)

Book V

Linsey Lanier

Edited by
Donna Rich

Editing for You

Gilly Wright
www.gillywright.com

Felicity Books

ISBN: 1941191169
ISBN-13: 978-1-941191-16-3

THIN ICE

The fifth book in the popular Miranda's Rights Mystery series.

A woman's right to respect.
A woman's right to be strong.
A woman's right to her child.

One determined woman.
One irresistible man.
One talented girl.
And one psychotic killer.

Can they stop him before he kills again?

Thirteen years ago, Miranda Steele's abusive husband stole her baby and gave it up for adoption. Now she's about to find out exactly what happened to her daughter.

THE MIRANDA'S RIGHTS MYSTERY SERIES

Someone Else's Daughter
Delicious Torment
Forever Mine
Fire Dancer
Thin Ice

THE MIRANDA AND PARKER MYSTERY SERIES

All Eyes on Me
Heart Wounds
Clowns and Cowboys
The Watcher
Zero Dark Chocolate
Trial by Fire
Smoke Screen
The Boy
Snakebit
Mind Bender
Roses from My Killer
The Stolen Girl
Vanishing Act
Predator
Retribution
(more to come)

OTHER BOOKS BY LINSEY LANIER

Chicago Cop (A cop family thriller)
Steal My Heart

THE PRASALA ROMANCES

The Crown Prince's Heart
The King's Love Song
The Count's Baby

For more information visit www.linseylanier.com

CHAPTER ONE

He stumbled along the dreary path in the dark, groping his way. His limbs ached. His flesh felt as if it would fall from his bones. The air reeked of something putrid. The decay of his own body.

He had been here so long. So very long in this murky hell.

He stopped. *What was that?* Something behind him. A voice? He spun around and peered into the thick, muddy air.

He couldn't see anything.

Who are you? He didn't dare ask aloud.

There was nothing.

He turned around and began to plod forward again. But now he felt a presence behind him. And after a moment, he heard the voice. This time clearly.

I'm disappointed in you.

"Who are you?" Now he said it aloud.

You know.

And he did. "What do you want with me? I'm dead."

I'm disappointed.

He spun back around, stared into the dark emptiness again and saw nothing. Disappointed. At that wretched word, his chest nearly collapsed in on itself. He fell to his knees, raised his hands over his head to shield himself from the blows. They didn't come. They would later.

Disappointed? Why?

You know why.

His mind raced. He thought as hard as he could until stray bits of memory formed in his mind. The mission. He'd had a mission. But he'd done everything right. Everything as it should be. As instructed.

You failed me.

No, I did everything right. It was perfect.

You. Failed. Me.

And he knew that was right. "Give me another chance. I'll do better. I promise."

That's why I'm here.

Another chance? His heart began to beat. Could he really have another chance? He would do it right this time. He would not fail again.

Can you do it?

"Yes. Yes, I can do it. I will do it. Will you help me?"

There was no answer. He reached out, trying to find the voice. But there was nothing. No, he wasn't reaching out. He couldn't move his arm. Couldn't move his legs. Couldn't move at all.

Where was he?

His eyes flickered open. He saw flashes of light. Tubes. He heard beeping. People were moving him, turning his paralyzed body over. Nurses? They were—washing him? Where was he?

Then his eyes closed again and he felt nothing.

CHAPTER TWO

In the backseat of the Parker Agency's neutral-colored surveillance sedan, Miranda Steele shifted her butt uncomfortably.

They were on Freedom Parkway heading toward Scottdale, Georgia, about nine miles from the office and she was crammed in the backseat between her team members Janelle Wesson and Dave Becker.

Short, stocky, thick-browed Becker had been her buddy since the day she started on the job. Tall, thin, flame-haired Wesson was—well, until recently Wesson had pretty much been a bitch. But she'd mellowed some since Miranda beat her in a martial arts competition.

She could call Wesson a coworker. One who just now had her elbow digging into Miranda's ribs.

"You'd think we could take two cars," she muttered under her breath, nudging Wesson's elbow aside.

In the front seat her other buddy and Becker's sidekick, tall and lanky Curt Holloway, turned and gave her a cocky smirk. "You're just spoiled because you're married to the boss."

At that remark, she twisted her lips and scratched at her dark, unruly shoulder-length hair.

Yeah, she was married to the boss all right, she thought, her heart fluttering embarrassingly. She was married to Wade Russell Parker the Third. The super handsome, super sexy CEO of the super successful Parker Investigative Agency in Atlanta—where they were all employed.

She didn't quite know how that had happened, but Miranda had had to endure a lot of ribbing from her co-workers since she got back from her honeymoon. Most of it good-natured. Besides Becker and Holloway worshiped the ground Parker sauntered across.

A tease in her voice, she curled a lip at Holloway. "And you used the excuse of your long legs to sit up front next to Detective Tan."

At the wheel, Parker's chief assistant, Noreen Tan, turned off the highway onto a side street, glanced over her shoulder with a groan and arched a black brow. "Knock it off, you two. Remember you're on duty."

Tan had been as tough on them as a drill sergeant with hemorrhoids when they were trainees. Now that she was their supervisor, she'd mellowed into a drill sergeant with gas pains.

The four of them had graduated from the Agency's training program almost two months ago and had been selected for field work. They worked together since they were still learning and not billable yet, so Tan was in charge. There hadn't been any big cases for a few weeks, so Tan kept the team busy with assignments like insurance fraud surveillance and serving subpoenas.

Today was a subpoena and their current target was a slippery one.

The team had been tracking him for a week now but had only ended up traipsing all over town to a string of fake addresses. This morning they had a hot lead and were following it.

As they cruised down a shady street just off East Ponce De Leon, Miranda scanned the small frame houses. A swing set stood in one yard, a gazebo in the next, beside another house a lone woman gardened. Miranda's stomach tightened, her mood turning gloomy.

Her daughter could be growing up in any one of those homes—or none of them. For all she knew, Amy could be in Bora Bora. She had searched for her daughter for over thirteen years now and come up with zip. Parker had searched for months and come up with zip. She had no idea where Amy was or who was raising her.

But she might find out soon.

Miranda rubbed her eyes. She'd had another nightmare last night. Fourth one in the past three weeks.

She dreamed her ex was coming at her with a bloody knife, just the way he'd done the last time she saw him. In her dream, she'd scrambled up the stairs of their old house to get away from him and ended up in Amy's room.

Her baby was gone. Just like she'd been gone thirteen years ago when Leon stole her out of her crib and gave her up for adoption. But she could hear her calling out to her.

Mama, Mama.

Which was crazy. Amy was only three weeks old when Leon took her. She wasn't talking yet.

In the dream, Miranda had turned around to face Leon and he'd slashed at her with his knife. She'd kicked and punched, but she kept missing. He cut her arms, her face. Blood spurted everywhere. She woke up screaming and had bawled into Parker's shoulder for an hour until they both fell asleep again. Sheesh.

Absently she touched the real life scars on her chest that Leon had given her. Why did she keep dreaming about him? He was lying in a coma in Brandywine-Summit Memorial Hospital. Four months after she'd put him there. Maybe her shrink could tell her. She was seeing Dr. Wingate that afternoon.

"We're here," Detective Tan announced, pulling the car over to the curb.

Miranda shook herself out of her thoughts. "So is this the real deal this time?" The house looked pretty much the same as the others they'd been to.

"This is the location Holloway and Becker dug up. I've got a hunch they got it right."

Beside her, Becker blushed. "Thank you, ma'am."

"Ellsworth Digby," Wesson read from the file on her lap. "Divorced. Two young kids. A boy six and a girl four. Wife has custody. Five months behind in his child support."

Nothing they didn't already know. That was why Digby was being commanded to appear in court for a hearing. And why the Parker Agency had been hired by the wife's law firm to serve him papers.

Miranda scrutinized the russet shingled, one-story house. Cozy brown shutters at the windows. One or two bedrooms at most. Small yard. Screened-in porch on the far side. Shades covering the windows.

"At least two entrances," she said. "Cyclone fence in the front, cedar one in the back. Look over there." She gestured to a shiny red Ford F150 sitting in the driveway. "Has enough scratch for a nice new toy for himself but not enough to pay for his kids to eat. Sonofabitch."

"Nothing worse than a deadbeat dad," Holloway agreed.

"Could be a drug dealer," Becker said. "Income would be off the books."

Wesson nodded. "I had an ex who dealt drugs. He was always buying sharp rides. When I found out, I dropped him fast." Wesson seemed to have a past as rocky as Miranda's, but she never talked much about it.

"Let's check it out." Tan opened her door.

They got out of the car and made their way across the sun-parched pavement.

Business attire in the office was required at the Parker Agency, as well as for some field work. Tan was all in herringbone gray, Becker and Holloway were in their standard dress shirts and ties, Wesson had on a white and peach colored thing, and Miranda was clad in a charcoal jacket with matching slacks that went with her dark, wiry hair. If Digby was peeking out his window, he might think he was about to get a visit from a church group.

They marched through the cyclone fence, up the drive and across the yard to the front door.

"Let's split up," Tan whispered as they reached the stoop. "Holloway, you take the entrance at the porch. Becker, go round the back. Steele, take the other side. Wesson, you're with me. If Digby's in there and he runs, whoever gets to him first, jump him."

"Yes, ma'am." Grinning like a schoolboy about to score a winning goal in his first hockey game, Holloway trotted off toward the porch. Miranda shoved her hands into her pockets and tried to look casual as she strolled with Becker to the opposite side of the house.

She planted herself behind a small shed under a shady oak while Becker crouched below a window at the back corner of the home.

As she scanned the backyard, she heard the doorbell ring. Silence.

After a minute or two, she heard Tan knock. "Ellsworth Digby?"

No response.

Tan knocked with more demand. "Mr. Digby. I'd like to speak with you about your insurance coverage."

Still no response.

For a long moment there was more silence. Birds chirped happily in the branches overhead. The sun beat down on them. A dog barked in a neighboring yard. Then suddenly a back door banged and a figure shot out of the house and across the grass.

Becker ran after him. "He's back here."

Miranda took off and passed Becker in seconds.

Digby was tall and skinny as an anorexic fashion model—with tattoos. Dressed in jeans and a wife beater T-shirt, he streaked across the yard, his long, black hair streaming after him. He was fast. Miranda really had to hustle, but she caught up to him just before he reached the cedar fence.

With one big leap, she was on his back and they both tumbled to the ground. "You're not getting away from us this time."

"Who the hell are you?" Digby squirmed and struggled, dragging Miranda over the grass, skinning her knee through her slacks.

She held on. "Take it easy, Digby. We just want to talk to you for a minute."

"Get off me, bitch." He twisted again and turned his head, trying to get a look at her.

It couldn't have been the name he'd called her. She was used to that. Her knee throbbed, but she'd had a lot worse. It must have been the look in his mean black eyes, the sneer on his narrow face. The way his greasy long hair fell over his forehead.

Somehow, it reminded her of Leon.

Before she could think, Miranda drew her fist back and popped Digby hard on his bony jaw.

Blood spurted out of his lip. Jeez, she hadn't hit him that hard, had she? She should apologize. Ask him if he needed help or a band aid. Instead, she reared back again for another punch.

Someone caught her arm from behind, pulled her up and off the deadbeat. "That's enough, Steele." It was Tan. Miranda didn't know the woman was that strong.

Digby scrambled to his feet. He spun around, about to take off.

Holloway stepped in front of him, blocking his move. "Are you Ellsworth Digby?"

"Who wants to know?" he drawled.

"The *National Enquirer*," Miranda sneered and Tan gave her a glare.

Digby swiped at his cut lip with his bare, tattooed arm. "Yeah, that's me. And who the hell are you? I want to tell the cops who to arrest for assaulting me."

Unmoved, Holloway took Digby's hand and slapped the papers into his palm. "Consider yourself served."

"What the hell?"

"You're due in court on that date. Be there."

"Oh yeah? I'll be in court, all right. When I sue y'all's asses. Now get off my yard before I call the cops."

"Be happy to, sir." Holloway gave the deadbeat a cocky salute and they all turned and tromped back across the yard to the Mazda. Their job was done here, though Miranda would have liked to get another lick in.

"Steele?" Tan called behind her.

"Yeah?"

"When we get back, I need to see you in my office."

Uh oh.

Miranda sat in the corner and watched Tan pace in front of the floor-to-ceiling window that formed the back wall of her office. She looked like she wanted to scream at her the way she used to in the gym when the trainees were running laps.

Instead she stopped and put a hand to her forehead. "What on earth possessed you to hit that guy, Steele?"

Miranda raised her palms. "Because he was a jerk?"

Tan rolled her eyes. "Of course a deadbeat dad is a jerk. Don't you think I would have liked to sock him, too? But we can't afford to let our emotions get out of hand. Not as employees of the Parker Agency."

Miranda swallowed. She knew why she'd hit him. The way the guy had sneered at her reminded her of Leon. So now she was seeing her psycho ex in people she ran into, not just in her dreams? Great. She could hardly explain that to Tan.

It had been a stupid move. It would be even stupider to try to blame it on a bad dream or a—hallucination. She had no excuse. "I apologize, Detective Tan. I know I acted inappropriately."

"Inappropriately? Do you realize the weight of what you did?"

Miranda rubbed at the grass stain on her slacks. There was a small tear. Her knee throbbed. "Weight?"

"What if Digby does press charges? What if he sues the Agency? Do you know what that might do to our reputation?"

She hadn't even thought of that. Shame flushed over her. She wasn't a rookie anymore. She'd solved four murders. Eight if you counted all the victims. She should have known better.

Had she really done it because he'd reminded her of her ex? Or she was worried about Amy? Or was it just from lack of sleep?

She nodded in agreement. "Again, I apologize. It won't happen again."

"It had better not."

"It won't."

"I'm going to make sure it doesn't."

A chill went up Miranda's spine. "What do you mean?"

"I'm taking you off field work."

Miranda grabbed the arm of her chair. "What?"

"You'll be on background checks for a week. After that, we'll see if you can go back to the field."

She felt sick. Dizzy. Miranda despised paperwork. The only reason she'd stayed in this job was to work on the street. "You can't mean that."

"Do you want me to make it two weeks?"

Miranda opened her mouth, shut it again. Not long ago, she would have walked out the door and never come back. Or she might have gone to Parker and pitched a fit. But now she was a professional. One week. It would be hell, but she could handle it.

She rose, straightened her shoulders, and looked her supervisor straight in the eye. "All right, Detective Tan. I'll be ready for field work in one week." And with that, she turned and went back to her office.

A stack of folders had already been delivered to her desk when Miranda reached her cube. Just like when she was a trainee. Oh, goodie. A week of boredom and drudgery. She wanted to let out a string of cuss words.

Instead she sat down and got to work. By the time she looked up again, she saw it was after three and time for her appointment with her shrink. Man, did she ever need it.

CHAPTER THREE

"He came at me with his policeman's baton this time."

"What did you do?"

"I ran. Like I always run." She had been such a wimp once upon a time. "But I couldn't get away from him. The blows were like shockwaves. On my back, my head. Then somehow the baton turned into a knife." Miranda felt her throat go tight as she remembered the feel of the real-life knife he'd cut her with.

"Take a deep breath. What happened next?"

"What always happens. I ran upstairs to Amy's room." She stopped as she remembered her dream more clearly. "I could see Amy in her crib. She reached out to me with her little hands. I could even see the mark." She touched her throat and fingers trembled.

"The birthmark?"

She nodded. The dark mark on the side of her baby's neck. It was as big as a dime. "Then she was gone. Just like she'd been gone thirteen years ago. But I could hear her calling for me."

Mama, mama.

Ridiculous. Her baby was too young to talk the last time she'd seen her. She rubbed her hands over the fabric of her slacks and fought back the stupid, embarrassing tears. She'd cried enough over the things Leon had done to her.

"Then what?"

"Leon came up behind me. He had the knife in his hand. Like the last time I saw him." Automatically, her fingers went to the scars on her chest. "I screamed. And I woke up." Her throat constricted again as her hands moved to the arms of her chair to squeeze the soft leather.

Her spineless cries had woken Parker up last night. He'd held her close and told her everything would be all right, just as he always did. It was comforting and humiliating at the same time.

And just as before, he was the one who insisted she come here today. But she hadn't argued with him.

"Breathe."

Miranda inhaled and looked into the kind, youthful face of Dr. Valerie Wingate. Behind her square-shaped glasses the shrink's steady brown eyes exuded compassion.

"I was such a wuss in my dream." She tried for a smirk, but a tear escaped and rolled down her cheek.

Dr. Wingate reached across her tidy oak desk for a box of tissue. "You're still working through those issues."

Yeah, she guessed she was. Miranda took a tissue, wiped her face, blew her nose, and stared at the medical texts on the bookshelf in the wide, friendly office.

Leon Groth. Her ex-husband. She'd like to resolve him. Once she'd snuck into his hospital room and had almost done just that. But that douchebag wasn't worth going to prison for. At least, not at the moment.

It wasn't that she was afraid of him anymore. She was over that. She just wanted to make sure he never hurt anyone else again. And she'd like to stop having nightmares.

"Why can't I get over this, Doctor?"

Dr. Wingate studied her a moment. The young psychologist was wearing a cream-and-tan summer suit with no frills or jewelry and as usual had her blond hair pulled back in an unadorned clasp. Except for color, her taste in clothes was a lot like Miranda's. Plain and simple.

"Is there anything going on in your life that might trigger these dreams?" she asked softly.

Hell, yeah. Her daughter.

Her stomach still clenched tight, Miranda stuffed the tissue into her pocket and once more rubbed her hands over the thighs of her dress slacks. The last time she'd faced Leon, he'd killed two young girls and an older woman in Pennsylvania. He'd been stalking her for years and she hadn't even known it. But that wasn't the trigger.

"Would you like to talk about it?"

Miranda could only grunt.

Dr. Wingate folded her hands and sat back in her chair. "How was your honeymoon?"

Changing the subject to get her mind off Leon. Good move. It helped a little and Miranda let herself grin a bit. "Pretty good."

"Only pretty good?"

She lifted a shoulder. "Only as good as you'd expect with a man like Parker."

Now Dr. Wingate grinned. Besides being a top-notch private eye, wealthy and well-bred Wade Parker, with his to-die-for face that matched his to-die-for, muscular body, was the sexiest, most desirable catch in Atlanta.

"You went to Hawaii?"

"Yeah, but we ended up in Italy." Miranda didn't want to talk about what happened in Maui. Or the murder she'd solved there. Or her brother whom she couldn't save. "We drove some fast cars around the countryside and ate lots of Italian food." Her favorite was the *Saltimbocca alla Romana.* Veal with sage and prosciutto. "And spent a lot of time in the sack."

Dr. Wingate laughed. "I should hope so on your honeymoon. It sounds like you both had fun."

"Yeah, we did." If you didn't count Maui. But they'd been back three weeks now and she'd had four nightmares. She'd never had them so often before. Miranda's hands moved from her slacks back to the arms of her chair, rubbing again.

"How's the relationship?"

She made a circle on the arm of the chair, watching the diamond-and-sapphire ring on her finger sparkle and felt suddenly self-conscious. The first time she'd come to see Dr, Wingate, it had been about Parker. He'd just given her that ring. He was getting serious and she didn't see how things could work out between them with all her baggage.

And yet now, for the first time ever she was beginning to believe it just might. "It's good. Really good."

"Wonderful." The doctor was silent for a long moment. Then in a quiet, steady voice, she asked, "So, is there something else you'd like to tell me about?"

Miranda blew out a breath. Distract the patient then bring her back around to the disturbing question. Pretty good shrink trick. Dr. Wingate was almost as bad as Parker at reading her mind. She'd keep on until she wheedled it out of her. Might as well get it over with.

Before she wore a hole in the arm of the chair, Miranda rose and strolled over to the tall arched window. She stared out at the willow tree. In about a month its leaves would start to drop. And the oaks and elms would turn colors. She'd heard fall in Atlanta could be gorgeous. She wondered if she'd be sharing it with her daughter.

"You know I've been looking for Amy," she said without looking back at the doctor.

"For a number of years."

Thirteen. "We recently got some data and we've appealed the judge's decision. We've requested him to open Amy's adoption records."

"Oh? That's good news."

"It might be. He could still deny the petition." Probably would. The knot in Miranda's stomach felt like she'd swallowed a handful of gravel.

"How long have you been waiting for the decision?" The doctor's voice was somber now.

"Three weeks. Parker filed the papers the day we got home. We could hear tomorrow or two months from now."

Dr. Wingate paused a moment, then spoke as gently as a mother to a crying child. "I'd say that's the stressor provoking your dreams."

Miranda pressed her lips together, forcing herself to admit the obvious. "Guess so."

"Is there something else?"

She hugged herself, trying to settle her stomach. "I don't know. I haven't seen my daughter since she was three weeks old. I have no idea what she's like now. I don't know who's been taking care of her. I don't know—anything. She'll be a stranger." She thought of the presents she still kept in her closet. Gifts she'd bought for Amy over the years and hauled around in boxes in the trunk of her car when she'd moved. They seemed silly now.

"I'd say those feelings are very normal. But they'll all work themselves out in due time. Whatever happens with Amy, I'll help you get through it. We'll take it one step at a time."

Miranda nodded. She made it sound so easy.

"If you practice the relaxation techniques we talked about, eventually your anxiety will lessen. And the bad dreams will stop. Especially once you hear from the judge."

"Yeah." Maybe.

Almost six months ago Miranda came to Atlanta because of a letter she thought Amy had written. Back then she knew—just *knew*—Amy was in this town somewhere. She thought she was close to finding her. When things didn't turn out that way, she'd told herself she'd been wrong. And yet—she still felt as if her daughter were here in this town. As if Amy might be around any corner. As if she might run right into her and not even know it.

She thought about the nightmare she'd had on her honeymoon. She turned to face the doctor and decided to ask the question that had been gnawing at her ever since. "Dr. Wingate?"

"Yes, Miranda?"

"Do you believe somebody could be—psychic?"

Her attractive brows knit together. "Why do you ask?"

Miranda took another deep breath and spat it out. "I had a nightmare when Parker and I were in Hawaii. It was kind of prophetic."

"What do you mean?"

She drew a hand through her hair. How did she say it without sounding crazy? "I dreamed something and then found out it had really happened. Around the time I had the dream, I think."

The doctor considered that a moment. "Could be coincidence."

"Yeah." She also got those strange sensations when she investigated murder scenes that seemed to point her in the right direction. But if she mentioned that, Dr. Wingate might want to have her committed. "So what do you think?"

The doctor's skeptical look told her what she'd feared. "I can't say I put much stock in paranormal phenomenon. In my opinion, the body of evidence can be explained by natural occurrences such as trauma or hallucination."

Miranda nodded. She'd certainly had her share of trauma. The doctor was probably right. She should just forget it, drink a beer before bed or something.

"We still have a few minutes. Would you like to go over some of those relaxation techniques again?"

Slow breathing and imagining yourself in some serene happy place had never worked for her. "Thanks, but—" Feeling suddenly ridiculous, Miranda glanced at her watch. "Gosh. Look at the time," she said with a nervous laugh. "I'd better get going or I'll be stuck in traffic half the night." She left the window and crossed to the door.

As she passed, the doctor rose. "Miranda."

"What?"

"You know you can come and see me anytime. However it turns out with Amy, I'll help you get through it. Please know that." She looked so kind.

"Yes, I do. Thanks—again," Miranda stammered, her hand already on the knob. Her stomach tighter than ever, she opened the door and escaped.

Miranda couldn't wait to get home. The escalator was being serviced so she had to take the elevator. She was hurrying across the marble floor of the medical center's lobby when her cell rang. She dug it out of her pocket and glared at the display.

Iris Van Aarle? Now there was a shocker. She ought to ignore the call, but her fingers pressed the button before she could stop herself. "Steele here."

"Miranda? Did I catch you at a bad time?"

"Iris?" What did she want? Had she seen Miranda's text messages on her daughter's phone?

"Well, I—a business meeting came up at the last minute here at the house and Wendy's at the ice rink. Do you think you could be a doll and pick her up for me? I'm so sorry it's such short notice."

Business meeting?

Iris Van Aarle was the busy CEO of Iris Rose Cosmetics, a company she'd founded in her kitchen and built into a small dynasty. But some of her business meetings were excuses for a little hanky-panky on the side. Or so Miranda suspected.

A flood of emotions tearing through her, Miranda stopped so short, a dude with a briefcase ran into her from the back. As he cussed and hustled away, she stepped into an alcove, secured herself next to a potted fern and stared at her phone.

Of course, Iris was asking for a favor. The only reason the woman ever called.

But for the past month the woman had forbidden Wendy to have anything to do with Miranda. Miranda was too dangerous for a thirteen-year-old, she'd said. Now she was all sugar and sweet tea? Right. The last time she had Miranda chauffeuring her daughter, she was fooling around on her husband.

Miranda was pretty sure she was fooling around. After all, Iris had done it before and she almost couldn't blame her. Golf pro Shelby Van Aarle was always away at some tournament and was as much of an absentee husband as he was an absentee father.

Miranda couldn't stand what that did to Wendy.

Warm, maternal-like feelings fluttered in her chest. When she first came to Atlanta, she'd felt such a strong connection to that kid, she thought Wendy was her daughter. A month ago, they'd really gotten close. She cared about her. More than that. She loved her.

Then Iris decided Miranda was a pariah and forbade Wendy to have anything to do with her. So what was up with this one-eighty? Miranda had a good mind to tell Iris to find another babysitter and hang up. She was tired and wanted to get home.

Instead she heard herself mutter into the phone, "Okay. I'll be there. What time?" Jeez what a pushover she was.

CHAPTER FOUR

Wade Parker sat at the desk in his sun-drenched office on the fifteenth floor of the Imperial Building and stared at the manila envelope in his inbox that had just arrived. He hadn't expected a response from the court so soon and he feared the worst.

A quick answer usually meant rejection.

When he first met Miranda Steele, her whole being had been focused on finding her lost daughter. She'd even gotten herself arrested because of it.

The first time he laid eyes on her in that jail cell, he'd fallen in love with the feisty, irascible woman. Despite her torn, muddy clothes, her wild dark hair, the fury in her deep blue eyes.

Behind the fury he'd seen yearning.

And rage and hatred and a thousand other emotions her turbulent past tormented her with.

She'd grown since then. They'd grown together. Become a unit. Miranda was turning into one of the best investigators the Agency had ever produced. And his love for her grew deeper and more multi-faceted each day.

When his first wife, Sylvia, died three years ago, he thought he might as well be dead himself. Now he was full of zest and vigor. Miranda had given him back his life. And that vitality, among other things, had him making plans to branch out his business.

Using the connections he had all over the world, he intended to offer investigative consulting services to any entity that needed him. Law enforcement, FBI, even organizations overseas.

And Miranda would be at his side.

Once more he eyed the envelope from the judge. What would a final denial do to his wife? She'd been through so much lately. She'd had such a bad night. He despised the nightmares she suffered because of that bastard in the hospital, that pitiful excuse for a husband, who refused to die.

He could open the envelope first. That way he could create some sort of emotional buffer for her. But Miranda wouldn't want him to. She'd want to open it herself. Besides, he might be tempted to hide the truth from her and he'd promised there'd be no more secrets between them.

She'd gone to her appointment with Dr. Wingate and wouldn't be back in the office today. He'd take the envelope home and give it to her tonight. He picked it up and started toward his briefcase.

There was a knock on his door and a familiar feminine voice. "Working late?"

Parker put the envelope down and looked up to see a stunning redhead in his doorway. The middle aged woman wore an ivory silk suit with a beaded jacket, a form-fitting skirt that hugged her curves, and the fresh, country girl smile he'd known from his youth.

"Patricia," he said getting to his feet. "Come in. Please."

"Hello, Wade," she said in a low, rich accent that didn't hide her aristocratic Southern heritage. "Gen let me in. I hope I'm not disturbing anything."

"No, of course not. I was just catching up on paperwork." He extended a hand as she slipped into the room with the grace of royalty. She was royalty of sorts. Her family was one of the oldest in Atlanta. As was his. They'd fairly grown up together.

"Please have a seat." He held the chair in front of his desk as she lowered herself with the fluid moves of the expert horsewoman she was. Parker used to ride with her when they were children.

"I was in town seeing my accountant and doing some shopping and I thought I'd stop by."

"It's been ages since I've seen you."

"Last spring." Her slim fingers skimmed over the tasteful jewelry around her long neck. "And you're looking more dapper than ever. You've even got the remnants of a tan."

She always knew how to flatter. "I've been on vacation. What have you been up to?"

"Oh, this and that. I've been splitting my time between the farm and the family house in Peachtree Heights." Patricia raised horses. "Ever since the Steeplechase last June. Oh, that business with the Langford sisters was so dreadful." She waved a hand over her face.

"Yes, it was." Parker had been involved in that case, thanks to Miranda. One of several she'd solved since joining the Agency.

"Without Harold around, it's just so much upkeep." Patricia's husband passed away about a year before Parker lost his first wife. "Well, you know that. You're living in your family home as well, aren't you?"

"In Mockingbird Hills, yes."

"Oh, and you're remarried now."

Parker smiled. "Yes."

"I'm so sorry I couldn't make it to the wedding. I was in Europe with a client. Though I heard it didn't come off quite as planned."

"No, it didn't. Unavoidable circumstances." Parker had been apologizing to friends for the disaster of his wedding for weeks. Most of them understood.

But Miranda was alive and that was all that mattered to him. He didn't care to elaborate. "Did you come to see me about something specific, Patricia?"

She gave him a warm, full-lipped smile. "You are a good detective."

He met her smile and her wily gaze. "What is it?"

She sat forward, looking like she was a little out of her element. "Do you remember the fundraiser at the governor's mansion last spring?"

"Vaguely."

"You captured a jewel thief."

"Ah, yes. Thomas Jameson."

"Everyone talked about it for weeks. Even with the news about Jackson's daughter."

"Hmm." Parker laid a crooked finger against his lips as he went back to that spring night. That was the evening Madison Taggart had gone missing. His best friend's daughter. A few weeks before he'd met Miranda.

"Wade?"

"Yes, Patricia? I'm sorry. It was a difficult case."

"I'm sure. Well, my circumstances will probably seem trivial to you."

He was being rude. "Not at all. Tell me."

She bit her lip. "I seem to be having a teeny problem with the staff at the homestead. You know how difficult it is to find reliable help."

"Oh?"

"I keep a lot of my good pieces in the master bedroom of the family mansion. Necklaces, brooches, rings. Some have been in the family for generations." Hesitating she rubbed her hands in her lap.

He sat back. "Go on."

"Well, lately, I've been missing a few pieces. One set of earrings in particular. Diamonds with tiny emeralds. They belonged to my grandmother. They're antiques, really. Quite valuable."

"And you think the staff is responsible?"

"Well, that's what I don't know. I hate to accuse anyone. But they're the only ones who have access to the room."

"Have you questioned them?"

She blinked at him as if the thought hadn't occurred to her. "I wouldn't know how to go about doing that. I wouldn't want to accuse anyone who's innocent. Lily, she's been with me for years. And then there's Grace. And Stephen. Can you help me, Wade?"

Of course, he could. "You'd like to hire the Agency?"

"Yes, that's exactly what I'd like." Her green eyes sparkled with anticipation. "I know you'd be discreet."

"Certainly. I'm happy you came to me. I can have a man out to your estate tomorrow."

She looked devastated. "Oh, I—"

"What is it?"

She wrinkled her nose. "I really wanted to keep this between us."

"My people know how to keep things confidential."

"Oh, of course. And it's not that I don't think one of your people would do an excellent job. But we're such old friends." She gave him a shy smile. "Can't you do it personally, Wade? I know you're the best of the best."

He was warmed by her flattery. After all, they did go back as she'd said. Her father was a judge and had been mentored by his grandfather. Their mothers had been friends before his passed away.

Slowly he smiled. "All right, Patricia. I'll stop by tomorrow afternoon."

"Oh, thank you, Wade. This is such a relief." With what seemed like reluctance, she rose. "Well, I'll leave you to your work."

"I do have a few things to finish up." He got to his feet, escorted her to the door.

"Thank you again," she murmured at the threshold, smiling at him just the way she did when he'd come to visit when they were children.

"You're welcome, Patricia." He smiled back.

"Well, I'll be on my way then." She turned and glided out the door, a spring in her step.

Parker returned to his desk. He made a quick note in his appointment book and turned back to his inbox.

Time to head home.

He reached for the manila envelope and put it tenderly into his briefcase. He'd have a special meal prepared for Miranda tonight. Something with the hot spices she liked so much. They'd share a bottle of vintage wine. He'd make love to her. And when she was relaxed and calm and sated, he'd give her the envelope.

It still wouldn't be a good time if the news was bad, but he couldn't think of a better way to do it.

He was just about to head for the door when his cell buzzed in his pocket. He pulled it out. A text from his father.

Don't forget the get-together at your house tonight.

He had forgotten it. What with Miranda's nightmare and the envelope arriving, it had completely slipped his mind that his father had arranged for a small party at the Parker estate this evening.

He'd said it was a celebration but had refused to tell him what they'd be celebrating. He could cancel, but what excuse could he give that would satisfy his persistent father? He didn't want to reveal even a whisper of Miranda's personal situation to his father or their friends until she was ready to. Besides, his father would only reschedule the party. Might as well get it over with now.

The envelope would have to wait until it was over.

As he picked up his briefcase, the office phone rang. What now? He was about to let it go to voicemail when he saw it was Antonio.

He picked up. "Hello, son."

"Papa," In his rich Hispanic accent Antonio sounded solemn. "I wanted to ask you about the party tonight."

"What about it?"

Antonio, of course, was on the guest list. He was bringing the singer he'd been dating whom Miranda had befriended. The food was being provided by Joan Fanuzzi, another friend and former coworker of Miranda's who'd recently opened her own catering business. Parker's father was bringing the champagne.

"I was wondering if you and Miranda are still up to it, now that she knows her daughter is—" Antonio uttered a name.

Parker set down his briefcase and sank into his chair. He put a hand to his forehead. Had he heard that right? "Excuse me?"

Antonio repeated the information.

Parker drew in a tense breath. "Your courier just delivered the documents. Miranda had an afternoon appointment. She hasn't opened them yet."

There was a pause. "And you haven't either. I'm so sorry, Papa. The courier picked up the envelope several hours ago. I didn't mean—"

"It's all right, Antonio."

"I only thought you might want to be alone tonight."

He did want to be alone and Miranda would, too. But canceling the party a few hours before the event would be sure to generate questions. Questions neither of them wanted to answer.

He'd stick to his former plan and get it over with.

"No, we'll go ahead and have the party, Antonio. I don't want to deal with your grandfather tonight."

He gave a sad laugh. "*Abuelo* can be stubborn. Very well, I'll see you there. Again, I'm so sorry for my slip."

"It's all right. I'm glad I know." Parker hung up.

He stared out the window at the bright blue, late summer sky as the name Antonio had just revealed echoed in his mind. Dear Lord. How could it be her? This was almost worse than a rejection of their petition.

What could he expect from Miranda when he gave her the envelope now? An angry tirade? Disbelief? She might want to fly to Chicago and talk to the judge in person.

He let out a slow, weary breath. Miranda would not be happy about this. Not happy at all. And even though he now knew the answer she'd been looking for all these years, there was little he could do to help. But determined to do what he could for her, once again, he picked up his briefcase and headed out the door.

It would be a long, painful evening in the Parker estate tonight.

CHAPTER FIVE

As Miranda trotted up the steps of the Marietta skating rink—after a fun-filled hour of fighting her way through rush hour traffic—the image of Wendy camped out on this very spot came to her.

A month ago the kid had run away because she thought no one cared about her. Miranda had found her here on this stoop in the middle of the night.

Sudden tears stung her eyes. That night she'd told Wendy she loved her. That she couldn't care about her more if she had been her own daughter.

That was still true.

But Wendy wasn't hers and never would be. And with parents as fickle as Iris and Shelby Van Aarle, she didn't dare get her hopes up for a long term relationship of any sort with the kid. Hell, Iris could take her daughter and up and move to Paris tomorrow and Miranda would never see either of them again.

Brushing away the embarrassing, ridiculous tears, Miranda opened the door and stepped into a blast of cold air.

Inside, shouts and the sound of skates slicing into ice echoed to the gymnasium-like rafters overhead. Down below kids glided around the large rink while parents and peers stood on the sidelines cheering or giving advice. Everyone was in coats and hats and scarves—a good way to dress if you knew ahead of time you were going to be refrigerated.

Blinking under the fluorescent lights, Miranda shivered in her thin office clothes—with the grass stain and the tear in the knee—and scanned the spectators for Wendy.

Before she could spot her, a nerdy looking girl wearing horn-rimmed glasses and carrying two cups of soda approached with a friendly grin. "Hello. You're Miranda Steele, aren't you? Are you here to pick up Wendy?"

The girl seemed to be about Wendy's age. She was thin and plainly dressed for that age, wearing ankle-high boots, dark knit slacks, and a rather utilitarian-looking parka. Her dark brown hair fell in a long braid down her back.

Miranda eyed the drab green knit scarf around her neck. There was a time when she'd studied the necks of every dark-haired girl she met, hoping to see a mark on the side of it and find Amy. A pointless habit.

"Yes, that's me," she said. "Wendy's mother had a meeting. Do I know you?"

"I saw you a few times when you used to come here before, but I never got a chance to introduce myself. I'm Jordan McFee." She set one of the sodas down on a nearby bench and extended a hand.

Oh, yeah. Jordan McFee. Daughter of the third partner of the law firm of Chatham, Grayson, and McFee. Wendy had mentioned her in her surreptitious texts.

"Good to meet you." Miranda shook Jordan's hand, noting her grip was pretty confident and businesslike for a thirteen-year-old.

"Wendy used to tell us about how smart you are. She said you're an awesome detective and she was learning a lot from you."

Miranda had kept Wendy at the Parker estate for a while and even taken her to work. But the arrangement hadn't lasted. "I think she's lost interest in becoming an investigator."

"Probably. But I'm thinking of majoring in Criminal Justice. Though my father wants me to study law and come to work for him." Behind her glasses, Jordan's brown eyes danced with enthusiasm.

Bright kid. Miranda liked her. A good friend for Wendy.

"Was there an emphasis on forensic science where you went to school? Chemistry is my favorite subject." She grinned showing a row of straight white teeth.

School? No, there was no forensic science in the school of hard knocks. Until she'd met Parker, she'd worked mostly construction jobs. Nobody needed to know that. Especially not a kid. "Uh, my experience is mostly on the job."

"Oh, that's right. At dinner the other night, Mr. Estavez mentioned you'd solved several murder cases recently."

Small world. Antonio Estavez was what Miranda referred to as Parker's surrogate son. Parker had taken the young man off the streets when he was sixteen and raised him in his own home. Now Estavez was a successful defense attorney at Chatham, Grayson, and McFee. Apparently he was doing well enough to be invited to the one of the partners' houses for dinner.

Miranda shifted from foot to foot and rubbed her arms, hoping she wouldn't get frostbite. "Is Wendy around? I'm supposed to pick her up today."

"She's over there." Jordan nodded toward the end of the rink.

Miranda gestured at the soda in Jordan's hand. "Is one of those for her? I'll take it to her."

"Thanks." The girl handed her the drink and picked up the one she'd set on the bench. "I need to get back to Kaylee. I'm helping her with Algebra and she'll get distracted and start talking to a boy if I'm gone too long. Hope to see you again, Ms. Steele. It was a pleasure."

"Me, too."

The kid pivoted and strolled away, a youthful skip in her step, toward the opposite end of the rink. Yeah, Miranda liked Jordan McFee. She'd find out how close Wendy was to her and encourage the friendship.

She turned around and spotted Wendy right away.

Near a group of other girls at the edge of the rink, she hung over the boards like an eager puppy. Her dark hair was pulled up into a tidy bun and she had on a pink jacket with fake fur around the neck. An expectant smile shone on her pretty face.

Miranda wasn't prepared for the tumult of feelings the sight of the kid brought on. Longing and sadness and a little bit of annoyance.

Wendy wasn't looking Miranda's way. She was fixated on the skater on the ice.

Dominating half the rink, another young girl deftly skated backwards, making figure eights as she went. Over what looked like a one-piece of black tights and turtleneck, she wore a short, deep red circle skirt that flowed with her moves as she swirled.

"Speed. More speed," a woman shouted from the sidelines. Must be her coach.

Increasing her pace, the girl circled, spun, raised her arms and lifted into the air, twirling like a top, red skirt flaring. After what seemed like a full minute, she landed on the ice again without a wobble in a perfect ballerina-like pose.

Applause came from the onlookers. Wendy bobbed up and down, her face ecstatic with pre-teen enthusiasm.

The skater ignored them all.

With a frown of concentration, she whisked away stray strands of ebony hair and began to skate fast again. Another set of swizzles and spins earned her more applause from her audience. Again, she ignored them.

Miranda noticed her hair was caught up in a bun like the one Wendy was sporting. Of course, Wendy was imitating the hairstyle. The figure skating diva was Mackenzie Chatham.

Wendy's latest obsession.

Mackenzie was an up-and-comer on the ice. She'd won a big contest a few weeks ago and was headed for a national one soon, according to the texts Wendy had sent Miranda.

But Miranda didn't like the girl. She treated Wendy like her servant. Last Miranda had heard, she had Wendy polishing her skates.

The crowd oohed as, moving backwards again, Mackenzie began to skate in a wide circle once more. Round she went, narrowing the circle until it was only a few feet wide. Slowly she raised her arms.

"Watch your footwork," the coach warned. "Crossovers."

With one leg lifted behind her, Mackenzie rotated and began to spin. Faster, faster. She bent her knees into a sitting position, lifted one arm in front of her and became a blur.

"Not too fast. Slow down before you rise."

This time, the direction seemed to confuse her. Mackenzie wobbled, tipped over, caught herself with one hand before falling on her bum.

The crowd gave a sound of dismay.

Her face burning, the skater got up and glided to the edge of the rink. "I'm done for today," she shouted over her shoulder at the coach.

She stepped off the ice and into the arms of a tall, majestic looking woman with perfectly styled dark hair with classic touches of gray, whom Miranda recognized as her mother.

Mackenzie shook off the hug and headed away to the locker room, anger flashing across her youthful face. So the little *prima donna* had a temper, huh?

Wendy took off after her and, trying not to spill the drink she was still holding, Miranda hurried around the crowd and followed the girls into the locker room.

Young voices crackled in the air as she stepped inside.

"It'll be okay, Mackenzie. You'll do better next time."

"You shouldn't talk about something you don't know anything about, Wendy," Mackenzie sneered.

Stopping behind the concrete block wall that opened into the room, Miranda gritted her teeth. That was uncalled for. Wendy had learned a whole lot about figure skating in the past few months.

"But, Mackenzie, you're so good and—"

"Good? I can jump fine, but my sit spins suck. I have to be able to do a sit spin if I'm going to win the Junior Interstate. You do know that, don't you?" she snapped.

"Of course, I do. I'm just saying—"

"Don't. Say. Anything." Mackenzie's words were sharp and brutal. "As if I needed advice from *you*. Just be quiet and take care of these skates."

That was all Miranda could take.

She stepped around the corner just as Mackenzie shoved her skates into Wendy's arms. She wanted to cuss. Instead she forced a smile. "Hey, girls."

Wendy spun around and glared at her, whether more in shock that Miranda was here or mortified at what she might have overheard, Miranda couldn't tell.

"What are you doing here?"

Miranda turned her gaze to Mackenzie. The kid looked like she had no doubt about what Miranda had overheard. The little diva straightened her shoulders and gave her a haughty, you're-not-good-enough-to-kiss-my-skates look.

She was pretty. Maybe even beautiful, with delicate features, dark, nicely arched brows and a pink blush on her flawless cheeks. She was thin and fit, as you'd expect a top figure skater to be, and graceful as a swan, even off the ice.

Dismissively, she turned away, pulled the band out of her hair and shook it out, letting it fall to her shoulders in rich dark waves.

Miranda wanted to shake the little snot. Instead she set the drink cup she was carrying on the counter, shoved her hands in her pockets and returned a gaze colder than the air, which Mackenzie caught in the mirror. "Last time I checked, this place was open to the public." She turned to Wendy. "Your mother sent me to pick you up."

"Really?" Wendy almost smiled.

"Yeah." Miranda shrugged. "Go figure. That's your drink, by the way."

"Okay, um." Ignoring the cup, she frowned and smoothed her dark hair, which was still in the bun.

"What?"

"I need to dry these blades first." She reached for a towel on a shelf along the wall.

Anger prickled the back of Miranda's neck. Wendy wasn't this kid's slave. "I think Mackenzie can take care of that."

Wendy gave her a look of pre-teen panic. "They'll rust if I don't dry them right away."

Miranda narrowed her eyes at the princess. "Aren't they *your* skates?"

Mackenzie gave her a superior scowl. "Of course, they're mine."

"Then why can't *you* take care of them?"

"Miranda!" Wendy wailed in horror as if Miranda had just slapped her.

Mackenzie straightened her shoulders and marched over to Wendy. "Very well. If you don't want to do it, I'll find someone else."

Wendy hugged the skates to her chest. "I didn't say I wouldn't do it."

Mackenzie rolled a shoulder toward Miranda without looking at her. "But she did. Give them to me." She held out her hands.

Wendy looked like she was about to burst into tears.

"C'mon, Wendy," Miranda said softly. "We need to get going."

Looking as helpless as a lost kitten Wendy shoved the skates into Mackenzie's arms. Tossing Miranda a glare of sheer hatred, she snatched her backpack off a bench and hurried from the room.

Outside in the parking lot, Miranda winced as Wendy climbed inside the hot red Corvette ZR1 Parker had given her for a wedding present and slammed the passenger door.

Sliding behind the steering wheel, Miranda ran a hand over the black leather of the bucket seat. "Pretty nice upgrade from my old Lumina, huh?"

Without as much as a "cool!" Wendy turned and gave her a venomous look that stung like yellow jackets. "You had no right to do that, Miranda."

"Do what?"

Wendy rolled her eyes and uttered a guttural groan that sounded like a cow in heat. "Do you really not know what I'm talking about? Really?"

Struggling to cool her own temper, Miranda started the car and headed out the parking lot. "I'm sick of that girl treating you like crap. That's all," she said at last.

"Crap?" Wendy squealed. "Do you know how lucky I am that she even speaks to me?"

Oh, brother. Miranda waited for a car to pass, then turned onto the side road that ran alongside the rink. "You shouldn't let her push you around like that."

"Push me around? Miranda, it's *Mackenzie Chatham*." She waved her hands dramatically, sounding like she was talking about Justin Bieber, or whoever the current heartthrob *du jour* was. "She's only the coolest girl in school. She's only the best skater in the region. She's only going to be in the Olympics someday."

"Maybe, maybe not." Miranda braked as they came to a red light. And okay, maybe she shouldn't have butted in. But who else was going to stand up for Wendy while her mother was off boinking her website designer?

Wendy's whole body tensed as her eyes moistened and flashed with rage. "You know, you really should mind your own business." Nice of her to point that out.

"I thought you were my business. I thought we had an—understanding."

Wendy didn't answer. Her arms tight around her, she stared out the window. Silent. Brooding.

A horn blared behind them. The light was green. Hissing out a breath, Miranda turned onto the main road and headed for the Interstate.

They inched along, the silence almost as unbearable as the heavy traffic. After traveling about fifteen miles in forty-five minutes, Miranda spotted their exit. Not that much farther, she consoled herself.

Out of the corner of her eye, she watched Wendy pull the band out of her dark hair. It fell to her shoulders in the same style as Mackenzie Chatham's. She'd colored it to match the *prima donna's*, too. This wasn't good. Wasn't healthy.

Miranda thought about asking if Wendy had seen Dr. Wingate lately. The therapist had treated the girl for PTSD after their shared ordeal last spring. But she didn't feel like having her head bitten off and spat out at her just now. Jeez. Why couldn't the kid be reasonable? Why couldn't she be more like Jordan McFee?

If Wendy were hers, she'd—

But she wasn't hers. Maybe Amy would have a sweeter disposition. If she ever got to meet her daughter.

Another half hour and they were cruising through Mockingbird Hills, the ultra wealthy Buckhead subdivision where they were neighbors, of sorts.

A slew of luxury estates and updated mansions from the Old South lined the streets, displaying styles as varied as their owners incomes. Ignoring the homes and the rolling, manicured lawns that had dazzled her when she'd first come here, Miranda turned onto Sweet Hollow Lane and pulled up to the curb in front of the enormous Van Aarle estate. Iris's BMW SUV was parked in the driveway.

I live in a big mansion in Buckhead, Georgia. My mom's an executive and my dad's always away. They are never home.

The words from the letter that had brought her here last spring. It had been a really bad night the first time she came to this house. Then again, that was the night she'd met Parker.

She was calmer now. She switched off the car, turned to her sullen passenger and tried again. This time, her voice was soft. "You know, Wendy, you and I are a lot alike."

"I don't have the foggiest idea what you're talking about," Wendy sniffed, her nose in the air. That sounded like something Mackenzie would say. It would break Miranda's heart if Wendy started acting like that stuck-up little snot.

"I'm talking about the way we handle humiliation. As in not very well."

That must have really hit a nerve. Wendy spun around with a cold glare in her dark eyes. "Miranda, are you supposed to pick me up again?" she asked in a tone as icy as her figure skating idol.

"I don't know. Why?"

"Because you don't have to bother. I can get a ride from Jordan's mom." And with that, she reached for her backpack, got out of the car, and raced up the drive.

CHAPTER SIX

Feeling bone weary, Miranda opened the majestic front door of the Parker estate and stepped onto marble tiles of its regal foyer. She eyed the sparkling chandelier overhead casting its elegant light onto the tall oil paintings, the grand mahogany staircase leading to the vast upper rooms, the ornate furniture that looked like it belonged in a museum, and wondered for the umpteenth time how she'd ended up here.

But here she was. Mistress of the manor. Ha.

Well, it wasn't all class and luxury. The sitting room off to the side had been boarded up and its furniture had been donated to a museum.

Parker had wanted to obliterate the memory of the horror that had gone on there a month ago and Miranda hadn't argued with him one bit. That was the start of the remodeling they'd done since they came back from their honeymoon. Or rather the start of making some decisions and Parker hiring a crew to do the work.

Next had been the dining room. There they'd obliterated the amorous love cupids on the walls—remnants of Parker's flirtatious father.

Dining room. Was that garlic and basil she smelled? Italian?

She started to cross the hall and heard voices coming from one of the nearby rooms. And music. Uh oh. She remembered her cell had buzzed when she got in the car with Wendy and she'd been too upset to look at it.

She did now and saw Parker's text.

Party tonight. Our house. Don't forget.

Oh, crap. She had forgotten. Mr. P had called last week and insisted on having a get-together tonight. Something about a celebration. Double crap. She didn't want a party tonight. She wanted to unload on Parker about Wendy and that awful Mackenzie Chatham. She wanted to kick and scream and cuss and throw things.

She considered going upstairs to change first, but decided it might be too tempting to stay up there. Heck, nobody would notice the grass stain on her charcoal dress slacks and the rip wasn't that big. It wasn't as if she were in jeans and a tank top. Good thing the Agency had a dress code.

She followed the chatter to one of the front drawing rooms—one they hadn't re-done yet. With its off-white walls, its crown molding, rosy print drapery, and matching overstuffed French-style chairs, this room always reminded Miranda of something out of Versailles. To cut down on the posh, she'd suggested to Parker that they put a pool table in the middle of it.

"There she is!" cried a voice, thick with Brooklyn. "Hi ya, Murray."

Joan Fanuzzi, Miranda's old road crew buddy, scampered across the Persian rug and gave her a hug. She was in a good mood.

"Hi, Fanuzzi. Sorry I'm late."

"Just glad you finally made it." The gap between Fanuzzi's teeth displayed in an ear-to-ear grin. She'd styled her black hair, which was currently shoulder-length, and was wearing a lacey, lime green party dress with matching heels that might have brought her up to five three. And here Miranda thought she hated dressing up.

"Evening, Steele." Wearing a suit and tie, Miranda's buddy Becker from the Agency, who was also Fanuzzi's new husband, raised a glass from the corner.

Miranda tossed him a salute. "Hi, Becker."

She scanned the room. Looked like everybody was here.

"If it isn't my favorite female investigator." In his trademark white suit, the wealthy local real estate mogul who was Parker's father grinned at her from behind a sheer glass coffee table where he was pouring champagne.

"Hi, Mr. P."

"Hello, Miranda," said a woman with a foreign tilt in her voice.

Along the wall near a credenza that dated back to the Revolutionary War stood Tatiana, Mr. P's new bride from the Ukraine, in a silky flowered dress. She was talking to Gen, Parker's only daughter and office manager at the Agency, who grunted a greeting at her.

As usual, Gen was wearing an impatient look of annoyance. Realizing she was the only one in the room without a partner, Miranda wondered if that was why she always had a stick up her ass. Especially since matrimony had been so thick in the air lately.

Mr. P picked up a flute, strolled over to Miranda and put it in her hand. He gave her a peck on the cheek. "Delighted that you invited us all here tonight, my dear." He'd invited himself. As well as everyone else.

"Sure, Mr. P. What's this about?"

"You'll know in a moment." He winked across the room at Estavez. "Antonio, are you ready?"

The hot Hispanic lawyer didn't look ready at all. He looked a little uncomfortable. Beside him, looking shy and dainty, stood her singer-piano-player friend Coco. Her pretty blond hair was in an upsweep, and the sequins across the top of her light pink dress glittered under the wall sconces.

She wiggled her fingers at her. "Hi, Miranda. Thanks for having us."

"Don't mention it." If everyone insisted on giving her the credit for this soiree, might as well take it.

"Oh, wait," Mr. P huffed. "Russell's not here. Now where did he get off to?" His thick white brows knitted together as he scowled and rocked back on his heels with irritation. "Gen, go get your father."

"He's right here, Granddaddy."

With classic Parker confidence, the man himself sauntered through an archway and into the room. He'd had a shower, Miranda saw, and had changed into a silk suit with a dark blue sheen that had to cost at least a couple thousand. A hundred-dollar-or-so silk tie of deep red was at his neck. His dark hair with its touch of salt-and-pepper around the temples was a little longer these days and a stray wisp fell temptingly over his forehead.

As his father went to him and put another champagne flute in his hand, Parker scanned the room with those heart-stopping metallic gray eyes of his. They were the color of a handgun and matched the sexiness of a face that made every woman in Atlanta stop and do a double-take.

His gaze caught Miranda's in one of those penetrating stares that made her stomach do cartwheels and her knees buckle like a swooning ingénue from the eighteen century. But tonight he seemed a tad edgy.

She suddenly had the urge to kick everyone out, dash across the room, and tear that suit off him.

Mr. P picked up his own flute and raised it. "All right, everyone. Are we ready?"

"As ready as we're gonna be," Fanuzzi beamed.

"Antonio?"

Estavez cleared his throat. "Papa, *Abuelo*." He nodded toward Parker, then Mr. P. "Coco and I have an announcement to make."

Miranda watched Parker stiffen. "What sort of announcement, Antonio?"

Estavez took Coco's delicate hand in his, kissed it gently. Gazing at her with a smile filled with desire and affection, he said, "Coco and I are engaged to be married."

Silence. It went on for what seemed like ten minutes.

At last Tatiana clasped both of her hands to her chest. "That is wonderful news, Antonio," she said as if she hadn't known all along. Mr. P had to have spilled the beans to her.

Fanuzzi grinned with approval. "Isn't that just too cool?"

With a look of shock, Gen raised her glass. "Congratulations. To both of you." Her voice betrayed a touch of disappointment, but she made the effort to hide it. Looked like Gen, Miranda and Parker were the only ones in the room who hadn't been in on the secret.

Mr. P raised his glass and took a sip. "We all wish you a long and happy life together."

Miranda drank, but she didn't know what to say. Coco had recently been divorced from a wife-beating psycho. A divorce you could call very messy. Her ex was dead.

Sure, she knew something had clicked between Estavez and Coco the minute they met. She knew they'd been sleeping together for a while now. Still, it was just too soon for an engagement.

"Congratulations!" Laughing, Fanuzzi danced across the room and gave Coco a big hug. "I wanted you to wait until I brought out the cake, Antonio. But that's okay." She swiped at her cheeks. "Sorry I'm so emotional. I'm Italian, you know."

Everyone wished the two love birds well and broke into chatter about the wedding, the date, which hadn't been set, and how the Latin lawyer had proposed.

"There's going to be another party at Ay Chihuahua's tomorrow night," Coco said. Ay Chihuahua was owned by Estavez's mother. "Everyone's invited. And of course, I want all three of you to be in my wedding party, if you're willing. We're going to keep it simple."

Miranda didn't say anything. Hadn't they just done that a month ago? She didn't think she could take planning another wedding, even if it wasn't hers. She cast a longing look at Parker, wishing again she could kick everyone out and be alone with him. He looked like he was thinking the same thing.

But the thought of her wedding reminded her of Wendy, who'd also been in her bridal party, and that made her think of the stuck-up Mackenzie Chatham. If only she had some ammo to get Wendy away from that girl.

Swirling the bubbly in her flute, she decided she might as well make the most of this opportunity and sidled up to the lawyer. "Congrats again, Antonio."

He gave her a grateful, pure white smile. "Thank you, Miranda. It's because of you Coco and I met."

Miranda looked down at the hardwood floor. If she could have prevented that at the time, she would have. But she wanted to change the subject anyway. "So how are things at work?"

He seemed surprised at the question. "Fine. Why?"

"I hear you're getting along pretty well with your boss."

"With Mr. Johnson?"

"No, with the partner. McFee. I saw his daughter at the ice rink tonight. She said you had dinner at their house recently."

He cleared his throat and suddenly seemed uncomfortable. "Ah. Yes, I did. Jordan's quite a precocious young girl."

"Yeah, she is."

Across the room Parker's brow rose. "What were you doing at the ice rink, Miranda?"

"Iris Van Aarle called and asked me to pick up Wendy."

"Oh, how is Wendy?" Coco wanted to know.

"She's fine. But she's fixated on one of the skaters. Mackenzie Chatham." She turned back to Antonio. "She's the daughter of one of your other partners."

He gave her a measured smile. "Yes, I know. She's quite the figure skater. She seems to have a bright future."

"So I hear. But what I want to know is what her parents are like."

Estavez looked uncomfortable. He exchanged a look with Parker that Miranda couldn't read.

"Is there a problem?"

"No, no. Oliver and Colby Chatham are fine people. Some of the most generous, giving people I know, in fact. Colby founded a charity for crippled children. Both of them sponsor fundraisers every year."

"Yeah?" She studied her glass. "Then why is their daughter so stuck up?"

Estavez's dark brows shot up. For a moment, he seemed speechless. Kind of odd for a defense attorney. "I'm afraid I don't know what you mean, Miranda."

"I mean, Mackenzie treats Wendy like dirt. Talks down to her. Has her cleaning her skates, for Pete's sake. And Wendy worships her so much, she thinks that's some kind of honor."

Parker set his drink down on a table and made his way over to them. "Pardon me, Antonio, but I've just realized I haven't said good evening to my wife. How are you, my darling?"

Miranda opened her mouth, but before she could say anything, Parker bent his head and laid his lips on hers in a sensual kiss that took her breath. His strong arms went around her, pressing her close to his muscular chest while his mouth kept working.

She breathed in the shower-fresh scent of his skin and her knees went weak. She heard a whistle and applause from Mr. P.

"Bravo, son."

She pulled away, her cheeks flaming. "Uh, hi, honey." Wiping her mouth, she glanced around the room and saw Fanuzzi's eyebrows were up to the ceiling.

"Wow," her friend mouthed. Good grief.

Parker glanced down at the grass stain and rip in her slacks. "Would you like to change?" She could read his tone.

Jeez Louise. Detective Tan must have blabbed to him what happened with that deadbeat this morning and Gen had probably rubbed it in. Miranda looked at her friends, then turned back to whisper. "I'm sorry about the Digby thing."

"I know you are."

"It won't happen again."

"I'm sure it was just an oversight." He sounded like he meant that. He was really starting to trust her, wasn't he? "Now run upstairs and put something on that knee."

No dressing her down? Well, he wouldn't do that in front of guests. That would come later. But it would be nice to escape for a few minutes. She'd get back to Estavez later.

"Sure," she said and headed through the archway to the staircase.

Grumbling to herself over her stupid attack on Digby and the too-good-to-breathe-your-air Mackenzie Chatham, Miranda took a quick shower, washed her knee, slapped some salve on it, and threw on a half-way decent dress. By the time she went back downstairs, everyone was in the dining room and Fanuzzi was dishing out gooey slices of lasagna from a huge pan on the long dining table.

Under a low-hanging chandelier sat flowers, a stack of the good china, and a big bowl of salad.

Fanuzzi handed Miranda a plate and told her to sit down and eat. Miranda obliged, hoping if she stuffed enough food in her mouth, she wouldn't have to discuss the upcoming wedding. Turned out she didn't have to say much.

The lasagna was out-of-this-world delicious and everyone chowed down and made small talk and told Fanuzzi how good her cooking was. When the dinner was over, she brought out a cake. A gorgeous creation, adorned with lots of white swirly icing and pink and blue flowers. As Fanuzzi sliced into it, everyone oohed at the rich chocolate inside.

Fanuzzi began passing out the pieces and it didn't take long for half of it to disappear. But not long after that, the conversation died down.

Gen excused herself saying she had an early day tomorrow, and Mr. P and Tatiana said goodbye as well. Miranda walked them out to the foyer. When she returned to the dining room, she found Coco and Fanuzzi cleaning up and Becker carrying leftovers out to the car.

Miranda ran a finger along the edge of the demolished cake to scoop up a bit of icing. The lettering on it now read "Congratulations Coco and Ant—."

"You really outdid yourself tonight, Fanuzzi."

"Thanks."

"You ought to go into business."

Fanuzzi grinned. "Full-time as of last week."

"Really? Good for you. No more road crew."

"Don't miss it a bit."

"You don't miss eight hours of breathing asphalt in the hot Georgia sun?"

Fanuzzi laughed.

"Me, neither."

Coco stacked what was left of the plates, her diamond engagement ring flashing like police lights. "Thanks so much for catering this party, Joan."

"My pleasure." Fanuzzi grinned at Coco while she spread plastic wrap over a pan. She winked at Miranda. "Don't you think they make a cute couple? Coco and Antonio?"

Miranda blinked at her and pulled her finger out of her mouth. "Sure. Adorable." They really did but that was no reason to rush into things.

Coco's baby blue eyes glowed. "Will you two help me plan the wedding?"

"Be happy to," Fanuzzi cooed, waving a box of plastic wrap. "I've already got some ideas for the color scheme. Where are you going to hold it?"

"We're not sure yet. What do you think, Miranda?"

Miranda swiped up another bit of frosting. "You're asking me?"

"Of course. You just had a wedding, didn't you?" Coco pointed to the cake. "Do you want another piece?"

She shook her head. "No, thanks. Let me think on that. Where's your, uh, fiancé?"

"He's in the kitchen talking to your husband. Why?"

She found one of the pastel paper napkins and wiped her hands. "I didn't finish my conversation with him." She turned and headed down the hall.

The black granite and stainless steel kitchen was about twice the size of the apartment Miranda used to live in when she first came to Atlanta. Dishes and glassware were soaking in the sink, but the room was empty. The door to the back deck was open and low male voices trickled through.

She tiptoed up to the door and heard Parker's voice.

"It isn't that I don't accept her, Antonio."

"Isn't it?" Estavez snapped. He sounded more upset than she'd ever heard him.

"No, it isn't. It's just that I thought you would choose a woman with talents more akin to your own."

"She's a musician, Papa. I'm a poet."

"You're a lawyer and a damn fine one."

"And you're a fine one to talk."

"If you're referring to me and Miranda, Antonio, our situation is entirely different."

There was a long pause and Miranda almost thought she could smell chili peppers burning. Then Estavez's words echoed through the door, dark with anger. "Are you sure it isn't that my fiancée's blood isn't as blue as yours, Señor Parker? Because if that's the case, I should remind you. Neither is mine."

Footsteps sounded on the deck's wooden floor. Miranda spun around and scampered over to the sink. She'd just turned on the water when Estavez stormed into the room.

"A woman's work is never done," she grinned.

He eyed her suspiciously, then came over to her and took her hand. He had to see it wasn't soapy but instead of giving her the third degree, he put his lips to it.

His face was full of suppressed Latin rage. "I apologize, Miranda, but Coco and I must be going. We'll see ourselves out."

Then he turned and left.

A moment later, Parker stepped inside and closed the door behind him.

"Fun night, huh?"

He scowled at her. "What are you doing over there?"

"All this marriage talk has put me in a domestic mood." She grabbed a sponge and waved it in the air.

He almost smiled.

Antonio's words had hurt him, but the lawyer was dead wrong. Parker didn't have a snobby bone in his body.

She put the sponge down and pretended to dry her hands. "For what it's worth, I agree with you."

He looked at her in surprise. "You do?"

"Sure. It's too soon for Coco to think about tying the knot. She met Estavez when she was still married to that jerk, Dexter. She hasn't had time to heal."

"I agree. I like the young woman, but I just don't see her with Antonio."

Miranda thought they were good together, just not yet. But now wasn't the time to say that. She plopped down on a stool at the island, remembering the vicious fight she and Parker had had here once. You never could tell where life would lead you.

She shrugged. "Not much we can do to stop them. People in love don't listen to reason."

"When did you get so wise?"

"I've had some recent experience in that department."

Parker smiled at the woman he adored. Antonio didn't understand. She might not be anything like the sophisticated socialites he'd used to date. Or Sylvia. She didn't resemble his refined first wife in the least. And Gen would probably never be happy that he'd married her. But Miranda Steele was everything he needed. And to him, she was more beautiful than any woman he'd ever known.

He drank in her dark hair flowing to her shoulders. Her lean and sensuous body that never failed to arouse him. Those deep blue, fiery eyes. She had changed into a ruby, form-fitting dress he'd picked out for her that showed off her best features and she looked lovely in it.

He stepped to her, took her hair in his hand and brushed her cheek with his lips. She smelled of fresh soap and raw desire. "Come on," he murmured in her ear. "Let's see Dave and Joan out and go upstairs."

CHAPTER SEVEN

As she hurried through the door of the mansion's master bedroom, Miranda's heart was already beating in double-time. She stepped onto the soft carpet of the huge blue-and-plum room with its tall windows and humongous luxury bed and caught the fire in Parker's eyes.

The smoldering in her stomach burst into full flame.

Parker took off his coat and tossed it on one of the chairs in the corner. Before she could say a word he picked her up, flung her onto the huge bed and pounced on top of her. She squealed with delight when his mouth crushed into hers and he pinned her to the silky comforter.

"You're frisky tonight," she giggled, coming up for air.

"Must have been something in the cake." And he took her mouth again and began to work her fancy dress off with his hands.

Something within her ignited like a Fourth of July firecracker. She dug her fingers into his thick hair, buried her mouth into his and turned him over on his back to straddle him.

He laughed aloud in surprise. "I see you've been into the cake as well."

"More like the champagne."

"Oh? Then let's see just how well that's working." He reached for her dress, but she batted him away.

She fumbled with the buttons, grunting as she struggled. The thing was gathered at the front and fastened with a long row of covered ones all the way down. With eyelets, for Pete's sake. What was she thinking when she'd put it on? But the jagged full skirt was nice for straddling.

Now it was his turn to bat her hands away. "I think my fingers are a bit steadier."

"I don't see how. You had more champagne." But she let him go at the buttons while she attacked the ones on his dress shirt. Now these were a lot more sensible. "I'm going to beat you," she singsonged.

"Oh, no you're not."

"Oh, yes I am."

"I don't think so. You're not wearing any underwear?"

"Nope." She felt his arousal grow beneath her but kept her focus on the buttons. "See?" She got the last one open and ran her hands over his delicious chest, watching his muscles quiver as he groaned.

"Not fair."

"Oh, yeah? How about this?" She traced a finger over the scar on his abdomen, then started to lower her mouth to him.

"I'm almost finished." He was only halfway down.

"Too bad, buster. I win."

He gave her a dark look. "Do you like this dress?"

"Not especially."

A good enough answer. He grasped the material in his strong hands and ripped it open until the buttons flew everywhere. One bounced off his chest and landed someplace on the floor.

She snickered. "I hope we don't end up sleeping on any of them."

"Not what concerns me at the moment." He raised his head and took her breast in his mouth.

"Now that's not fair," Miranda gasped as he turned her over and began to work her with those deft, nimble fingers of his. She shuddered, trembled as his hands moved over her, teasing, caressing, making her gasp.

Then he moved down, over her sides, her stomach, lingering, sending shivers straight through her until he reached his goal. He had to break his touch to move over her dress, which was tangled around her waist, but her center, his bull's-eye, was wet and open for him and she parted her legs, almost daring him to make her even more delirious than she already was.

She knew he would.

His hand began to stroke her. She sucked in air and dug her mouth into his. As he worked his magic below, their tongues flayed against each other as if in mortal combat. She reached around him, let her fingers slide down his back to his belt.

"You still have your pants on," she gasped coming up for air.

"Mmm," he murmured as if he didn't care and pressed his mouth to hers again as he worked her harder.

She reached around him, groped for the buckle of his belt. Just as she went over the rise she got his zipper down and reached inside for him.

They cried out together as she came.

It took every ounce of control Parker had to keep going, to let her ride out the full pleasure of her orgasm while she had her hands on him. Did the woman not realize what she was doing to him? As soon as he was sure she was finished and the desire sparked again in her lovely blue eyes, he reached for his slacks pulled them off in one tug and plunged into her, not caring that her poor dress had never come off or that it was in tatters.

He'd buy her a dozen more tomorrow as long as he could have her tonight. Now.

They were both too aroused for finesse. He plunged into her, watching her eyes go wide, loving the sound of her gasps.

Hearts beating madly they pounded together, her hips meeting his with every thrust. More. More. More. Dear Lord, he thought his whole body would burst. His shudder seemed to rock the earth as he felt her release with him.

Gasping, sweaty, he fell beside her. They couldn't speak. All they could do was pant and puff and stare at each other, amazed at the miracle they had together.

When at last his heartbeat quieted, he pulled her close to him. She was the dearest thing in his life. "I love you, Miranda."

"I love you, too." She smiled at him, watching the happy gleam in his sexy eyes.

The words came easy for her now. A miracle in itself. Something she never thought would ever happen. This wonderful man had given her more happiness than she ever thought possible.

Soon she might know who her daughter was. Life seemed brighter than it ever had.

He drew the back of his hand across her cheek. "You make me complete."

"You, too."

He studied her face, so lovely and complex. He thought about what she'd said about Coco needing time to heal. Miranda needed time to heal, too. And yet, the news he had to tell her would hinder that healing. It would hurt her, set her back. If only he could hide it from her. Perhaps he should wait until tomorrow. But if he did, tomorrow he'd find another excuse to put off telling her.

But there might be a way to soften the blow. He took her hand, traced a finger over her palm. "I have a proposal for you."

She rolled and grinned at him. "You want to go up to the Taj Mahal room?"

He had to smile. "Not exactly."

She waggled her lovely dark brows. "The last time we went there was pretty intense."

"It's something else."

"What?" Her lovely face grew serious.

He studied his mother's ring that she now wore on her finger. The sight of it there always gave him a surge of joy. "I've been thinking about this for some time."

"And?"

"You know I have professional connections with many organizations."

She laughed. "Yeah, like all over the world."

"I'd like to start branching out the business. Offering services to some of these organizations on a case by case basis."

Her expression turned contemplative. "Sort of like consulting?"

"Yes, exactly. Cold murder cases, kidnappings. Anything where there's a shortage of manpower."

"What kind of organizations are you talking about? FBI?"

"I know a few people there. And in the CIA. And in local law enforcement in various states."

Miranda lifted her head and studied him, apprehension quivering in her stomach. "Sounds like travel. Extended travel."

"Yes, it would involve that."

Her mind started to race. Parker had been away before. She could be on her own if he needed to stretch his legs this way. Or was he getting tired of her and her problems? Maybe he just wanted a good night's sleep without her nightmares plaguing him. "Is this really what you want?"

"I think so."

She inhaled deeply. "Okay. I can handle some time alone. I've got things I'd like to do, too." She rolled over and stared at the wedding cake ceiling. It could get awfully lonely in this big house by yourself. Maybe she'd rent an apartment in town while he was away.

He sat up, took her in his arms. "I think you're misunderstanding me."

She tensed. "What am I misunderstanding?"

"I want you to come with me."

Her mouth opened and closed. So this was the "proposal?" She wasn't sure what to think. "As your trainee?" She wasn't sure she wanted that.

He grinned knowingly. "As my partner."

She scoffed. "I'm only a Level One."

"You learn well on the job."

She thought of how she'd attacked that deadbeat this morning. "You don't think I'm too much of a hothead?"

He frowned.

"After what happened this morning on that subpoena job?"

His face took on the look of the wise sage and teacher. "I'm sure it was merely a temporary slip in judgment that you won't let happen again."

"You've got a lot of confidence in me."

He took her hand, brought her knuckles to his lips. "Always more than you've had in yourself."

That was true. Most of the time. She cocked her head at him. "When do you want to start this 'proposal?'"

"Anytime you'd like."

She grinned in disbelief. "Right away? Am I really ready, Parker?"

"The only thing you're lacking is experience. This opportunity would provide plenty of that."

Yeah, it would. She'd certainly had some experience other trainees at the Agency didn't. And Parker's idea sounded great. Traveling all over, taking on all kinds of tough cases. Cases that had other professionals stumped. Wow.

The most alive and fulfilled she ever felt in her life was when she was working a case. And working at Parker's side would be a dream job. But—what about the nightmares that haunted her?

What about Amy?

She smoothed the silk comforter over her legs. "Maybe after we hear from Judge Rozeki."

His face turned to granite.

Her stomach tightened into something just as hard. "What is it?"

She watched his nostrils flare as he exhaled, then inhaled a slow, deep breath.

"Oh, my God. Did we get a reply?"

Without a word, he rose, slipped on his silk robe and marched into the huge walk-in closet.

She rolled up and wrapped the sheet around her and hopped toward the door. "Parker! What are you doing in there? Have you heard back from Chicago? From Judge Rozeki?"

He returned a moment later, a stern, pained look on his handsome face. At his side he held a large manila envelope.

Her heart began to pound. This couldn't be good. "Don't hide this from me. Tell me what's going on."

She watched him stiffen his broad, muscular shoulders to steady himself. "Oh my, dearest darling. I'd like nothing better than to hide this from you. But I know I can't do that."

"You know what it says?"

"Antonio let it slip."

What in the world was in there? She held out her hand to him and felt it tremble. "Let me see it."

"I have to warn you. I don't think you're going to like what's in this envelope. You don't have to know. We can leave it unopened."

Her stomach suddenly felt like she had swallowed cleaning fluid. "What do you mean? Is she being abused? Are her parents drunks? Drug dealers?"

"No, nothing like that. Are you sure you want to open it?"

"Yes. Yes, of course, dammit." She got up and snatched the envelope out of his hand. She sat back down on the bed and turned it over, hesitating.

Thirteen years of searching.

After Leon beat her up and tossed her out, she'd wanted to die. The thought of finding Amy again was all that had kept her alive back then. Back then she'd begged the courts to open her daughter's adoption records. She'd told them Leon had forged her name, had stolen her child.

But no one had believed her.

She'd registered with adoption reunion organizations. She'd searched neighborhoods all over the country. She'd begged everyone she could think of for help and no one would. No one could.

Except Wade Parker.

And now, here was the answer. Right in her hands was the key to where her daughter was. Who she was.

How could she not open it? How could she go on any longer not knowing?

She lifted her hand, began working at the clasp. Her fingers shaking so hard, she could barely move them.

She could hear Parker breath in and out as he stood watching her. This was at the limit of even his patience, but he knew better than to help her.

At last, she got the clasp open. Slowly she drew out the papers. And stared at them.

There was a letter from Judge Rozeki. She remembered him as a kind, elderly man who'd wanted to help her. And now, as he wrote, he was happy he could.

He was helping them. It wasn't a denial.

The next page was her motion. Her heart hammering, she skimmed over the legalese. "The Court, having examined the pleadings.—It is therefore ordered—"

She turned to the next page and saw her name neatly typed, her forged signature. A few lines down were the names of the adopting parents. The people who were Amy's parents now.

Wait. What?—What?

Right in the middle of the page was the name of the child after adoption.

She stared at it, hardly able to breathe. Pain stabbed at her stomach lining like she had the flu. Or she'd drunk a gallon of acid. Tears welled in her eyes. The letters on the page blurred. She thought she might throw up.

"Is this some kind of joke?" she croaked in a whisper.

Parker was beside her now, his hand stroking her back. "It would be a cruel one, but I wish it were."

No, Parker wouldn't joke about this and neither would Antonio. He'd helped draw up the papers. Her mind shot back to the scene in the living room tonight and the questions she'd peppered the attorney with. Parker had distracted her with a kiss. Now she knew why.

"This has got to be wrong. Judge Rozeki made a mistake."

Parker's tender look told her all he could do now was humor her. "We both know this isn't a mistake."

"But how—? Why—?"

Wiping her cheeks, she sniffed and stared down at the name again. How could it be possible? Thirteen years of agony and pain for *this*?

Her voice shook as she spoke the name printed on the page aloud. "*Mackenzie Chatham?* Mackenzie Chatham—is *Amy*?"

Parker rose and took her hand. "I'm so sorry."

Slowly, she got to her feet, though she didn't know how she could stand. The bed sheet was still wrapped around her.

She took a deep breath, steadied herself.

So that was that. That was it, huh? This was who her Amy was. A high and mighty, swollen-headed *prima donna* who'd be about as thrilled to learn Miranda was her real mother as she would be to swallow a cockroach.

"What do you want to do, Miranda?" Parker asked in a soft murmur.

She'd never known what she'd do if she ever found Amy. She'd never let herself think about it. It was too painful to dream, to hope.

But now she had. Now she knew.

She put the papers back in the envelope, crossed the room and tossed it on the dresser. "Nothing."

"Nothing?"

"The judge passed the health information we had onto the family. There's no need to make contact."

"Are you sure?" He didn't sound convinced. He came to her, put his arms around her. His handsome face was riddled with concern.

She laid her head on his strong chest. "She'd only hate me, Parker. I couldn't live with that."

He held her a long moment, rubbing his strong hands over her arms, her back. "Very well."

She heard him sigh in resignation and suddenly her whole body felt heavy. All her energy seemed to drain out of her like an emptying bathtub. She felt achy and more tired than she'd ever been in her life.

She put her hands on his chest and pushed away. "I just want to go to sleep. I'm exhausted."

She plodded back to the bed, sank down onto the mattress, stuffed her head into the pillow. She felt him lay down beside her and pull the covers over her. She closed her eyes and let herself drift. She wanted to be far away. Somewhere in another galaxy. Another lifetime.

Parker's arms slipped around her, but she couldn't face him. She could barely move.

"Leon always told me I had no right to Amy," she murmured wearily as sleep overtook her. "Guess he didn't know how true that was."

CHAPTER EIGHT

The dark tunnel closed in on him. It grew narrower and blacker as he crawled through the muck. He could barely stand the stench now, could barely keep going. Was he condemned to wallow through this rotting hole forever?

Was this hell? Or only his hell?

He pushed forward and the low ceiling of the tunnel scraped across his back. The passage became smaller, forcing his head down and into the filthy mud. His chin dragged along the ooze. He wanted to vomit.

"I'll do better next time," he cried out.

There was the usual silence. And then, the voice!

Will you?

"Yes. Yes, I promise." He started to cry. The voice. It had been so long since he'd heard it.

But last time you failed me.

"This time will be different. I won't fail you this time. Just give me a chance."

Silence. It seemed to echo into eternity.

At last the answer came.

I think you're ready now.

Ready? He was ready?

And then there was a jolt that shot through him like a searing lightning bolt. Was he being burned to death? In atonement for his sins?

With a loud gasp, he opened his eyes.

He blinked.

More darkness. But there was light this time coming from—somewhere. He lifted his head to turn toward it and pain shot up his neck.

He touched his face. Something coming out of his nose. Tubes. Beeping. He heard beeping. The air was—medicinal.

He touched his arms. There were tubes there, too. IVs. Monitors. Hospital. He was in a hospital.

He was alive.

Giddy with joy, instead of lifting his head, he rolled to the side. His vision was blurry, but he could make out a thin strip of light. From a hallway. Under a door.

He tried to raise his arm, but it felt like lead. The beeping grew quicker. His heartbeat. Was he paralyzed? No. Please, no. He clenched his fist. His fingers moved. Relief flooded him.

He breathed, waited for the beeping to slow. He couldn't attract attention.

Once more he tried to raise his arm. It was slow, shaky. But this time he did it. He placed it over his chest, lifted the other arm. He dropped it on top of the other one and began to feel with his fingers. He found the tube in the crease of his elbow, the tape. Gritting his teeth, he began to tug at it.

It took forever. Damn forever. But at last the tape came loose. Slowly he pulled out the narrow tube.

Pain rushed through him. He was so weak. So very weak.

Patience. Breath. His will would take him through it. He was a man, after all. Had a man's will. He reached out, touched the railing on his bed. He grasped onto it. Slowly. Carefully. It took every bit of strength he had, but he managed to pull himself up.

He felt around, found a button and got the barrier down.

Excited, he swung his legs over and let his feet dangle over the side of the bed. He stretched and they touched down on the cold linoleum. Slowly he forced himself to stand. He was standing.

He let go of the rail. And wobbled and fell.

Damn.

Something ripped as he groped for the bed. It was only his gown.

He was prone on the floor now. One hand holding the bar of the railing that had imprisoned him. Shadows of footsteps passed under the door. His heart banged in his chest. If they found him—No, no.

And then the shadows stopped. He exhaled. With a mighty effort, he pulled himself up to a sitting position. He touched his face, his head. His hair. Where was his hair? Someone must have shaved him.

He pulled off the Velcro, the rest of the tubes and the wrappings. Pain shot into his groin. Catheter. Get rid of it. He ground his teeth together, reached between his legs and pulled out the tube. Liquid dribbled on the floor. Urine and blood.

He wiped it up with his gown and pulled one leg under him. Holding onto the bed, he kneeled, raised himself up. Slowly, carefully he stood. He still wasn't steady, but this time he didn't drop. He was standing.

He moved his feet, turned.

His eyes were used to the darkness now and he could make out a form that looked like a closet on the opposite wall.

He shuffled to it without falling.

Breathing hard, he steadied himself against the door, then opened it. A dim light illuminated the contents. Blinking from it, he reached inside. There was a suit of clothes. Black. For a funeral. His funeral. Not his clothes. Where were his clothes?

A twitch of pain pierced his shoulder blade. And he remembered. The wine cellar. The blood. The knife.

Her.

Rage pummeled his insides. What had she done to him? Did she think she could get away with that? No, he'd show her. He'd teach her a lesson she'd never forget.

Shakily he bent and retrieved the shoes on the bottom of the closet. There was a pair of socks, underwear—a wallet.

His wallet! Cash, credit cards. Yes.

He carried everything back to the bed, used it to lean on as he dressed. It took so long, he feared someone would come in and try to stop him. But he kept his eye trained on the light under the door.

No one entered the room.

His hands shook. His arms were weak. So very weak. But he forced them to move. He had to hurry. They'd be coming for him soon.

At last he was dressed and ready. He stuffed the wallet into his pocket and began to walk. One foot after another. Slowly. Easy.

He made it to the door of his room. His heart pounded with joy and exhaustion. He was alive.

He put his hand on the knob. Turned.

The light was blinding. He raised his arm to shield his eyes. His lids didn't work. Blink, dammit, blink. Finally, he did and after a minute or so, he could see.

He looked down and started. There was a man in a chair. A uniform. A *guard?* They were guarding him.

But the man's head was leaning against the wall, his eyes shut. A gentle snore came from his open mouth.

He grabbed the door jamb as his stomach roiled. Too much exertion. He should go back and lay down. He managed to shake his head. He had to go on. Had to leave here.

The guard might try to stop him. No, he could handle the guard if he woke up. He had to get out of here. He had a mission. He had to save them. He could save the young ones.

He smiled and peered down the hall. An arrow pointed to the nurses' station. Go the other way. Find the exit.

He turned and shuffled down the hall. No one stopped him. No one was here. It must be late at night. Everyone was asleep.

The passage made a turn. He rounded it and stared down another hall. No one was here, either.

But at the end of the corridor stood a big heavy door. Exit. How could he even open it? He should go back. Crawl into that bed. Sleep until he was stronger. But they'd know he was awake.

His shoulder twitched again and he thought of *her.*

Anger welled inside him. Fury and murder fumed in his brain. Letting his rage fuel him, he hobbled to the end of the passage and shoved the door open.

By the time he got into the stairwell, he was gasping for breath. His heart pounded against his ribs. Pain ripped at his sides.

He looked at the dozen or so steps beneath him. How could he ever get down them?

Do not fail me.

The voice.

No, I won't fail you. Not this time. I promise. He grabbed onto the thick rail, felt its cold metal and forced himself to descend.

Do. Not. Fail.

I won't fail. I'll do it this time. I will. I promise, Mother. I promise.

And now it was fear that propelled him down to the door that led outside.

CHAPTER NINE

Miranda sat at her desk in her cube staring at the form on her computer screen as if it were the first time she'd seen one.

The file on her desk lay open, unprocessed. The words in them were gibberish to her. It was already past ten. She'd been at work over an hour and hadn't done a thing.

She closed the file and put her head in her hands.

Mackenzie Chatham was Amy? How could that be possible?

She'd known, hadn't she? Deep down she'd known her search for her daughter wouldn't end sweetly with kisses and hugs and happily ever after. How could it after the beginning she'd had?

She'd told herself that all she ever wanted was to know that Amy was safe and happy. That she was in a good home, being raised by good parents.

But it had been a lie.

She'd wanted more. She'd wanted to be part of her daughter's life in some way. She'd wanted Amy to know her. To forgive her for what she'd let happen to her. To love her. And maybe even, just once in awhile, to call her Mother.

No way any of that would happen now.

Miranda picked up the photo of her father and his family, all of them in Aloha shirts. She and Parker had kept in touch since they left Hawaii, just as she'd promised.

She ran a finger over her father's tan, smiling face.

Well, Dad, you've got a granddaughter. She's a beautiful, talented figure skater. But if she knew you, she'd think you were lower than dog piss.

The thought made her stomach twist with anger. Mackenzie Chatham would never know her grandfather. Or Miranda. Maybe it served her right.

She put the photo down.

She had to think about something else. She should call Coco and arrange for lunch together so she could tell her to cool it with Antonio. Yeah, that would go over great. She was a real relationship counselor. Coco would be thrilled with her advice. She'd probably drop Miranda from the guest list.

She could call Fanuzzi and ask her to talk to Coco. But Fanuzzi was even more excited about the wedding than the bride to be.

She'd always been able to talk to Fanuzzi. Maybe she should tell her about her daughter.

No, she'd just chat a little with Coco and feel her out. It would get her mind off things for ten minutes, at least.

She was about to reach for the phone when a window popped up on her computer screen. It was a text from Parker. "Can you come in here for a moment?"

Uh oh. Was she in trouble? Maybe he'd changed his mind about the Digby matter. Maybe he'd come up with an idea for handling his surrogate son and his fiancée. Or maybe he was going to talk her into going home since she wasn't worth squat today. He hadn't wanted her to come in, but what was she going to do in that big house all by herself?

"Sure," she typed and got to her feet.

CHAPTER TEN

Miranda stepped into Parker's blue-and-silver corner office and found him staring out one of the floor-to-ceiling windows at the cityscape beyond. The warm sunlight gave him an other-worldly glow.

He had on a suit of deep charcoal today, but the jacket was slung over the back of one of the fancy chairs. His white shirt had red pin-stripes that matched the silk tie of the day. His arms were folded over his broad chest. He looked weary.

"Close the door," he told her without turning around.

Uh oh. She was in trouble. "If Detective Tan has—"

He held up a hand then gestured to the speaker phone on the large glass table that reflected the light like a huge diamond in the middle of the room. "I have Lieutenant Erskine on the line. He has something to tell us."

She frowned at him as she closed the door. "What does he want?"

Lieutenant Erskine was a lead detective in the Atlanta Police Department. Did he have a case for them? That would be a first. Usually, he wanted to kick Parker's ass for poking his nose into an investigation.

Instead of answering, Parker pressed a button on the phone. "She's here now, Hosea. Go ahead."

The Lieutenant cleared his throat and the dark voice that could put the fear of God into an MMA champion came through the speaker.

"I'm very sorry to inform both of you that just before three a.m. this morning, as far as we can ascertain, Leon Groth left the premises of Brandywine-Summit Memorial Hospital."

Parker's face turned to granite. "What do you mean he left the premises?"

Miranda's heartbeat sputtered. "Is he dead?"

"No, he's not dead. He regained consciousness. The guard found his bed empty at approximately 3:20 a.m. Apparently, the guard had fallen asleep and didn't see him leave."

Miranda laughed out loud, but she grabbed the back of a nearby chair. "What a prankster you are, Erskine. What are you trying to pay Parker back for?"

There was a pause, then Erskine spoke again, his voice even darker. "This isn't a prank, Ms. Steele. I'm afraid I owe you both an apology."

She heard herself laugh again. "Are you talking about the Leon Groth that attacked me and Parker last spring? The one that's been in a coma since then?"

"Yes, Ms. Steele, I am."

"You mean he just woke up?"

"That's exactly what I mean. He roused out of his coma, found his things and made his way out of the hospital. As I said, the guard was derelict. He's been let go."

At last, Erskine's words sank in. Leon? Awake? Alive?

The light from the windows was suddenly blinding. Everything went white. Then dark. Her whole body felt like rigor mortis had set in. Her heart seemed to stop beating. Her stomach felt like it was crawling with lice. Her knees buckled beneath her and she sank into a chair.

She couldn't breathe. She couldn't breathe. Leon? Alive?

"How can that be?" she heard Parker demand. His voice sounded like an echo. "Jackson told me there was blood loss, lack of oxygen, possible brain damage."

She remembered him saying that, too. Jackson Taggart was Parker's best friend and Chief of Staff at Saint Benedictine. He would have known. He wouldn't have lied to them.

"I recall Dr. Taggart saying there was a slight possibility he could rouse."

Parker leaned over the phone and spoke as if Erskine were deaf. "Infinitesimal."

Erskine huffed in frustration. "But apparently not zero. I apologize again, Parker. I take full responsibility." But the hospital guards weren't under Erskine's jurisdiction.

Parker ran a hand through his hair, paced to the window and back. "Groth is still in a weakened condition. He couldn't have gone far."

That was right. The doctors had done surgery when they first brought Leon in to repair the holes in his lung from the knife she'd plunged into his back. They'd also had to take care of his face and remove about a million shards of glass from his body from the fight Parker'd had with him in that wine cellar. All that had probably healed by now. Still, he had to be pretty weak after lying in a hospital bed for four months.

"We're doing everything in our power, Parker." Erskine said, trying to sound reassuring and failing miserably. "We're sending out BOLOs. We're releasing the story to the news. We're organizing a manhunt with the GBI. We'll find him, Parker. I promise you. I promise you both."

Parker stared at the phone, looking as white as a sheet. "What do you want us to do?"

"Stay out of it. This is police business. It's not for civilians."

Somehow Parker managed to find his cavalier chuckle. "Hosea, do you really think we can do that after our personal involvement with Groth?"

"That's exactly why you need to, Parker."

Parker ignored the comment. "We'll do better if we work together, Hosea."

There was a long silence.

"Or would you rather I go to the Governor?"

"Suit yourself, Parker."

"I intend to. Keep us informed of your progress."

"That I can do." And he hung up.

Miranda stared at Parker for what seemed like a year. He stared back, saying nothing.

Finally, she shot to her feet, began to pace. "This can't be right. It just can't be." She stomped across the carpet to the far corner where the solid wall met the glass of the window. She raked her fingers through her tangled hair.

"It can't be," she said again. "I just called the hospital."

She turned around. Parker's face was unreadable. Confession time.

She licked her lips that had gone dry as salt. "I called after my nightmare night before last. Every time I dream about that sonofabitch, he feels so real, I've got to check to see if he's still in a coma."

"I know." His voice was gentle.

"You—know?" It was the last thing she wanted him to find out about.

"I heard you. The first time was before our wedding. I decided to let you be. Let you get it out of your system."

"You heard?" Normally, she would be furious, feeling invaded. Now she didn't feel a thing. How could this be happening? "I dream about that bastard. I dream he's coming after me. With his fists. Or a belt. Or a knife. And now he's awake. Parker—"

"What?"

She searched his deep gray eyes for answers, for sanity. "Am I psychic?"

He looked like the question surprised him. "I think you have highly tuned instincts. You're a fine investigator, Miranda."

It was the best thing he could say to her right now. And if it was true, she'd better use her skills to find that bastard.

She forced herself to snap out of the hysteria. "What are we going to do?"

"He can't have gone far in his condition. We'll find him." As he spoke, he moved to his desk, sat down, began to type. "I'm sending out an email for all employees to be on the alert for Groth. I'll have Judd and Tan form a team to coordinate with the GBI while you and I start at the hospital."

That sounded good. She felt the first trickle of relief. "Go to his room?"

He nodded. "Interrogate the staff, confirm this report, the details."

"And figure out how he left."

"And where he might have gone."

And what would happen when they did find him? If—no, when—she had to face Leon Groth again? She stared out the window, hugging herself, digging her fingers into her own flesh.

The last time she faced Leon, she'd fallen to pieces. Despite years of training and toughening herself up, when she saw him she'd turned back into the whimpering weakling she'd been when she was married to the jerk. Until she had managed to pull herself out of it.

She remembered his oily black hair hanging in his eyes, his hollow cheeks, his scraggly beard, those mean, black eyes.

One look from them had her shivering like a child.

He'd been dismissed from his job after a psych eval. He'd had to move to Texas, back in with his mother, who was about as cruel and crazy as he was. He'd found her in Texas. Then his mother died and he started following Miranda. He'd been stalking her for years. She'd felt his presence.

She thought of Wendy lying bound on the tasting table in her father's wine cellar. She thought of the two young girls Leon murdered. He drugged them. Performed what he called "purification rites" on them with oils and herbs. Tied a white ribbon around their necks.

Then he strangled them.

What had he called it? "Releasing" them. Before they were "defiled with femininity." By age thirteen, she guessed. It was almost October. Amy would be turning fourteen in November.

Her hand went to her throat. She couldn't swallow.

He said something about his mother's last wish. She wanted him to atone for what he'd done. And what he'd done was to—let Amy live.

"I want the same thing you do," Leon had said.

He wanted Amy. He said he'd find her. And now he could.

"Oh, my God. He's going to go after Amy, Parker. I mean Mackenzie," she corrected. "He'll get to Wendy and use her to get to Mackenzie, just like he did last time."

Parker studied her, she could see the alarm in his eyes. But he shook his head. "Groth doesn't know who Mackenzie is. The adoption records aren't accessible to the general public."

Like that would stop him.

She began to pace again like a trapped tiger. "What if he finds out anyway? It's what he wants. What he's intended all along. What if Mackenzie and her mother are walking around, going to the rink, going to the mall, oblivious to all this and he finds out who she is and nabs her? He'll kill her. That's what he wanted. That's why he went after Wendy. Why he stalked me."

He came to her, put his arms around her, brushed his lips against hers in a soothing kiss. It helped calm her nerves a little.

"I can put a guard on the Van Aarle house. The Chathams', too."

She studied his face a moment. It was grim and intense. He'd do everything he could. She knew that.

But she broke from his embrace and paced again. "Will that be enough? Will it stop him? You can't make sure a person's okay twenty-four-seven. Look what just happened." She gestured at the phone. "I know our people are better than that hospital guard, but still."

She came to a halt in front of his desk, watched him reach into a drawer, pull out the shoulder holster that held his Glock and slip it on. He strolled to the chair and put on his coat. He turned and gave her a knowing look. "What do you want to do, Miranda?" he said softly.

She rubbed her cheeks with both hands. What did she want to do? She'd wanted to keep this a secret. She never wanted Mackenzie Chatham to know who she was. She pulled at her hair as hot tears stung her eyes. Mackenzie was going to hate her. Despise her. Treat her like a leper. She didn't know how she was going to bear the cold stares the girl would no doubt give her. And how would Wendy take all this?

But that wasn't important now. Saving their lives was all that mattered.

She sucked in a breath and straightened her shoulders. "We have to let them know. We have to let the family know. Somehow."

"Are you sure?"

"We don't have a choice, Parker. There's no other way."

"Very well. I'll talk to the Chathams. You don't have to see her."

That was a relief, even if a small one. "Do you know them? Will they see you?"

"Only socially. I can contact Antonio and arrange a meeting with Oliver and Colby."

Oh, God. Why couldn't that bastard have just died? Why didn't she kill him when she had the chance? If she'd gone to prison for the rest of her life, at least it would have spared her daughter and her adopted family.

"I'll meet with Judd and Tan then we'll head for the hospital. Be ready in fifteen minutes. I'll meet you at the back exit."

She nodded and hurried to her desk to shut down her computer and fetch her Berretta.

CHAPTER ELEVEN

The security at the hospital was tighter than the Pentagon. As soon as Miranda hit the metal detector, all hell broke loose.

Well, people didn't usually bring weapons and an investigator's field kit when they visited their sick aunt.

Parker spent an hour sweet-talking and schmoozing the staff and they still wouldn't budge. Finally, he threatened to call someone on the Board of Directors. It wasn't until he actually pulled out his cell that somebody went to get the head honcho.

"I apologize, sir, ma'am." A short woman in a dark blue business with a thick Southern accent hurried toward them from a lime-colored hall. "After what happened last night, the guards are extra cautious."

"I understand perfectly, Ms. Franklin," Parker smiled his suave, charm-her-off-her-feet smile as he eyed the name tag that, in addition to her name read, "Head of Operations." "In fact, that's the matter we're investigating. We're helping the police find the patient who disappeared last night." He handed her his card.

That was smooth.

"Oh, well then. I'm sure there's nothing amiss." She turned to a tall, bony female in pale blue scrubs, who hardly looked of age. "Jan, please escort Mr. Parker and Ms—"

"Steele," Miranda supplied.

"And Ms. Steele to the second floor."

Without a second's hesitation, Nurse Jan, as her name tag read, led the way down to the elevators at the end of the hall and they made it through Level One of the Hospital Red Tape game.

They rode up in silence and when the doors opened again, Jan took them to the nurses' station.

Two harried-looking workers were behind it, one on the phone, the other busily typing on a keyboard. It took a few minutes before they even noticed someone was waiting.

From her not-so-secret phone calls Miranda knew Leon had been moved to the second floor a few weeks ago. She wondered whether he'd have been able to get out so easily if he'd stayed in ICU.

"I'm so sorry. I didn't see you there," one of the nurses said at last and smoothed back her dark blond hair with her hand as she stepped to their side of the counter. "How can I help you?"

Jan made a quick gesture at the visitors. "Emily, this is Mr. Parker and Ms. Steele from the Parker Investigative Agency. They're here looking into the—incident that occurred last night."

"Oh." Emily's eyes went wide. But she managed a half-smile as she took in Parker's good looks. She wasn't bad looking herself. And she seemed young, too, though the lines under her eyes were dark and crying out "overworked."

"Ms. Franklin requests that you help them any way you can."

"Certainly."

Jan turned to Parker. "Is there anything else you need from me?"

"I think we're set here now. You've been most helpful. Thank you."

"You're welcome, Mr. Parker. I'll leave you to your work then." And with a brisk nod at Miranda, she turned and swept back down the hall to the elevator.

"What do you need to know?" Emily asked.

Parker set down his investigator's kit and turned back to the laminated counter with an ingratiating smile. "Let's start with who was on duty last night."

She nodded and reached for a clipboard. After flipping a page, she frowned. "Tony was the head nurse last night. Ginger was scheduled, but she didn't come in. Priscilla's the aide. She was here."

So they were short handed. Parker leaned an elbow on the counter as if he were shooting the breeze about the weather. "How often did they check on Groth?"

Emily stiffened her shoulders. "We check patients every hour round the clock. We check vitals, IV, and in a case like Mr. Groth's, we reposition the patient at least four times a day."

Miranda nearly choked at the way she referred to the asshole. "When was he last checked?"

Again Emily consulted her clipboard. "Just before two a.m. Priscilla recorded his vitals right here." She turned the clipboard to them.

Feeling a little nauseated, Miranda glanced at the numbers.

"And when was it discovered that he wasn't in his room?"

"That would have been about three. When the next check was due."

Or not. There was no proof other than the signature of a nurses' aide.

"Do you have any idea how he might have left the building?"

"No, I'm sorry, I don't. As far as I know, no one saw him leave."

Still smiling, Parker straightened. "Can we have a look at the room?"

"Certainly."

She moved around the desk, gestured for them to follow as her noiseless nurses shoes plodded across the institutional linoleum down the hall to room two-twelve.

It was near the end of a long stretch of rooms. Yellow tape across the door told Miranda Lieutenant Erskine or some of his minions had already been here. And a new hospital guard stood at the door, since the old one had been let go.

The burly, broad-shouldered man stepped in front of the opening to block their path as they approached, like some medieval giant guarding a secret treasure. "I'm sorry. No one's allowed in here. Orders of the Atlanta PD."

This time Miranda did the honors. She dug in her pocket for her card and handed it to him. "We're from the Parker Investigative Agency. We're helping the police find the suspect who escaped from here last night."

She caught a touch of a smile at the corner of Parker's mouth at her direct approach.

The big man folded his arms. "My orders are not to let anyone in there. I'll have to clear it with one of the officers. He's due to check in in about an hour."

Miranda drew a breath, forcing herself not to get testy. "In an hour Leon Groth will be that much farther away. Do you want to be responsible for what he does during that time?"

The guard looked from Miranda to Parker to Emily.

"It's all right, Gerald," Emily assured him. "They've been cleared by Ms. Franklin."

"Are you sure?"

Miranda really couldn't blame the guy for being stubbornly cautious. All the staff must be antsy about their jobs. But she'd sure like to give him a kick to help him find some balls.

"I'll take responsibility," Emily added.

Parker cleared his throat. "I'm a personal friend of Lieutenant Erskine. I'll see to it that you don't get in any trouble."

That did the trick. Gerald gave a quick nod and loosened one end of the tape. "Don't forget I'm standing right here keeping an eye on you," he warned them as they stepped inside.

Emily crossed to the bed and pulled a switch to turn on the florescent light.

The room looked like any other hospital room.

Walls painted in a shade of greenish-blue that made you just a little queasy. A single bed. Machines and carts crowded around it. IV stand. A single visitor's chair. The bed was unmade and the tubes were still scattered on the floor.

"The police wouldn't allow us to clean and change the sheets. This isn't the usual state of our rooms," Emily said in an apologetic sigh.

Parker reassured her with a warm smile of sympathy. "I'm sure it isn't."

Her skin crawling, Miranda stepped over to the bed and eyed the tubes. "He pulled them all out, didn't he?"

Emily raised her hands. "That's our best guess."

"Didn't that make the monitors go crazy?"

The nurse put a hand to her forehead and squeezed her eyes shut. "I don't really know what happened last night, Ms. Steele. The Head Nurse is calling a meeting this afternoon of the entire staff to try to find out."

Miranda looked at Parker. He gave her an almost imperceptible head shake. They weren't here to interrogate the staff. She nodded and crossed the room to a tall white piece of furniture that looked like a closet and opened the door.

"Was there anything in here?"

"Clothing, his personal effects. Someone donated a suit and shoes. I understand his own clothes were ruined when he came in. I've only been on staff in this unit two months."

The clothes bloodied by the awful fight and the knife she'd plunged into him. "Did he have a wallet?"

"I believe so. We would have used the contents to ID him and get him recorded in the system when he came in. The police must have, too, I suppose."

Again Miranda's gaze met Parker's. That meant he probably had cash. Maybe credit cards. If he tried to use them, it would trigger an alert.

"Is there anything else? I really should get back to my station."

Parker studied the bed again. "One more question. In your professional opinion, what sort of condition would the patient have been in?"

"It's hard to say. He'd had time to heal from his initial injuries and the surgery. It's very rare, but some people do awake from a coma and go on to lead full lives."

"But he'd be in a weakened condition."

"Oh, yes. All his muscles would be atrophied. We do some limited physical therapy for the comatose, but in his case—" Her voice trailed off.

She didn't have to say it. In Leon's case, everyone thought it was hopeless so why bother?

Parker turned to Miranda, she nodded. Emily had told her all she could.

They stepped outside the room and she heard the big guard grunt in relief as he replaced the tape.

"Thank you, Emily. You've been most helpful." Parker gave the nurse one of his famously ingratiating grins and gestured down the hall. "Do you mind if we look around outside the room?" He was so smooth, so good at what he did.

She hesitated for only an instant. Hard for any woman to resist that magnetism. Parker could charm an overworked iceberg and Emily was far from that cold.

"No, that's fine," she said, smoothing her hair again. I'll be at the desk if you have any more questions." And she turned and left them to themselves.

That was easy.

CHAPTER TWELVE

Miranda gave Parker a knowing smirk. "What now?"

He took her arm, moved across the hall out of earshot of the guard and spoke softly. "It's late at night. You just woke up from a four-month coma."

"Uh huh." It certainly wasn't Miller Time.

"You're weak. Not feeling your best."

She tried to put herself in his place. "How much did he remember?"

"Depends on how much brain damage he had. We can try to confirm that with the doctors, but obviously their opinion isn't conclusive."

"Yeah. He could have total recall, full use of his faculties. He'd just be weak like Emily said."

"We'll assume that's the case until we have evidence to the contrary."

She nodded.

Leon wasn't a big man, but he always kept in shape when she'd known him. He'd been a cop, after all. He was pretty strong. She knew from personal experience he could break bone with his fists.

Thinking it through, she ran her tongue over her teeth. "You wonder where the hell you are and how you got here. You try to get out of bed, but your body is shaky. Despite how crappy you feel, something makes you want to get the hell out of here. So you pull out all your tubes, find your things, get dressed, and leave."

Parker gazed at the door. "You stand in the doorway, see there's a guard and that he's asleep."

"The guard at least had to give him a clue why he was here."

Parker nodded, he looked at the wall they stood near. There was a sign with an arrow pointing to the nurses' station.

Miranda followed his gaze. "Don't want to go down there."

"So you go the other way." He strolled down the hall to the corner.

"There's no trail of blood or fluid on the floor here," she noted.

"It might have been cleaned up."

"But we'll assume he wasn't bleeding. At least not much. His wounds had healed."

Reaching the next hall that crossed the first one in a T-shape, Parker stopped. He nodded, squinting as he peered down the passage. "And that's where you go next."

Miranda smiled at the big red Exit sign over the heavy door at the end of the hall. "Bingo."

Parker started for the door. "You're groggy, no doubt winded by now from the exertion you're not used to."

She kept close to his side. "So you move slowly, but you keep going. Something's spurring you on. You have to get out."

"No one sees you here."

"Everyone's in bed. Maybe the staff is watching TV in the break room. Or snoozing."

"Or occupied with another patient. They were short-handed." He reached the door. "At last, you're here. The door is heavy. How do you get it open?"

"Nobody here to manage it for you. So you stop, catch your breath, look around." She mimicked the movements. "You've got to get out. You don't dare stay here long. You find a way. Dig deep and find the strength." She bent, pressed the door with her shoulder and hand.

The door open, she stumbled into the stairwell, caught herself on the rail. "That wasn't easy, but you made it." She gazed down at the concrete steps. "Somehow, you have to get down those stairs."

Parker gestured to the number painted on the wall. "You can see you're only on the second floor, so there isn't far to go."

"Right. So you use this." She leaned over on the railing and dangled a foot over the first step. "And make your way down as best you can. Crawl if you have to."

She mimicked the movement, while Parker studied the stairs as he descended. "Wait. There's blood here," he said.

Miranda halted as Parker put his investigator's kit down on a step, opened it and drew out a cotton swab. He dabbed it on the concrete, then bagged it.

"Good thing we've got our own lab." And access to national databases for a match.

He grinned that sly Parker grin. "Of course, I'll tell Hosea about this but there's no harm in double-checking."

"Especially when we're faster." She walked down to the first landing. "I don't see any more fluid. Maybe he noticed it and stopped to wrap up whatever was leaking. Okay, so he got here. There's just one more set of stairs to go. By now, he's got to be dizzy and gasping like an asthmatic."

"It might have taken a full hour for him to get this far."

"Probably. The staff is still distracted. And he's probably having second thoughts about going back in and getting some medical attention."

Parker's face turned grim. "But by now, he's remembered our altercation and what he's done. He knows what sort of trouble he's facing if he tries to get help and the staff detains him."

Jail, a trial, and most likely a death sentence. "So what's he got to lose? Maybe he sits down here on the last step awhile, lets himself recover a bit from the exertion. And then?" She looked around.

There was another heavy door marked with the number one. It had a window covered with wire. She skipped down the last few steps and peered through it. "There's a door to the outside right there." She pointed off to the side where there was another Exit sign.

Parker stepped up beside her, put a hand on her shoulder as he got a look, too. It was the first steadying touch he'd had time to give her and it felt good, gave her an extra boost. If Leon could push himself through this, she could, too. "Does this door open?"

She pushed the thick handle and it unlatched. "Yep." She stepped through.

At the far end of the hall was another opening. It was painted bright blue and had large silver strips for handles. Two people in scrubs approached from a side hall, pressed the lever and the doors opened to a large room loaded with equipment. No one paid attention to them.

"There couldn't have been much activity down here last night," she whispered.

"Or everyone was too busy to notice a single person standing here."

"So he didn't linger here long."

The door to the outside was glass and she could see street traffic, trees, and buildings across the street. At night it would have been lit well enough to tell whether there were people around. Probably wasn't too many.

"You look out and when the coast is clear, you go." She pushed through it and stepped outside.

Parker came up beside her. "Not difficult at all, even with the weakness."

"Security's a lot tougher getting in than getting out."

"This isn't the best of areas."

She smirked at Parker's gift of understatement as she recalled going for a motorcycle ride with a badass gang member in a scary part of town.

Parker rubbed his chin as he studied the street. "It was warm and calm last night, so you're not inhibited by the weather."

"Fresh air probably felt good. Probably helped him revive some more. So now what?"

"Depends on what you're after."

If he was after what she thought, he'd be planning, scheming. Where would he go to do that? She blew out a breath. "If Leon kills again, the victim's family could sue this place."

"They did let the guard go."

"After the fact. Lot of good that did."

"It was an oversight we made ourselves. No one thought Groth would wake up." He gazed up at the towering structure with its beige and brown stone façade and gray tinted windows. "This hospital has been here over a hundred years. My grandmother was born here. It provides a vital service to the community."

Parker and his objectivity. He was right, but he'd have to give her a pass on this one.

They stood scratching their heads, staring at the foot traffic. The vagrants loitering under the trees in the cement divider along the sidewalk, the hospital personnel in scrubs walking this way and that on their way to lunch or the next surgery, a couple of locals on the other side of the street walking a dachshund.

She folded her arms and forced herself to think it through. "So you're out here alone, in a weakened condition."

"There's the risk of being attacked or of a police car driving by."

"You know they'll be coming for you soon so you've got to keep moving." She scratched at her hair. "Leon had to have a place somewhere when he came to Atlanta. Erskine's men never found it."

Frowning, Parker nodded. "Let's assume that's where he's headed."

She raised her palms. "How do you get there? MARTA?"

He shook his head. "Buses and trains stop running after one thirty."

"He could have jacked a car."

Again he shook his head. "Too risky. And it would have been reported by now."

Right. That would draw way too much attention. So how did the jerk get to his hidey hole? He couldn't have walked. That was too much of a stretch. She was out of ideas.

She was afraid they'd come to a dead end when a siren screamed down the street and a big white-and-red ambulance barreled toward them, then made a sharp turn.

"That's it!" She took off and trotted to the corner.

Parker watched her a moment. He loved the intensity in that frown between her brows, the flash of fire in her deep blue eyes, the dogged determination in her stride. As well as the loveliness of her lean and fit thighs, her hips, her whole body. No wonder he'd seen total strangers stare at her. And she was as oblivious to their attentions as she was to her own charm.

On the other side of the building, Miranda came to a stop and sucked in her breath.

Under a red metal awning marked "Emergency," she saw the ambulance had stopped and EMTs had the doors open and were pulling out a gurney with a bleeding man on it. In two seconds, they had the poor guy through the doors and inside.

The truck pulled away.

She rubbed her arms, feeling awful for whoever that was. Life was rough all over, she guessed.

Parker came up beside her. "And so?"

She turned to him. "Middle of the night, some people come to the emergency room like that." She gestured to where the truck had been. "Some come in their cars, maybe leave them open and run in the doors."

Once more, he shook his head. "Even at that hour there'd be too many people around to risk taking a car like that."

Probably. She looked at Parker. There was a slight breeze that ruffled his hair making him look sexier than what ought to be legal. They'd been through so much together. In her opinion he was the best investigator on the planet and she always wanted to make him proud of her whether she had a personal stake in a case or not.

But right now, she was drawing a blank.

What was she going to do? They had to find Leon. He'd be going after Wendy as soon as he could. And if he found out who Mackenzie was, he'd kill her for sure.

She took a deep breath.

He'd always hated her baby. He'd hated Miranda the whole time she'd carried her. She suddenly remembered the night her water broke and the labor pains started. He sat in his chair reading a book and refused to take her to the hospital. She'd had to take a cab.

Cab. That was it. She gasped out loud.

Alarmed, Parker grabbed her arm. "What is it?"

"Pregnant women take cabs to the hospital sometimes."

His eyes widened. "When the husband is away or they're on their own."

"Some people don't have anyone."

"Or the child comes earlier than expected and the planned help is away or sick."

"He had to have cash in his wallet so he could pay for the ride."

Parker let her go, rubbed his chin as he stared at the emergency door. "If we assume he did, and further assume it took him at least an hour to get to this spot, we have a time frame between two and four in the morning."

"Perfect time for a baby to come."

"Or some other emergency." Amazing how some sections of the same building could be dead quiet and others wild with activity at the same time.

"Right." She exhaled again, the wind out of her sails. "But how do we find the cab?"

"There are about thirty or more cab companies in the city."

Great. They were still at a dead end. She groaned out loud.

Parker was undaunted. "We'll have to find out from the hospital staff if any patients came in by taxi during that time frame. We'll talk to the patients and try to get the cab companies from them."

That sounded like fun. "From the patients? How can we get to them?"

"I have my ways."

"So we'll have to go back inside?" She almost groaned at the thought.

"And hope we can find some assistance." He started for the emergency entrance.

"Oh joy." But at least it was something, she thought. Sucking it up, she caught up to him.

The double doors opened automatically as they approached and they slipped back into the building.

CHAPTER THIRTEEN

They had to battle their way through Security again. Then almost bribe someone to let them talk to someone in Admissions. Parker had to dial up his charm to ultra-sexy—not that hard for him—to wheedle the information they needed out of the staff along with permission to speak to a few of the patients.

But it paid off.

Four hours after arriving on the hospital premises, they had talked to three patients and had the corresponding names of three local cab companies who'd dropped said patients off at the emergency room between two and four this morning. Now on to the next phase.

Which one of those companies had picked up Leon?

Miranda was raring to get to the first place of business, but when they were outside again and heading for the parking lot, Parker heard her stomach growl.

"It's been too long since you've eaten," he commented drily.

Him, too. "Been a little busy."

"I'll find a place."

"Make it fast food," she said as she trotted back to the car.

The non-answer let Miranda know Parker had other ideas. They were near Ay Chihuahua, but she knew he wasn't in the mood for another party for Estavez and Coco. Besides they had a good excuse for not showing up, so she didn't even mention it.

Instead they hit a fancy restaurant in one of his father's hotels in the heart of the city. Parker had enough clout with the valet and waitstaff to get them in and out in a hurry so it was faster than waiting in line for a cheap burger at a drive-thru.

She shook her head at the chateaubriand and the lobster tail on the menu. Too many old emotions were grinding away in the pit of her stomach to make room for much else. It was only the knowledge that this was going to be a very long day and Parker's gentle prodding that made her force down a gourmet chicken sandwich, while Parker made do with the London broil.

The meal did rejuvenate her, but she was glad when they were back in the car after thirty or so minutes and heading for the first place on their list, the Steadfast Cab Company.

On the twelfth floor of an office building near Auburn, they found a short, wide little balding man gnawing a thick wad of gum and answering phones.

His bright blue cotton T-shirt was stained under the arms and sweat poured from his forehead, which he daubed with a red bandana as he verbally directed drivers this way and that.

It took ten minutes before they could even get the harried dispatcher's attention, but finally they asked him if one of their cabs picked up a guy at the hospital last night.

After searching records while still answering phones, he located the driver. "Here it is. Cab twenty-three picked up a passenger at 3:42 a.m. this morning and took her to Brandywine-Summit Hospital. Balu, the driver, notes the passenger was a pregnant young woman."

Miranda leaned over the desk, feeling satisfied her guess was right. At least the first part of it. "Did he pick up another passenger at the hospital?" she asked again—the original question.

The dispatcher frowned and studied the computer screen. "Nope. Balu returned the cab to the depot and clocked out. Shift was over. Sorry."

Strike one. On to contestant number two.

They got back in the Mazda and zigzagged a few miles through heavy traffic down to Logan Street near I-20 to Standard Taxi.

There they found a middle-aged woman with a sour disposition and about the same information. Except her cab driver's passenger was a man who had cut off a finger with a band saw and she had to spend five minutes cussing about the blood on the cab's seat that would have to be cleaned. When Parker patiently asked for the third time if the driver had picked up a passenger at the hospital, all he got was a grunt and a, "Nope."

Strike two. Back in the car.

Three strikes and you're out. Miranda pulled at her hair as they backtracked to Piedmont. "What if this turns out to be another dud, Parker?"

She watched him set his jaw as he steered the car onto the Downtown Connector. "Then we'll find him another way."

She glanced at the clock on the dash. It was after six. The traffic on the interstate was murder. It would take them an hour to go the three miles. "How late are these places open?"

"Would have to be twenty-four seven."

How could he sound so patient? She'd never have his calm serenity under stress. Tapping her fingers on her jeans, she gritted her teeth and counted the city buildings along the skyline as they inched their way along, exit by exit.

Finally, their ramp appeared and Parker made a left, only to be stopped by a traffic light. He'd been right to take the highway. It was worse on the side streets. Now she stared at pedestrians until she thought her eyes would bleed. Finally, they turned onto a semi-residential street.

Down a steep, tree-lined hill and just past a smoothie shop she spotted a bright pink building set back from the road, with a gaudy sign reading "Triumph Transportation."

Parker pulled into the small lot.

"Here's goes nothing," she murmured under her breath as he helped her out.

This office looked about like the others. Cheap linoleum on the floor, cheap furniture, buzzing fluorescent light flickering overhead, outdated equipment.

"So how 'bout I pick you up around eight when I get off, sugar?" A skinny young man who couldn't be older than college age sat wiggling his high-top clad feet on the desk in the corner of the small office, as he murmured into a cell. "Oh yeah, darlin'. I know what you like." He snickered into the phone without seeming to notice there were visitors standing right in front of him.

Parker cleared his throat loudly.

"That's right, honey pie. I'm all over that." His thin lips spread in a sickening grin. Didn't acknowledge Parker at all.

Her eyes narrowed, Miranda marched across the room, swung her arm and knocked his feet off the desktop. "Hey, bud. You got customers."

The young man shot up with a start. "Gotta go, baby," he said into the phone and clicked off. He stared at them, looking first at Miranda, then at Parker, then at Miranda again with wide, too large eyes behind a pair of glasses.

His brown hair fell to his shoulders in curls and his T-shirt, that sported a Georgia Tech logo, fell past the desk. She'd already seen the jeans and running shoes. Must be a student who worked here after classes. And he looked too nerdy to be the flirt he'd been posing as on the phone.

"Are—are you from the Inspector's office?" he stuttered.

Parker strolled over to a filing cabinet and ran a finger over it pretending to look for dust. "And what if we are?"

"Mr. Smiggles says we're okay. He's paying the fee for the license tomorrow. He didn't mean to get behind." He smiled and nodded.

Taking the lead from Parker, Miranda smiled at the kid. "What if we don't say anything about that license in exchange for some information?"

His eyes grew even wider. "What kind of information?"

"About one of your cabs. We think one of them dropped a passenger off at Brandywine-Summit Memorial Hospital last night and picked another one up."

Now his eyes went beady. "You're not from Inspections." Bright kid. Must be getting straight As.

"We're private investigators. We're after a killer who escaped from the hospital last night."

"The guy on the news?"

Erskine's press release must have hit the air already. "That's right. If you can give us the information, you'll help us catch the suspect."

"Sure, I'll try. What do you need?"

Parker gave him the details. It took awhile, even though this guy wasn't on the phone, but at last, he came up with something. "Yes, yes. The Buick made a stop at Brandywine-Summit last night. Just before four."

"And?"

"He took an orderly whose car had broken down to work."

"Did he pick anyone up there?"

The guy squinted at the screen through his glasses, paged down a few times, frowned.

Miranda thought she could hear her heart hit the floor as it sank. They had struck out again.

"Oh, yeah. It's right here. He did pick someone up. No details, though."

She leaned on the desk, trying to get a look at the screen herself. She wasn't at the right angle. "Does it say where he took the party?"

Again he squinted at the small monitor. Miranda held her breath. Couldn't someone from a technical college read faster than that?

"Oh, I see it now. Right here. See?" He pointed as if proud of himself.

Miranda grunted through gritted teeth. "What. Does. It. Say?"

"Oh, sorry. He took the party to the Uptown Inn. Hey, that's right near my cousin's dorm. I'm not a student, but the girls dig the nerdy look. Know what I mean?"

"Was the passenger a man?"

He read again. "Yeah. He didn't have any luggage, either. Did the driver charge for that anyway?" he mumbled half to himself, then grimaced at the screen. "He did. I'm going to have to report that to Mr. Smiggles. Oh, wait. They stopped at a fast food place on Fifteenth. And a convenience store."

To get food and necessities. That was Leon, all right. "Thanks." Miranda spun and headed for the door.

"Thank you for your time," she heard Parker say curtly behind her. Then he was at her side. She was already opening the door. "We don't have a moment to spare," he murmured as they hustled down the hall. But she already knew that.

"If you are from the Inspector's office," the kid called out from his office doorway as they exited the building, "remember you promised not to report us."

CHAPTER FOURTEEN

It was seven p.m. by the time they got back to the car and traffic was a little lighter, thank God. Still, Miranda thought she was going to have a heart attack if they didn't get to that hotel in another five minutes.

Would they really find Leon there? What kind of showdown was it going to be?

Leon had to be too weak to fight them, but he could have gotten a weapon on the street in the wee hours of the morning. She started to fantasize about what she would do when they found him. What Parker would do. She could never bring back Dr. Taggart's daughter or Wilhelmina Todd's little girl. But she might be able to even the score just a little. If she could just get another chance at that bastard, she'd—

"We're here."

Miranda came out of her reverie and realized Parker was pulling the car over to the curb. The sun was starting to go down and the slash of sky between the buildings overhead was ablaze with color, but the traffic down below was still pretty heavy.

They were lucky to get a parking spot.

She got out of the car without waiting for him to come around and open the door, and gazed up at the eight-story red-brick building in the shape of a badly made wedding cake. Uptown Inn, huh? Probably one of the cheaper places to stay down here.

Was Leon really somewhere in that building?

Her heart pounding, she crossed the street and fairly ran to the entrance. Parker caught up to her just in time to open the door for her.

"Easy," he said under his breath.

Yeah, she had to calm down. She needed her wits about her. She didn't need to do anything stupid.

Taking a moment to inhale a calming breath, she smoothed her clothes and strolled across the lobby to the front desk.

A woman with caramel colored skin dressed in an uncomfortable looking black suit stood chatting on the phone to a customer and typing on a computer keyboard. "And how many nights would you like to book with us?" Her fingers paused in midair.

Evidently, the person on the other end was having trouble making up his or her mind. Something that felt like nails scraped at Miranda's stomach lining as she waited.

"Two? Friday and Saturday?" The woman hit some keys. "Oh, Sunday as well." She did some backspacing then hit some more keys. "Certainly." She had an accent that sounded Middle Eastern. Miranda couldn't place it.

But she'd sure like to delete that phone call. Instead, chewing her lip, she turned around and studied the tiled, high-ceilinged lobby, which Parker was already doing. His keen gray eyes swooped over the whole area, taking in every object and every person.

Not that there were many. An older woman in a chair near a potted plant reading a newspaper. A couple having a conversation at a simulated fireplace. A party of three heading out the door with a bellhop guiding a cart piled high with their baggage.

None of them were Leon.

"May I help you?" At last, the clerk was finished with the phone call.

Miranda let Parker take the lead on this one.

"Good afternoon, ma'am." He drew out a card from his coat, smiling that heart stopping smile. "I'm Wade Parker of the Parker Investigative Agency." He handed her the card as if he were giving her jewels.

The woman smiled back, a little flustered. "Yes, I've read about you in the papers, Mr. Parker. What can I do for you?"

Parker leaned on the counter and turned up the heat. "My associate, Ms. Steele, and I are on a case. We're looking for a missing person. We have reason to believe he could be residing in your establishment."

"Oh?" At first she sounded flattered, then her dark eyes went even darker. "It's not that man who escaped from the hospital last night, is it?"

Miranda looked at Parker. Erskine's press release was getting popular. "That's the man," she told the clerk. "We don't want to alarm your guests. If he's here, we simply want to take him into custody." Or maybe shoot him if he puts up a fight.

The clerk was rubbing her throat with her hand. "I don't know. I'm not sure what to do. I think I need to call the manager."

"Please don't, ma'am." Parker's voice was half command, half seductive plea. "First we need to determine if he's even here." He let out an almost causal laugh.

"Yes, I suppose so. His name is Groth?" Erskine's release must be detailed, then.

"We don't know if he checked in under that name, but he probably arrived here by cab between four-thirty and five this morning."

A deep frown between her brows, the woman turned to her keyboard again and let her fingers fly. Her shoulder rose and sagged. "Only one party checked in during that time span. A single man. Under the name Trevor Jones. He paid cash."

A credit card would mean he'd have to use his real name.

"What room is he in?" Miranda said, forcing her voice to sound steadier than she felt.

"I—I don't know if I'm supposed to divulge that information under the circumstances. If you let me get the manager—"

Parker leaned close to her, as if he were a spy on a secret mission. "As you may know, Groth is a suspected killer. Not someone your guests would welcome as a neighbor. If you'll help us, we can have Groth out of here without the knowledge of any of your other patrons. If the manager gets involved, I can't promise that."

Especially if he were the anal type who'd want to fill out forms or check everything out by calling the police first, Miranda thought.

The woman looked from Parker to Miranda and back again, weighing the risk. Miranda's gut twisted into a triple knot.

At last the woman nodded. "He's on the fourth floor. Room four-twenty." She grabbed a key, told another clerk to watch the desk, came around the counter and led them to the elevators.

The elevator had worn brown carpet, paneling that looked like it had been there since the fifties, and a faint musty smell. She'd been right, Miranda thought, hugging herself and resisting the urge to tap her foot as they creaked upward. Despite the fancy veneer of the lobby, this was a pretty cheap place. Leon would have to be watching his pennies.

She glared at the floor numbers as they flashed overhead. One. Two. Three. Four. At last.

The elevator slowly came to a stop and the doors eased open. She was through them in a flash, Parker and the now irritated clerk hurrying to match her strides.

The room was down the hall. Four-oh-two, four-oh-four, four-oh-six. Hell, why was it so far away? Round a corner. Four-ten, Four-twelve, Four-fourteen. Around another corner.

Four-sixteen, four-eighteen. At last.

Four-twenty.

Catching her breath, Miranda stopped and stared at the numbers. Her heart was beating in her ears.

The clerk stepped to the door and started to knock. Parker caught her arm. "Let us handle, this. Please."

She blinked at him in shock, then nodded.

"We simply need you to open the door," he said in a half whisper.

By her expression, she didn't like the request. She hesitated and for a moment, Miranda thought she was going to go back downstairs and get the manager. But at last, she slipped her card in the slot.

The door clicked opened. Parker put a finger to his lips. "Stay out here while we go in. If anything happens call 911."

Her eyes went wide, but she nodded and stepped back.

Slowly Parker drew his Glock and pushed the door open.

Behind him, Miranda slipped her Beretta out of the back of her jeans.

Together they went in. Silently, stepping lightly, sweeping the air with their weapons as they went. No one in the bathroom.

Miranda stepped inside the small space, pulled back the shower curtain. Tub was empty. Used towels on the floor. In the trash was a bandage, dried blood on the gauze. Her skin started to crawl.

She turned back to the tiny hallway. Parker was scouring the closet, but no one was hiding there. No clothes, either.

They tiptoed into the main room. A light was on, the bed unmade. Two chairs at the window, no one in them. She stared at the rumpled covers feeling queasy at the thought that Leon had slept here.

Parker strode to the bed and gave it a light kick. The mattress sat on a hard box so no one could be lurking under it.

They looked at each other and she read the irritation on his face that matched the frustration chewing her gut away. Then at the same time, they marched to the glass door leading to the patio. Parker slid it open with one swing and they stepped onto the small slab of concrete.

Nothing.

The tiny terrace was as empty as the room.

Miranda peered over the decorative railing, listened to the sound of traffic below, cars swooshing by in the dim twilight. "Long drop down," she murmured.

"He didn't go out this way."

Her throat tightened. He was gone.

"Is it safe to come in?" The worried desk clerk called from the doorway.

"Your guest isn't here," Parker told her as they both stepped back into the room.

"I don't understand."

Miranda glanced at the phone on the nightstand. "He might have called another cab. Do you have a record of outgoing calls?"

"Yes, we do. We also have a payphone in the lobby. It's rarely used, but the manager keeps it for some of our eccentric regular guests."

"Can you check the phone record for this room?"

"Yes. Yes, I will. But I think you'll have to contact the phone company for the payphone."

Parker had some connections there, but he might not be able to get hold of them at this hour.

"What do we do now?" Miranda whispered as they followed the clerk back down the hall to the elevator.

"We'll call Hosea. His men can comb the room, canvas the area for anyone who might have seen him."

Canvas folks on a busy city street and people coming and going in a hotel. Good luck with that.

"We can see what the phone records tell us. And Hosea will want to set up surveillance around the hotel in case Groth comes back. We can help with that."

"Yeah, that would be good." But she knew Leon wouldn't come back here and so did Parker.

When the squads arrived, they had a long talk with Erskine and told them everything they'd learned. He dispatched a team to gather the evidence from room four-twenty, as well as officers to interview the other guests and watch the entrances and exits front and back.

Miranda followed Parker back to the Mazda and they sat staring at the hotel's front doors until two in the morning. The phone records came back. Leon didn't make a single call.

Miranda rubbed her forehead in agony. "How did he leave? Where did he go?"

Parker let out a deep sigh. "We'll find out more in the morning." He gave her a tender look. "You're exhausted. Let's go home and get some rest."

She didn't have the energy to argue.

They drove back to the Parker estate in silence, showered and fell into bed. Feeling as if her whole body was made of lead, Miranda squeezed her eyes against the wave of dread that shivered through her. Wendy. Mackenzie. She had to save them from that monster.

The fact that Agency guards were at both houses eased her fears only a little. She was too tired to fight off the relentless anxiety. Too weary to think of anything more she could do.

As sleep came over her, all she could think was that Leon was out there.

Waiting.

CHAPTER FIFTEEN

He squinted through his sunglasses at the pot-bellied man coming down the walk of the white frame split level. Colorful flowers and well-trimmed shrubs bordered the green lawn. Took good care of the place. A good sign.

"Man, you're an early riser." The homeowner, who was dressed in jeans and a ball cap, had one of those thick, good-ole-boy accents he despised. Flesh jiggled under a wrinkled tan T-shirt and slippers flopped on his feet as he navigated the cement steps leading to the driveway.

"I'm glad I caught you at home."

"I'm usually here on Saturdays. Family's still asleep inside." He chuckled as he extended a hand. "I'm Gary, by the way."

"James," he told him forcing a smile. "Is that the vehicle?"

"That's her."

A nineteen-year-old Lexus sat parked along the curb. It was a nice midnight blue, almost black. The windows were shaded. Not as dark as he'd like but they would do. "Does it run?"

"Like a top." He dug in his pocket for his keys, sidled over to the driver side door, unlocked it and got inside. With one leg still on the pavement, he turned the key. The engine sputtered but started after a moment. "Wanna take her for a spin?"

Not really, but he'd better. "Sure." He got behind the wheel and the man ran around and climbed in next to him. Trusting sort.

They drove around the block, the motor choking like it had the whooping cough.

"She just needs a new set of spark plugs," the man reassured him with a fat-cheeked grin.

He'd like to pull over, tell this asshole to get out and take off, but he couldn't risk the attention of the police. Besides, he was a law abiding citizen. Instead he drove around the block and stopped the car in front of the split level again.

They got out and shut the doors.

"Well, what do you think?" the redneck said eagerly.

He needed wheels. He'd had to hitchhike last night from that flea-bitten hotel where he'd grabbed a few hours sleep to the house in the abandoned subdivision where he stayed before. After throwing up most of the junk food he'd bought, he'd slept the entire next day.

He'd woken before dawn today, feeling a little stronger. And he'd found the wad of cash he'd taped under the sink.

Once he had a vehicle, he could get to a health food store and stock up on protein drinks and vitamins. He'd get some exercise bands and weights and start working out. He would get his strength back.

He'd need disguises, too. Wigs, clothes. Sooner or later, someone would recognize him in this suit from the hospital. He'd found the clothes he worn before full of mildew.

He made a show of studying the Lexus. "I'll give you two thousand for it."

The man made a gagging sound. "You joshing me, James? It's worth three times that much."

"Your ad said twenty-two."

"My ad said twenty-five fifty."

He didn't want to spend that much. He had a good bit of cash now, but he'd need it for gas and some decent meals as well as his other expenses. And enough for a plane ticket if he had to run.

"It has a dent." He pointed to a long gash over the fender.

"That's just cosmetic. It can be rubbed out easy." He patted the hood as if it were a pet. "This baby runs real good. I took extra special care of her."

It did look well cared for. Except for the dent. He supposed he could replace the plugs. "Twenty-three."

"Come on, man. Twenty-four."

"I can't do that. I'm sorry." He turned to go, started for the sidewalk.

"Twenty-three fifty," the man called after him.

Hiding a smile, he stopped and turned back around. He had him now. "Twenty-three."

The man grimaced, took his ball cap off and scratched his head. "Aw, hell. Okay. I wouldn't do it if we didn't need the money so bad. Wife just got laid off."

"It's a deal then." They shook hands and he reached for his wallet.

CHAPTER SIXTEEN

Miranda brushed the hair out of her face, rolled over and stared out the tall bedroom window at the painfully bright blue sky. "What time is it?"

"Almost nine."

She turned her head and saw Parker standing alongside the bed already dressed in a power suit. An ensemble of dark blue and white silk shirt, with an understated tie that indicated clearly who was in control. He had his cell in one hand, a huge mug of coffee in the other.

He handed her the cup. "I spoke to Hosea about half an hour ago."

She sat up and took the coffee. It was that pricey, imported stuff he liked and it smelled wonderful. "Did he get anything yet?"

"They've verified it was Groth who stayed at the Uptown Inn last night, but they've found nothing to indicate where he might have gone. No witnesses remember seeing a man of that description."

She took a sip of the delicious dark liquid. "Yeah, that's about what we expected."

"Erskine has people surveilling the area within a ten-mile radius of the hotel. We can do the same after I finish my errands this morning."

Errands? She knew that was understated code for something but wasn't ready to ask what. "How likely are they to find him with so much ground to cover? How likely is it that he's still in that area?"

"The odds aren't in our favor. Nonetheless it has to be done."

Yeah, there was nothing else to do until they got a decent lead. If they got one.

Parker moved to the dresser, put his keys and wallet in his pockets. She eyed the shape of his body under those expensive clothes, the fluid movement of his muscles. "I've also spoken with Antonio."

"Yeah?" They couldn't have been discussing the engagement party she and Parker had missed last night.

Parker turned back to her, caught her gaze with those deep gray eyes. "He's arranged a meeting with the Chathams' this morning."

Her whole body tensed. "Oh," she whispered and tried to swallow with a throat going dry, despite the coffee.

"Mackenzie is riding with Jordan McFee and her mother to the ice rink today. Colby cleared an hour to see me." His voice was tender as a guardian angel's.

She put the mug down on the nightstand and smoothed the silky white covers as she forced down the emotions bubbling up inside her. "Sounds good."

"Miranda, do you still want to do this?"

She put her hands to her head, feeling a migraine coming on. "I don't want to. But I have to. Nothing's changed, Parker." She looked up at him, feeling helpless.

Parker's heart broke anew for her.

She looked so beautiful, sitting there cross-legged in her pale blue T-shirt, her dark hair more awry than usual, her intense blue eyes pleading with him. If only he could do something. If only he could fix this. But there was nothing to be done but go through the motions and pray they'd all come out on the other side.

They would find Groth. He or Hosea or someone from the GBI would put that psychotic monster away and then they'd be done with him forever. He had to believe that.

After that—well, then they'd figure out how to pick up the pieces of their lives.

He watched her lovely face grow determined, her dark brows draw together in purpose.

Enough of this wallowing around in self-pity, Miranda thought. She pulled the covers off and got to her feet. "If Mackenzie's at the ice rink, Wendy will be there, too. I'm going up there."

His heart sank. He'd been hoping he could talk her into staying here at home until he returned. Foolish thought. "I do have Agency guards on Wendy and Mackenzie, you know."

Her eyes flashed with annoyance. "Of course, I know that, Parker. I need to talk to Wendy myself. Tell her about Leon. Tell her—to be cautious. If I can get the kid to listen to me."

He came around the end of the bed, caught her by the arms. In only T-shirt and panties, with her long, muscular legs and bare feet, she was sexier and lovelier than any woman he'd ever known. She made his heart ache. He wanted to protect her, even though he knew she could take down a two-hundred pound man with the martial arts skill she had.

"What?" Her brow creased with irritation.

"I just want to hold you a moment."

She slipped her arms around his neck, gave him a quick kiss, then pulled away. "I've got to get dressed and you've got to get going."

Reluctantly, he let her go. "I intended to stop by the Van Aarles' and speak to Iris after I leave the Chathams' place. She may have already seen the press release."

"Do that. I'd rather not talk to the woman." She moved to the closet, began tugging on a pair of jeans.

He nodded, glanced at his phone. "After that I have another appointment with a client. I had to cancel yesterday and I rescheduled for just before noon today." Patricia had texted him four times begging him to stop by and help her with the missing jewelry problem she was having.

It seemed so trivial now. But she was an old friend. He had to honor his promise. Besides, if he didn't, she would keep texting until he did.

"Okay." Miranda pulled on a rust colored T-shirt, grabbed a brush and made the useless effort of raking it through her hair.

"Must you really go to the ice rink?" His voice was soft and low.

Miranda turned around, saw the concern riddling his handsome face. This was tearing him up as much as it was her. "I just have to, Parker."

He nodded, his expression understanding mingled with disappointment.

She hurried over to him, put her arms around his neck again. "I love you, Wade Parker. I can't get through this without you. But you have to let me work it out my own way."

"I love you too. And you have to let me worry about you." He touched her hair, ran his gaze over her face, gauging her, then bent his head and kissed her. It was deep and intense and for a moment, she longed to forget about Leon and Mackenzie and Wendy and everything and hop into the sack with him. But that wouldn't solve her problems.

She pulled away. "Deal."

"Be careful, Miranda."

"I will."

She watched him fight with his overprotective nature. "How would you like to meet me at Tamarind Gardens for a late lunch? Say around one?"

Change of subject. She had to grin. "That place with the extra spicy sausages?"

The distinguished looking lines in his handsome face creased as his eyes twinkled in a sly smile. "That's the one." He'd taken her there last week just to test the limits of her heat tolerance, or so he'd claimed. She'd loved the place.

He never would stop wining and dining her. Or taking care of her. She'd never wanted to be dependent on a man after Leon. She'd always taken care of herself. She'd been terrified she'd lose that autonomy if she got serious with Parker, that she'd get spoiled and needy and turn into something weak and easy to take advantage of.

Instead, she was discovering she kind of liked the attention.

"Okay. Tamarind Gardens sounds nice. Pharr Road, right?"

"Good memory."

"It's a date, then." She pulled on her sneakers, gave him a peck on the cheek and hurried out the door.

"What are you having for breakfast?" he chided at her side as they hustled down the grand staircase to the elegant foyer.

She had to laugh as she shook her head. "Don't worry. I'll grab a protein bar."

CHAPTER SEVENTEEN

The house looked the same as he remembered it.

An expansive castle of limestone and shale with tall gothic windows and a well-manicured yard. Emblems of people who had more money than was good for them. He remembered the back yard and its trees. He remembered the back entrance that led to the wine cellar.

His victory, his defeat. His shoulder tingled. Don't go there. It was only a temporary setback.

He reached for the green concoction he'd bought at a downtown health food store and took a sip through the straw. It tasted awful, but it seemed to give him a lift. He had to drink slowly though. He couldn't afford to be vomiting while he was working.

His gaze traveled across the street and he saw a nondescript sedan parked a few yards away. The windows were dark, like the Lexus, but it looked like someone was sitting in it.

Had that detective sent someone to watch the girl?

Well, he should have expected as much. The detective was smart and his escape from the hospital was already all over the news. He'd read about himself in the paper this morning. There was a picture, too. His face, enhanced with the weight loss and shaved head after his hospital stay.

He'd learned he'd been there four months and everyone, even the top doctors, thought he was as good as dead.

Well, he'd surprised them all, hadn't he?

But the police and that too-smart detective weren't going to make this easy for him. He'd handle it. He'd already had the spark plugs replaced in his vehicle so the engine wasn't as noisy. He'd been to a thrift store this morning and bought several sets of clothes, all different styles and colors.

He was wearing a baggy red sweatshirt and jeans right now. And he had on a long blond wig he'd found in a shop in a strip mall. Through his tinted windows, he must look like a woman. He started to laugh at that idea, but his ribs ached. He took another sip of the nasty drink. He was getting stronger.

The front door to the mansion opened and the girl bounded out.

There she was. The corner of his mouth began to twitch as he watched her skip down the walkway to the Mercedes parked in the drive. The mother was behind her looking annoyed and distracted. It would be so easy to take them both right now.

But that wasn't the plan.

He waited until they got in the car, backed out and started down the street. He waited longer until the sedan started and went around the block to follow them. He did likewise.

He kept back, slowly like someone lost in the neighborhood until they came to the main road that led to the interstate. He put on his signal indicating he was turning the other way and after the sedan had turned, waited until it was over a hill to turn left instead. He caught sight of the sedan again just as the driver was about to get on the ramp.

Once on the interstate there was more traffic for cover but he worried, wondering how long this trip would be. They were heading north. What on earth did these people do with themselves that required such an expedition?

Some trivial and useless pastime for females, like shopping, he supposed.

He thought they might be going to Chattanooga when the sedan took an exit and began winding its way along a series of two-lanes. After about fifteen minutes, the Mercedes pulled into a parking lot in front of a large beige brick building.

He read the sign. "Marietta Ice Rink."

Ice skating? What a ridiculous place to take a young girl. She should be learning how to cook and clean.

The lot was already crowded. The Mercedes pulled into the nearest space available to the front door, still several cars away. The sedan circled the building and after a moment he could see its headlight peeking around the corner.

Had to be discreet. Look like he belonged here. He steered the Lexus into a spot in the opposite row and turned off the engine. He adjusted the mirror so he could see both the Mercedes and the sedan.

The passenger door of the Mercedes opened and the girl got out. Her mother remained in the van.

Two girls about the same age came over to her and started talking. One wore a long dark braid and glasses. The other had lighter, curly hair. She was giggling like a silly hyena.

What on earth could they be jabbering about?

Some of the vehicles left, others took their place. More young girls got out of them, some in groups, some accompanied by an adult female.

He began to breathe hard.

Was one of them her? The one he was looking for? She could be anyone, anywhere. Anywhere in the world. What was he doing here?

His heart began to race. He grabbed the health drink and began to sip. He put it down. It was making him queasy now.

How was he going to do this?

You must do it. You must.

Yes, I must. But it wouldn't be easy. The child was almost fourteen now and he'd have to hurry.

He was almost gasping when he caught sight of a new red sports car that had just driven into the parking lot. He watched it pull into a space at the end of the walkway, shut off. The door opened. And a woman got out.

Her. It was her.

He took in her scrawny body, her ugly dark hair as untamed as she was. Someone ought to shave it off. She was dressed in jeans and a dark T-shirt. Form-fitting. Slutty. Like the whore she was.

His shoulder began to throb.

There were more young girls getting out of cars and going into the building. More mothers. Too many. Far too many of them. His head began to pound in time to his hammering heart.

He could smell their femininity. Their inferiority. Their wickedness. Oh, that awful stench of womanhood. He remembered how his mother would put his face in it when she bled.

His stomach roiled with it. He had to get out of here.

He put the car in reverse and managed to make it through the lot and onto the side street. He drove around the block. As soon as he was out of sight of the building, he pulled the car to the curb, threw open the door and heaved.

The green liquid from the health food store splashed onto the pavement until there was no more in him. He stomach convulsed without giving up anything else for what seemed like half an hour.

At last it stopped. His ears were ringing. But he could still hear her.

Are you going to do it, son? Are you going to release her?

Closing the car door, he wiped his mouth on his sleeve and nodded. "Yes, Mother," he whispered hoarsely. "Yes, I will do it. I promise." Somehow, he would. He had to. It was his destiny.

Miranda got out of the Corvette and leaned against its side after shutting the door. Right away she spotted Wendy talking to Jordan McFee and a couple of other girls beside Iris's Mercedes. Wendy was in black tights and a short teal and pink outfit with matching pink ballet slippers today.

Miranda didn't see Mackenzie. Too good to mingle with the lowlifes, no doubt.

A shudder went through her as she remembered who Mackenzie was. Still hard to believe. Impossible to believe. She'd never get used to it.

Squinting, she could see Iris inside the van. She didn't look like she'd seen the press release. She was talking on her cell through a headset, batting her hands in the air like an overly dramatic orchestra conductor.

That's right. Don't even pay attention to your own daughter when she's right there in front of you. Miranda's heart filled with tenderness for the kid.

Even with her mother and her obsession with Mackenzie, Wendy finally had something close to a normal life. She had friends and laughter and fun.

And now Miranda was about to shatter that with the news about Leon. News that would turn her normal life back into the nightmare she'd been living when Miranda had first encountered the girl in a schoolyard.

The thought made chills run up and down her spine. She scanned the parking lot, feeling as if she were missing something.

She'd seen the guard from the Agency parked alongside the building and it gave her some reassurance. Still, something felt off.

The lot was pretty crowded. Lots of coaches and "rink moms"—what else would you call the equivalent of soccer moms?—dropping their kids and their friends off or accompanying them inside. Vehicles coming and going, a few fancy, high ticket models. Lots of vans and SUVs. What else would a rink mom drive?

One caught her attention. An older Lexus, dark blue, with a gash in its fender. It was parked across the row about six or seven spots down. Its windows were dark, but the driver inside looked like a woman. Some single mother who'd managed to scrape enough together to give her daughter pricey skating lessons?

Maybe the good car was in the shop. Maybe this one belonged to the teen in the family. Still, something about that vehicle was unsettling. The engine turned over. Slowly it backed up and headed out the exit at the opposite end of the lot.

Miranda craned her neck. She couldn't see the plates.

Her gaze went back to Wendy. The kid had finally noticed her and was glaring at her with red hot anger. She broke away from the group and came trotting over. Uh oh.

"What are you doing here, Miranda?" she snapped as soon as she was near.

Miranda grimaced at her. "Good morning to you, too."

She ignored the comment and hissed under her breath so her friends wouldn't hear. "Didn't I say you didn't have to pick me up any more?"

Miranda looked down at her nails. Free country, she wanted to say. But this was too important. "I have something to tell you, Wendy. And it isn't good."

Wendy rolled her eyes. "What? Are you going on a trip or something? Do you think I'd miss you?"

That stung. The kid was obviously still royally pissed about the ice skate incident yesterday. But this ought to sober her up. "I hate to tell you this—" How could she say it?

Wendy groaned. "What? I have to get back."

"Leon's out of the hospital."

Her dark eyes blazed and her face twisted in disbelief. "What?"

"Leon Groth. You remember him, don't you?"

"Of course, I remember him." Her voice was shaky now. "But you're not making any sense. I thought he was in a coma and he wasn't coming out of it." What everyone had told her. What everyone had told Miranda, too.

"The doctors were wrong. Leon woke up early yesterday morning and escaped."

The noise of kids and cars seemed to go dead still. Wendy's eyes went wide, she gave a little gasp, then wrinkled her nose as her lips pursed out, flattened. She glanced down, kicked at the black pavement with her hot pink slipper.

All at once she glared at Miranda, eyes blinking like a police siren, as if Miranda were a total stranger. "You're lying."

Miranda felt her throat go tight. "No, I'm not."

"You are too." She spun around to go.

Miranda caught her by the arm. "I'm not lying, Wendy. Why would I do that?"

She turned back, teeth bared like an animal caught in a trap. Her eyes were wet now, her girlish voice breaking. "You're just jealous of how much time I spend with Mackenzie. You're trying to spoil things. You're trying to ruin everything."

Miranda lowered her voice. "I'm trying to keep you from getting hurt. I want you to be careful. He could come after you again."

Again Wendy stared at her, her deep brown eyes glistening like chocolate drops. Was the message sinking in at last? And what would it do to her when it did?

A car door slammed nearby.

Miranda looked up and saw Mackenzie moving away from another SUV, her back perfectly straight, her head high, her nose in the air. She didn't acknowledge any of the other girls who were staring at her in awe, but it seemed as if she were emitting an unspoken command to follow her into the building, which they all did, including the harried coach, who was laden with backpacks and equipment.

There was her daughter. A pompous, spoiled little brat. Miranda felt sick.

"I've got to go." Wendy jerked out of her grasp and with a final sharp glare that felt like a stick in the eye, she ran to catch up with the others.

Miranda stood hugging herself. She lifted a hand and pressed her fingers against her temple. Now didn't that go well?

She wanted to run across the lot, bang on Iris's window and tell her the news. She wanted to go inside and tell Mackenzie and her coach to be careful. But she knew she'd better let Parker handle it. People listened to Parker.

Feeling like she'd only made things worse, she got in her car and left.

CHAPTER EIGHTEEN

Miranda cruised down I-75, going faster than she should, punching at the radio buttons, trying to find some heavy metal rock to take her mind off her latest disaster. She had a couple of hours to kill before she had to meet Parker for their lunch date and she'd intended to stop by Coco's for that don't-rush-into-marriage talk she'd been meaning to give her. Wouldn't she be convincing in this mood?

She hit another button and caught a snatch of a newscast.

"Lieutenant Erskine further states that the police have some good leads and expect to capture Groth in a few days."

Yeah, right. That was an editorial stretch.

"In the meantime, if you have any information regarding the suspect who allegedly killed two young girls last May, please call the Atlanta Police Department." The newscaster gave the number, then another voice came on. This one sultry and feminine.

"Stay tuned right after the news for my own take on these developments. Have I got some juicy details for you today! This is Tanya Terrance. Join me in just a few moments for *The Talk of the Town*." Silly theme music played.

Tanya Terrance, huh? Miranda hadn't listened to her show in ages, but she remembered seeing the elegant, long-necked beauty at a fancy dinner months ago. And learning that she and Parker had been a number before she'd met him.

So what could this socialite-slash-talk-show-host have to say about Leon that was so juicy?

She waited through several boring commercials and a rather self-indulgent intro to find out. At last, the low, sultry voice kissed her eardrums again.

"Hello, everyone.Tthis is Tanya Terrance, your personal finger on the throbbing pulse of the most exciting town in the south—Hotlanta." Oh, brother. "What has everyone in town talking today? I'll tell you." Her voice grew lower and ominous. "The escaped serial killer, Leon Groth."

Miranda bristled. What did this blue-blood know about Leon?

Now the voice took on a whispery tone, as if she were sharing a deep, dark secret with her listeners. "As you know, the suspect is suspected of killing two young girls last May and may also be guilty of the death of a woman in Pittsburgh. As my regular listeners may remember, Wade Parker of the Parker Investigative Agency was involved in the altercation that led to Groth's injuries."

Miranda gritted her teeth. This bitch better not say anything about Parker.

"Here's what Dr. Stahl, an ER surgeon on the staff of Brandywine-Summit had to say."

A soft-spoken voice began to describe the procedure they'd performed on Leon when he first came in to the emergency room. "I can't really explain what happened to Mr. Groth or why he woke up after four months in a comatose state. His initial injuries were very severe. We had no hope for his recovery. All I can say is it would be a miracle, if the patient weren't so—notorious."

"Notorious, indeed," Tanya continued, her voice even more layered with secrecy. "But we all know how Groth wound up in the ER on that fine spring day, don't we? Miranda Steele."

Miranda's nostrils flared. She glanced in the side mirror to make sure she wasn't about to ram another car.

"As my listeners know, Miranda Steele married Wade Parker this past August and, well, wasn't that a bizarre event?" The low laugh took on a wicked edge.

Miranda thought her teeth would crack from gritting them. She was shivering all over.

"But listen to this! I've learned from a very trusty confidential source that Ms. Steele was once married to Leon Groth. Can you believe that? And that they had a very—well, let's just call it a *tumultuous* relationship."

Bitch! Miranda slammed on the brakes and jerked the Corvette onto the road's shoulder. The ZR1 screeched to a halt just as a pickup truck squealed past her, blaring its horn.

"Go to hell!" she screamed at the driver as she smashed her palm against the radio to shut it off.

She put her hands on her face, her head pounding so hard she thought it would blow up like a stick of dynamite. She'd been in the news after the fight with Leon, but all that was said was she was an employee from the Parker Agency and she'd discovered the man who'd been murdering kids in Buckhead. She'd been portrayed as a hero. Nothing had been revealed about her past with Leon. It was mortifying. Something she'd told only a few people. The last thing she wanted anyone to know.

And now everyone in the whole freaking place did.

Who? Who could have told Tanya Terrance about her relationship with Leon? It didn't matter. It was Terrance who'd gone public with it. She remembered the woman's glittering indigo gown at the fundraiser. A piece of scum dressed up in fancy rich-girl clothes.

Whatever outfit she was wearing today, Miranda would bloody it for her.

She punched at the GPS to find the radio station's address, swung back onto the highway and headed there. That bitch would be sorry. Let's see how she sounded on the air tomorrow with a fat lip and a couple of missing teeth.

CHAPTER NINETEEN

As Parker turned his Mazda into the steep, shady drive that led to the Pendleton estate, memories of his youth came back to him. He was eleven or twelve when his grandfather first brought him here for a Sunday lunch with the family and their young daughter.

His heart warmed at the sight of the ancient white oaks casting shadows over the wide, white veranda, with its tall ionic columns. He and Patricia used to play checkers on that porch and drink sweet tea or lemonade in the cool of a summer evening. A time of youthful innocence. A time before Sylvia, even before Laura, his first love. A time of slow, pleasant days that he could never recapture.

With a nostalgic sigh, he parked his car, got out and strode to the front door to ring the bell. It didn't take long for a familiar face to answer it.

The small woman in a demure black suit had short gray hair and a brilliant smile in her pale blue eyes. "Well, hello there, Mr. Parker. It's been a long, long time, hasn't it?" There was the familiar hint of an Irish brogue in her motherly voice.

"Hello, Maddie. How have you been?" Parker took her hand in his, shook it tenderly, remembering the sandwiches this motherly woman had served him on this very veranda along with that delicious homemade lemonade.

"As well as can be expected, as you see I'm getting on in years."

"Nonsense. You don't look a day over thirty."

Her musical laugh made him feel right at home. "What a liar you are, sir. But come in, come in. No need to stand on the porch. Miss Patricia is expecting you."

"I believe I'm a little early." He stepped into the expansive foyer and caught the fragrance of fresh-cut roses.

The entrance was similar to his family estate. The marble floor had been imported from the same foundry in Italy where his father acquired the stones for the Parker mansion's entrance hall. But with its twin staircases curving around the exterior, and its antique settees along walls covered with pastel murals of idyllic landscapes, the Pendleton home had a decidedly ethereal feel.

"Not early at all." Maddie strode across the floor to one of the drawing rooms, then looked up and stopped. "Ah, there she is now."

Patricia appeared at the banister overhead, adjusting an earring, her handsome face glowing. "Wade, I'm so glad you're here." That low, sultry voice floated down like an old Southern song.

He watched her descend the stairs with a liquid, not-too-hurried gait that flattered her every curve.

She wore a fitted satin peach blazer with matching slacks. Strings of small golden spheres adorned her graceful neck. The blazer was low cut, revealing her ample bosom.

He averted his gaze to her face and her rich red hair as he reached for her hand. "How are you this morning, Patricia?"

"Busy, but you couldn't have arrived at a better time. My, aren't we formal." Laughing, she bypassed the hand and tossed her arms around his neck in a welcoming hug. "So nice of you to stop by, Wade. Come, let's go into the sitting room." She drew a friendly arm through his and led him into the classically furnished space.

"No need for refreshments just yet, Maddie," she called to her head housekeeper. "Mr. Parker and I want to catch up for a bit first."

"Very good, ma'am."

He watched her reach for the golden handles and pull the tall white double-doors shut. She put a hand to her breast as she turned to him with a look of relief.

His brow rose as he spoke softly. "You don't suspect Maddie of stealing your jewels, do you, Patricia?"

"Oh, heavens, Wade. I hope not. I really don't know what to think. I can't believe it of any of my staff. They've all been with me forever." She looked lost and bewildered. His heart went out to her.

"Facts are the only way to sort something like this out and that's why I'm here."

"Yes, I need to keep my head, I suppose." She laid her fingers against her cheek, let the little one dangle to her full mouth. He noted the peach-colored gloss on her shimmering lips that matched her nails. "What do you propose?"

"A few well-placed surveillance devices should tell us what we need to know."

Shock colored her features. "Hidden cameras?"

"Precisely."

"Oh. I hadn't thought of that." Her brow in furrows, she crossed to the ornate fireplace under a large portrait of an eighteenth-century soldier on horseback. "How would they work?"

He gave her a reassuring smile. "I would discreetly position several units in the room where you keep the jewels. The units would be monitored from the Parker Agency."

She seemed both surprised and impressed. "Twenty-four-seven?"

He nodded. "The feed would be recorded. Someone would periodically check them."

"You?"

"Or one of my staff. And if you notice the incident occurring again, you can report it to us and we can zero in on the time frame."

"And that would show you who the thief was. Oh, I hate to even use that word." She rubbed the back of her neck as if considering the consequences of such a discovery. A frown crossed her brow. "What if the equipment malfunctions?"

"There's little chance of that. But if it does, someone will be out to fix it."

"You?" she said anxiously, then uttered a nervous laugh, twisting a strand of her thick red hair around a finger. "I can hardly explain a stranger in my boudoir to the servants."

And how would she explain him? Any Parker Agency employee would know how to make him or herself invisible. No use belaboring that point now. He didn't need to linger here any longer than necessary. "We'll decide that if the need arises. Shall we get started?"

She hesitated, biting her lip like a little girl. At last she lifted her palms. "What choice do I have?"

"I just need to get my kit from the car." He raised a hand as she opened her mouth. "Don't worry. I'll be discreet."

It took less than forty minutes to install the devices in the master bedroom. One in a desk lamp, a second behind a photo, a third in the smoke detector.

When he finished, he turned to Patricia with a confident smile. "That should do it. Everything is wifi and will be monitored digitally, as I said."

She nodded, a faraway look in her large green eyes.

"Displeased?"

"Oh, no. I just find this all very disturbing." She took his hand. "Come sit with me for a moment."

He needed to get downtown to meet Miranda for lunch, but he couldn't leave the woman alone in this state. He let her lead him into as small sitting room next to the bedchamber.

"I can stay only a few minutes more." He waited for her to be seated.

She lowered herself onto a diminutive couch upholstered in a fabric of jonquils and hummingbirds. He was about to take a seat across from her when she patted the spot next to her.

"Oh, please do sit over here, Wade."

He wanted to say the chair was fine, but it seemed rude and she was so upset by this ordeal. Acquiescing, he crossed to the couch and lowered himself beside her. "I'm sorry this business is so brusque."

"It is, isn't it? But I needed to take care of it. My schedule is so crowded over the next month. I've got several horse shows coming up. And there's the fundraiser I'm hosting at the Town Club in less than two weeks. A champagne reception," she added when he said nothing. "Dinner, dancing, and a silent auction. You'll be there, won't you?" She eyed him expectantly.

He'd heard about the fundraiser but hadn't thought much about it. He hadn't attended such an event in some time. Perhaps he should get back into the rhythm of the city's social scene, not that he missed the tedious affairs. But they could be good for business.

If Groth was captured soon, he might go. "I'll have to see. Miranda doesn't take to parties the way I do."

"Yes, I can imagine." She toyed with her earring and studied him, as if measuring her next words. "As a matter of fact—"

"What is it?"

"All the news lately has been full of that horrible man who escaped from Brandywine-Summit. That killer. You've heard about that, haven't you?"

"Yes, I have." He had nothing to say to her about the matter.

She waved a hand. "Oh, of course you have. You were involved with capturing him, you and Miranda."

"Yes."

She rubbed her arms. "It's just that—I just heard the strangest thing on the radio."

"What did you hear, Patricia?"

"That Miranda—your Miranda—had a relationship with that awful man. That she was *married* to him. It sounded like he beat her. Please tell me that's not true, Wade."

Parker's jaw tensed like a vice. It was all he could do to speak. "Where did you hear that, Patricia?"

"Why on Tanya Terrance's show. *Talk of the Town.* Tanya said she had a trustworthy source for the information. But there must be some mistake, isn't there?"

Parker felt a rumble in his chest that could rival the highest seismic activity along the San Andreas Fault. How dare that shrew publicly divulge Miranda's personal information?

Patricia blinked at him, curiosity in her liquid green eyes. "*Is* it true?"

He didn't answer. All he could do was glare at her.

"Oh, dear. I've offended you. I don't know what gets into me sometimes."

He got to his feet. "I really need to be going now, Patricia." He moved to the door.

She followed him. "I'm so sorry, Wade. I didn't mean to speak out of turn." She reached for his hand. "I mean it. I wouldn't do anything to damage our friendship for the world. It means far too much to me. Forgive me?" She dipped her chin and smiled that coy smile, her lips glistening.

He forced himself to breathe. To try to calm down. What Tanya Terrance had done wasn't Patricia's fault. She was an old family friend.

"There's no apology necessary, but I really must be going. I'll let you know if we get any results from the installation."

Her face fairly glowed. "Oh, thank you, Wade. I don't know what I'd do without your help. Are you sure you wouldn't like a nice tall glass of ice tea before you leave?"

"No, thank you. I'll see myself out. Don't worry. I'll make sure no one notices me."

He left her standing in the room alone and stole down the staircase and out the front door, wondering how he was going to break this latest news to Miranda.

CHAPTER TWENTY

Miranda stepped into Tamarind Gardens' sedated entryway, her stomach churning like a cement mixer with a bad set of ball bearings. How in the hell was she supposed to eat anything?

The smell of fresh ginger and exotic spices in the air had made her mouth water the last time she was here. Now? She only felt nauseated. Just another reason to kick Tanya Terrance's ass when she found that bitch.

At the station, she'd discovered the radio personality had pre-taped her Saturday morning show Friday afternoon and hadn't even come to work today. Well, she could run, but she couldn't hide. Miranda would catch up to her eventually.

A short man in a red silk jacket and golden pants approached, bowing when he reached her. "Mrs. Parker?"

"Yes." She hadn't taken Parker's name for business reasons, but she answered to it.

"Welcome to Tamarind Gardens. Mr. Parker has already arrived. Please follow me."

She did and found Parker seated at a cozy table shielded from the other diners by an archway of carved wooden columns. He rose as she reached him and studied her face. She watched him read her mind.

Great. They were trying to carve out an hour or so of relief from the hell they'd fallen into and now he couldn't enjoy his lunch, either.

"Glad you thought of this place. I'm starved," she lied as he held her chair and she sat down.

The maitre d' handed her a menu and rattled off the specials. Parker listened politely then told him they needed a moment to peruse the choices.

"What's wrong?" he murmured under his breath after the man had disappeared.

"Two words. Tanya Terrance."

Frowning with concern, he shook his head in disgust. "So you heard."

The hair on the back of her neck rose. "You heard her broadcast, too?"

"I heard about it. I'm so sorry, Miranda. I'm going to have a word with Tanya as soon as I can get a hold of her."

Giving him a smirk, she picked up her menu. If she got to her first, the bitch wouldn't be able to talk. "You think you can stop her?"

"I'll go to her station manager if I have to, but I think I can make her think twice before she does something like that again."

"What are you going to do? Threaten to have Erskine arrest her for obstruction of justice?"

He smiled as if he already had a plan in mind. "How did your visit to the ice rink go?"

She raised a brow at him. He was changing the subject but that one wasn't much better.

Miranda rolled her eyes. "Wendy's still pissed at me. I tried to talk to her. She might have listened to what I said. I don't know. But she stormed off in a huff." Miranda scanned the chef's selections on the menu, but everything blurred together. She closed it and laid it on the table. "I'm sorry I don't feel like eating."

"How about some lemon grass soup?"

She leaned her chin in her hand. She was pitiful, wasn't she? "Oh, just order me something. We'll take it home if I can't get it down."

"Very well."

He looked over the list, made his selections and hailed a waiter. After a few minutes, the man returned with hot tea, hot soup, and a plate of lumpy things wrapped in white.

She poked at one with her fork. "What is that?"

Parker poured some tea into a small cup for her. "Basil rolls wrapped in rice paper."

She shrugged and took a sip of the amber liquid. It did soothe her a bit.

With a look of determination, Parker cut off a bite of one of her rolls and dipped into a small saucer of brownish red liquid. "I think you'll enjoy this sauce."

"What's in it?"

"Hoisin sauce, cilantro. Oh, and most importantly, chili paste." He smiled wickedly.

Only because she knew he'd argue with her until she ate it and she didn't feel like causing a scene, she opened her lips and let him put it in her mouth.

She chewed, tasted. It was good. Shrimp and mango, mint and cashews, all wrapped in a sharp, almost painful tang that used to make her swell with pride that she could get it down and want to challenge some poor sap who couldn't to a contest.

Now all she wanted to do was take that sauce and pour it down Tanya Terrance's dress.

Instead, she dutifully got down a few more bites of roll and when the main dish arrived, nibbled at some of that, too. If she didn't, she knew Parker wouldn't tell her what she really wanted to know.

The entrée he'd order her really was nice. Dumplings and carrots and water chestnuts and chicken, again liberally ladled with curry and chili pepper. Parker had something with garlic and pork topped with colorful strings of vegetables, which he ate with chopsticks, the showoff.

Halfway through the dish, she couldn't take it any longer. "So," she said chasing a scallion around her plate with her fork. "I told you about my morning. How was yours?"

He eyed her with compassion and a look that said he could see straight through her. He stole a glance at her plate and since she'd eaten enough to satisfy him, he didn't beat around the bush. Much.

"Iris hadn't heard the news about Groth yet. When I related it to her, she seemed very concerned. She promised to keep a close eye on Wendy and thanked me for the guard I assigned to them."

Miranda set her fork down and blew out a breath. "That's a relief. I hope she means it."

"I think she does." Parker was a good judge of character. She hoped he was right.

She picked up her tea, swirled the remaining liquid around in the bottom of the cup. Her rib cage felt tight. A little like she was wearing a strait jacket. "And that other stop you made? The first one?"

He caught her gaze and she held her breath. Did the Chathams want to sue her for invasion of privacy or something?

"It was rather civil."

What the heck did that mean? "Be straight with me, Parker. I can take it."

Parker hated having to watch her endure any more blows. He eyed her plate again, knowing he wouldn't get any more food into her once they'd reached this part of the conversation.

He picked up his own teacup, took a swallow for fortification, wishing it were something stronger. "Colby and Oliver were shocked, of course. That's to be expected. They received the health information Judge Rozeki sent them but never expected to hear anything further about Mackenzie's birth mother."

"So you told them who I am."

"Yes."

"Go on."

"They hadn't heard the newscasts about Groth either."

She put her teacup down, drew in a breath. "Okay."

"And when I explained the details to them, they didn't want to believe it."

"But you made them see it, didn't you?"

"I tried. They're in denial right now, Miranda. They don't see how a madman who escaped from a hospital would come after their daughter."

She leaned forward. "That's just it. Because he is a madman."

"They're convinced the police will catch him soon. They're focused on preparing Mackenzie for the Junior Interstate Championships in Lake Placid next month. If she does well, it will bring her one step closer to the Olympics."

The back of her neck started to ache. "Hard to make the Olympics when you're dead."

"As I said, they're in denial. It will probably take some time for them to come around and see reason."

And what if Leon got to her in that time? "Are they going to tell Mackenzie—anything?"

Parker gave her a dark look, then slowly shook his head. "They refused to tell her about you. They don't see the need to upset or confuse her."

"She needs to know, Parker. She needs to understand why Leon might be after her. If he gets to Wendy again, she could lead him right to her. She'll be totally unsuspecting. Defenseless."

"I have a guard watching the Mackenzie estate."

"Will that be enough?'

His jaw tightened as he studied a spot on the table. "We have to respect their wishes, Miranda. We'll get Groth. Or someone will before he can do anything."

She ran a hand across the table's glossy surface, wanting to dig her nails into its finish. "Now you sound like the Chathams."

"Give them a little time. I gave them my card and told them to call if they had any further questions. They'll contact me once all this starts to sink in."

Her face felt hot. Her temples throbbed. Her stomach started doing spins like Mackenzie on the ice.

He was going to get her. Leon was going to get her daughter. She wiped her mouth, put her napkin on the table and rose. "I think I need to go powder my nose."

Parker shot to his feet, reached for her arm as she passed him. "Oh, my darling. I'm so sorry."

He was saying that a lot lately. There was a lot to say it about. It would be easy to blame him, but none of this was his fault. "I'm okay. I'll be right back." She broke away and hurried to the little room in the back.

It was hitting her hard now. Much harder than she thought it could. Her head pounded. The scars on her chest seemed to throb. Her stomach felt like it was going through a vegetable shredder. She thought she might puke on the polished hardwood floor before she got to the restroom.

She rushed inside, hurried into a stall and lost half of the nice expensive meal Parker had just bought her. She heaved several times more. Then it stopped. Shivering, she flushed the toilet and went to the sink to rinse her mouth.

She splashed cool water on her hot cheeks, leaned over the marble counter and stared at her own reflection in the mirror.

Her wiry dark hair stuck out in a fluffy mass that fell to her shoulders. Her blue eyes were bloodshot, her face drawn. She had on a cheap T-shirt and jeans. Why was she wearing that in a fancy place, dining with one of the wealthiest men in the city who was dressed in an expensive suit? She wasn't part of this lifestyle and never would be. She could hear the gossip among

Parker's social set. How did he wind up with the likes of her? With a psycho killer's ex-wife?

Bunch of stuck up snobs.

She wondered if the Chathams had heard Tanya Terrance's show? How could they ever tell Mackenzie the woman the talk show host was blabbing about was her mother?

But she had to know. How else could she protect herself?

If they wouldn't tell her, maybe she should. No, that would be too hard. For both of them. There had to be another way to protect her.

She grabbed some tissue, dried her face and hands and straightened her shoulders. The best way to keep her daughter safe would be to find that bastard and put an end to him at last. What was she doing in a restaurant when there was a killer on the loose?

She left the restroom and marched back to the table with new determination.

Parker was on the phone. "Yes. Yes, Hosea. I'll do that. Thank you." He clicked off and gave her a grim look.

She sank into her chair, gripping the table. "What is it?"

"The police got a tip from a man in Druid Hills who believes he sold Groth a vehicle this morning. He recognized his picture when he saw the latest newscast."

Miranda's blood froze in her veins. "Dark blue Lexus. Older model. Tinted windows. Gash in the left fender."

His eyes went wide with shock. "How did you know?"

"I saw that car at the ice rink this morning."

His face turned to stone. "And?"

"It drove away a few minutes after I got there." What did that mean? Had Leon seen her? Was he afraid of her? No, couldn't be that simple. "I'm pretty sure your man in the Agency car saw him, too."

"I'm about to alert the guards. The police are re-focusing their efforts to areas near the seller's home."

"We ought to scour those neighborhoods, too. Somebody might have seen him." And it was all they had right now.

He got to his feet, tossed some bills on the table. "That's just what we're about to do."

They drove to Druid Hills and interviewed the guy who'd sold the Lexus. From his description, it was Leon, all right. Gaunt, shaved head. Looked just like the enhanced photo the newscasters had been flashing around on TV. He was wearing the suit the nurse in the hospital described to them. Paid cash for the car.

"Where'd he get that kind of money?" Miranda asked when they were back in the Mazda. "He couldn't have had that much with him in the hospital."

Parker turned out of the subdivision. "If he went to a bank, someone would have reported it by now. The amount he paid was too much to withdraw from ATMs."

"Yeah, they have a limit. So he must have had a stash somewhere. Probably the place he stayed when he was after Wendy. Wherever that is."

Parker nodded. "That's where we'd find him. Let's try."

They drove around for hours. Through neighborhood after neighborhood. They searched under bypasses, behind strip malls, in parking lots. They talked to folks coming out of a grocery store, convenience store clerks, shop owners.

It wasn't that they couldn't find a dark blue Lexus. The model seemed to be everywhere. Miranda couldn't believe there were so many in Atlanta. It was as if they were crawling out of the ground like ants.

They searched and hunted until Miranda's eyes burned but there was no sign of Leon. The bastard knew how to hide.

A little after one in the morning, Parker decided to call off the search for tonight and go home.

As she sank into bed, feeling just as deflated as the previous night, Miranda thought of Mackenzie. The girl was preparing for that big ice skating event. Focused on her spins and jumps and whatever, she'd be totally oblivious to what was around her. Totally clueless that a dangerous man might be following her.

She'd be easy to nab.

Tomorrow was Sunday. Her only day off from practice at the rink, Miranda knew from Wendy. She'd be at home. Good opportunity for Miranda to take matters into her own hands. Parker wouldn't like it. No doubt the parents would pitch a fit. But none of that mattered. She didn't care what anybody thought or said. She couldn't stand by and do nothing.

She had to protect her daughter. Tomorrow she was heading for the Chatham place.

CHAPTER TWENTY-ONE

Married.

Some silly woman on the radio—who clearly thought more of herself than she ought—had said she was married. And to Wade Parker, no less. The head of that detective agency where she worked. The one who had beaten his face in. The one who had stopped him from ending her life.

Blinking in the sunlight streaming through the windshield, he touched his cheek, studied its hollow contour in the rearview mirror of the SUV he had rented this morning, recalling the pain.

He wouldn't let that happen again.

Focus.

Yes, he had to stay focused. But wouldn't *she* lead him to the one he was looking for? They were detectives, after all. They would know how to find a lost child. Certainly they had found her by now.

He'd tried to find her himself. He'd looked up the judge he'd bribed thirteen years ago to put the baby in the system, but the man had had the audacity to die in the meantime. He never should have given that child up for adoption. He should have smothered it and buried it in the backyard. But he hadn't known his calling then.

Now *she* was the key to finding the girl.

A little research at a library computer gave him a general idea of where they were living. It wasn't hard to deduce the rest. Just down the street from Wendy. How ironic. How perfect.

And now he sat parked along a two-lane road, facing the side street leading out of Mockingbird Hills. Waiting.

It was risky. They were looking for him.

He studied himself in the mirror again. A fake goatee, glasses, a light brown wig, a ball cap. With a dark checked shirt and worn jeans, the disguise had served him well in the bar he'd gone to last night. He'd watched a whole episode about himself on the news and no one had recognized him.

But the newscast told him that bastard who'd sold him the car had reported him to the police. Thinking of the newscaster describing the dark color, the gash over the fender, the tinted windows, he fought back the angry fire in his belly.

Early this morning he'd had to dig up one of the fake IDs he'd used before and go to a rental place. Now he was sitting in a tan, late model SUV that no one would recognize. No one would suspect the driver of that old Lexus, which he'd left on the side of a downtown road, was behind the wheel of this vehicle.

But it had been such a waste of time. If he had more time, he'd go back to that seller and give him what he deserved. He'd like to practice on a man. Watch his eyes go wide as he cut off his air supply. Watch him beg for—

Wait.

He tensed as the front end of the red Corvette he'd seen yesterday appeared at the intersection. It was *her*.

She signaled left, paused to let a few cars pass, then made her turn.

If she'd had any decent training as a detective, she'd be able to make a tail. If she was any good. But he'd been a cop and he was better.

He waited until the Corvette reached the top of the next hill and followed.

Miranda's skin tingled as she made her way down Ivy Street.

She'd slept late and found Parker at his high-powered computers, running searches of the area they had combed through last night, looking for places where Leon might be hiding. He'd wanted to make her breakfast, but she'd said no thanks.

Guilt trickled over her heart.

She'd told him she was going to see Coco and try to talk some sense into the girl—which she intended to do. But first she had another stop. And her stomach started doing the jitterbug inside her every time she thought of it.

She glanced down at the passenger seat. Beside a small purse she'd stuff with tissues sat a large canvas bag holding a half dozen presents. The bows were smashed on most of them, the gift wrap wrinkled, but she hoped that wouldn't matter.

Each year since she'd lost Amy, when November rolled around she'd bought a birthday gift. When December came, she purchased a Christmas present. Another one at Easter time. And others at various times of the year.

She'd kept them all, dragging around the growing box of toys from place to place whenever she moved, hoping to be able to give them to her daughter one day.

She'd left the baby things back home in the closet, but she'd carefully selected the ones a thirteen-year-old might like. A pink pony, a Barbie doll, a teddy bear, a stuffed rabbit. Maybe they would be some sort of peace offering. A token of—good will. Something.

She drew in a shaky breath. This was going to be harder than she thought.

Fighting back the nerves, she checked her rearview mirror. And blinked as a feeling like a cold wind made the hairs on the back of her neck stand up. A light tan SUV was several feet behind her. Wasn't that the car she'd seen parked along the curb a few blocks back?

Was it following her?

The nerves in her gut turned to anger. Did Parker have someone guarding her, too? It would be just like him to do that without telling her. She had a good mind to pull over, flag the car down and find out who that driver was. If it was Becker or Holloway, she'd be humiliated beyond words. Surely Parker wouldn't do that to her.

But before she could execute, the SUV turned onto a side street and disappeared.

She shook herself. She was getting paranoid.

Okay, maybe talking to Mackenzie like this wasn't the best way to handle things. Parker certainly wouldn't think so. She knew it would rattle the girl. To say what she had to tell her would be disturbing would be the understatement of the century. But it would be a lot less disturbing than getting nabbed by a psycho.

Parker was wrong. This was her only course of action. It was time to act. She couldn't wait around and take a chance Leon would move first. She had no choice. She'd just get it over with and tell Parker about it afterwards.

With renewed determination, she drove to Northside Drive, heading for West Paces Ferry.

CHAPTER TWENTY-TWO

The Chatham place off West Paces Ferry near the Governor's mansion was a sprawling stone-and-brick palace the Queen of England might feel at home in.

Gable upon gable of rounded clay tiles jutted over facades of creamy-white stucco. Must have been a real bitch to lay that roof. The house was set well back from the street and surrounded by an iron fence, which made Miranda exhale in relief. Except when she saw the gate was wide open.

It opened onto a broad expanse covered with trees and the manicured shrubbery and flowers she'd gotten used to seeing everywhere in the better neighborhoods of Atlanta.

She felt better when she spotted the Agency guard across the street, even if he might pick up his cell and report her to Parker.

She turned into the gate and made her way up the long drive that stretched across a lawn that looked like each blade had been cut to measure and was so green, her eyes hurt. At the majestic entrance, she stopped the car, grabbed her purse and the canvas bag holding the gifts and strolled to the front door.

A cathedral-like arch of dark brown loomed over her. It looked hand carved, its hardware specially made for royalty. It took her a minute to find the bell. When she did, she rang it without hesitation.

After a long moment, the huge door opened and a very tall, very thin, very surly-looking woman stood before her. She looked to be in her late forties by the lines in her face. Her mousy brown hair was in a tight knot atop her head and she wore a plain gray suit with matching pumps. Another one of the guard dogs rich folk hired to keep out the riffraff.

"May I help you?" British accent. Probably fake but intimidating to some. Not her.

"I'm here to see the Chathams."

"Do you have an appointment?"

"I thought so." Miranda pretended to look at her watch. "I think this is the right time."

"No, I don't think so. The Chathams are at church and won't be home for some time."

Church, huh? Maybe she was in luck. "I'm so embarrassed. I must have misunderstood." She pretended to hunt in her purse for the information.

The woman's smile was condescending as a monarch. "Come back when you figure out when your appointment is." She started to close the door.

Miranda put out a hand and stopped the door in mid-swing. "Is Mackenzie home? I'm really here to see her. It's about the, uh—" What was the name of that event? "The Interstate Championships."

Her long neck drew up her head like a suspicious swan. "Are you a representative of Ms. Evans?"

That sounded good. "I'm on the committee. There's been a misunderstanding about Mackenzie's—placement."

"Miss Mackenzie's placement?"

She should have browsed a book on skating before she came. "There's just been a mix-up at headquarters. But you're right. Her parents should be here. I'll come back later." She turned to go.

"Wait. What did you say your name is?"

"Ms—Brown."

"Come in, Ms. Brown. I'll see what I can do."

She opened the door and led Miranda down a long, arched, off-white hall to a large, octagon-shaped entrance hall. It too was all off-white and its walls rose to a glass dome overhead where sunlight streamed in. A series of arched hallways branched off from the center like a catacomb.

The guard dog led Miranda across the marble tiles to one. Down the hall they went passing paintings of stiff-looking men and women Miranda took to be family ancestors. There were side tables and chairs dotted about in a variety of styles. Asian, Egyptian, European. Eclectic tastes.

They turned a corner, went down another long hall and finally reached a sliding glass door that led to a patio.

Her escort opened it. "You can wait here, Ms. Brown. I'll see if Miss Mackenzie is available."

"Thank you."

As the door closed behind her, Miranda stepped onto the blue terrazzo floor, crossed to one of the wrought iron benches along the low stone wall encasing the space, and lowered herself onto a rose patterned pad. She set her purse beside her, the canvas bag on the floor.

Chewing on her thumb, she stared out at the wide lawn with its perfect blades of too-green grass and the willows and pines lining the yard in the distance. The trees were forest-thick and edged along the bottom with an assortment of even thicker hedges and flowering shrubs. Fence-like, the greenery ran all the way up to the building, giving the rear of the estate some security. Still, she couldn't help thinking about how Leon had trekked through the woods behind Wendy's house. And though it was warm out here, she felt an icy chill brush over her skin making her shiver.

Leon. How was she going to tell Mackenzie about him? How could she find the words to tell the girl who she was?

The long stretch of yard was flat and still, but suddenly her stomach felt like she was on an ocean liner in the middle of a typhoon.

Might upchuck any second.

She was about to see Mackenzie. Her Amy. And it wasn't going to be like anything she'd ever imagined it, was it? Had she imagined this day over the years?

Not consciously. Sure there were the toys, but she'd never let herself think about what it would really be like. Yet deep in some corner of her mind, there was a steady image of tears and hugs and murmurs of "I've found you at last," and "I knew you would come for me." That wouldn't be happening today. No, her life didn't play like that.

She heard the glass door slide open behind her.

Miranda sucked in her breath as footsteps sounded on the tiles.

"Ms. Brown?"

Slowly Miranda turned around.

She wore a pretty layered top and jeans with a sequined pattern of pink seashells at the knees. A lightweight scarf of pale blue was wrapped around her neck. Her rich, dark hair fell to her shoulders in waves. Her delicate dark brows twisted in confusion and anger. "You're not Ms. Brown. I know you. You're Miranda Steele. Wendy's friend."

The one who told you to polish your own skates the other day. "That's right," Miranda said, managing to sound a whole lot calmer than she was.

Mackenzie folded her arms, raised her eyes to the sky. "Is this about Wendy? Honestly, I don't see why—"

"It's not about Wendy. It's about something else. A very serious matter."

The girl huffed in exasperation. "This is ridiculous. If you have anything to talk to me about, you'll have to see my mother or my coach. I'm going to have to ask you to leave now." She turned away and reached for the door handle.

Miranda shot to her feet, ready to tackle the kid to keep her here. Then she spoke with as dark a tone as she could muster. "Mackenzie, I'm here about a matter of life and death."

The girl's eyes flashed. The drama of that statement was too much for a thirteen-year-old girl to resist, even one as cold as this kid.

She thinned her lips and slowly nodded. "Very well, Ms. Steele. You have ten minutes."

She crossed to the other bench and sat as far away as she could. Oh, so prim and proper. Her back perfectly straight, her hands clasped together in her lap, she waited for Miranda to speak.

Miranda sat down again and picked at a spot on her jeans. Her turn at bat. The ball was in her court. And whatever other stupid cliché applied. Where to start?

At the beginning, she guessed. She sucked in as deep a breath as she could and let the words come. "A long time ago, I had a little girl. A baby. She was so pretty. She had a shock of dark hair. Big eyes, so full of curiosity. Tiny little hands and feet." She remembered the feel and the smell of her soft skin. "I loved her very much. And then one day, I woke up and my baby was gone."

"Gone?" Ah, that got her attention.

Miranda nodded. "I learned my husband, who was a real—jerk, had taken her away and given her up for adoption."

"How could he do that?" She seemed genuinely concerned.

Miranda shrugged. "He had pull. He knew some corrupt judges. Probably bribed them."

"That's—too bad, Ms. Steele. But I don't see—"

Miranda shot up a hand. "Hear me out." She drew in another breath and went on. "And so I never saw my child again. I left my husband and got a job. I traveled a lot and during that time, I began to search for my daughter."

"Did you ever find her?" Was that a note of compassion in her voice?

"Not then." Miranda gazed into the girl's face. Her expression was expectant. Could she sense where she was going with this? Maybe not. "I searched for Amy—that was the name I gave her—for thirteen years. But I couldn't find her. Didn't have a clue where she was. Then last spring I came to Atlanta and went to work at the Parker Agency."

"Yes. You're an investigator there. Wendy's mentioned that."

"Mr. Parker took an interest in my case and joined my search. He discovered some information that allowed us to petition a judge in Chicago to open my daughter's adoption records." Man was that an understatement. But there was no need to go into those details.

Mackenzie gave her a kind smile that seemed genuine. "That's very nice. I'm sure you're looking forward to learning who your daughter is."

"I got the judge's decision three days ago. I know who my daughter is."

"Oh?" Her pretty dark brows drew together in apprehension.

Any doubt she'd ever had about her heritage, any question she'd ever had about how she got here was right there now on her smooth young face.

They locked gazes, stared at each other for an eternity.

Then all at once the words came out of Miranda's mouth in a hoarse whisper. "It's you."

Mackenzie cocked her head like a cute little puppy at a dog whistle. "I beg your pardon?"

"My daughter is you."

Her back went rigid as a metal brace as she choked out a laugh. "What?"

Swallowing to wet her dry throat, Miranda reached for the bag at her feet. "I used to buy Amy presents every year. For her birthday, holidays, you know. I kept them. I want to give them to you." She drew out the biggest one.

Mackenzie's blue eyes grew wide as she shook her head emphatically. She held up both hands. "I really don't want—anything like that."

Okay, if she wouldn't open the gift Miranda would do it for her. She began peeling back the wrapping paper. "I know this has to be a real shock to you, Amy."

"Mackenzie. My name is Mackenzie."

"Yes, I know your name. It's typed on the adoption papers the judge in Chicago sent me. Do you want to see them? I can get them for you." She had the ribbon and the paper off now. She put them in the bag and held the stuffed animal out to the girl. It was the blue bunny.

Mackenzie glared at it like it might have rabies. "No, thank you, Ms. Steele."

"Take it. Please." She got up and put it in the girl's stubborn hands and sat down again.

Holding the toy gingerly, Mackenzie coughed out another laugh. "I'm very sure you're mistaken, Ms. Steele. I'm not your daughter."

"I know this is a shock," she repeated. "But I really didn't have a—"

"It's no shock at all. How can I be shocked by something that isn't true?"

"But it is true. You have that mark on your neck. It's the same one my father has."

Shaking her head in disbelief, she began to stroke the stuffed rabbit. "Ms. Steele, this is the most ridiculous conversation I've ever had in my life. If you're looking for money, perhaps my father's firm can help you. You didn't have to drag me into it."

"I don't need money." Even if she wasn't married to Parker, she'd never asked for a handout and never would. Especially from her own daughter. Miranda smoothed her jeans and stared down at her own lap, forcing herself to calm down. There was only one reason she'd come here today. It was time to cut to the chase. "I have something else to tell you, Mackenzie."

She could feel the tension roll over the girl and felt terrible for her. She wished with all her heart she didn't have to do this. Her life had been so good and what she had to say would change it forever.

"What is it, Ms. Steele?"

This was the hard part. Do it and get it over with. "Did Wendy ever tell you about the man who nearly killed her last spring?"

She smoothed the toy rabbit's ear. "A little. I read about it in the papers. What does that have to do with anything?"

"That man was my ex-husband. The man who stole you from me."

Again her brow wrinkled. She went a little pale. "What are you talking about?"

"His name is Leon Groth. Four months ago Mr. Parker and I stopped him from hurting Wendy. He ended up in the hospital. In a coma."

She stopped rubbing the bunny. Her mouth opened and closed as shock invaded her eyes. "The man on the news? The man who escaped from Brandywine-Summit?"

"Yes, that's him. He's dangerous. Crazy. And when I last saw him—the day I saved Wendy—he told me he was going to find my daughter and kill her."

Miranda watched the shudder go through the girl as she stared at her, frozen in disbelief. This was too much. The last thing she wanted was to torment her own daughter with these facts. But they might save her life. "I wouldn't have told you all this. I would have kept it all a secret. But you have to know. You have to be careful."

They sat staring at each other in dead silence for what seemed like an eternal space of time. And in that space, Mackenzie's expression went from confusion to fear to rage. Then the girl's shoulders moved, stiffened. She raised her chin as gracefully as a debutante.

Her chest heaved in frustration. "I'm sorry you lost your child, Ms. Steele, but I'm not her."

"That's not what your adoption records say."

Still fingering the toy bunny, Mackenzie rose, fighting back tears of anger. "I don't care what they say. I'm a Chatham. I'm named after my grandfather and my father. You'll never make me believe otherwise. Never in a million years."

Oh, Lord why hadn't she prepared for this? She had to do something. She had to convince her or she'd be just as vulnerable as before. Miranda thought of the times she'd seen Mackenzie practicing at the rink. The picture of her Wendy had sent when she won the Regionals. She'd always had something around her neck. Just as she did now.

Miranda jumped off the bench, pulled the scarf off Mackenzie's neck and sucked in air at the sight even though she knew it would be there. The dark spot on the girl's neck was as plain as a polka dot. "There's the mark. That proves it."

Protectively Mackenzie's fingers flew to her throat. She shot to her feet. "It doesn't prove anything."

"Of course, it does. I saw that mark on your neck every time I put you to bed. Every time I held you, fed you."

The girl's eyes glistened with tears now. She moved toward the door, hugging the rabbit tight to her chest. "You're insane. You're just doing this to get back at Wendy because she's not interested in becoming an investigator anymore."

Miranda grabbed at her own hair in frustration. Why was she being so obstinate? Why wouldn't she listen? Why wouldn't she at least take some precaution?

Anger pounded through her. Miranda couldn't hold back her temper a second longer. "Do you know what the word 'shallow' means, Mackenzie?"

The girl's mouth opened in shock. Then her face went white with rage. "Do you know what the word 'paternity' means, Ms Steele?"

"What are you saying?"

"If you're my mother, who's my father? That madman they're talking about in the news?"

Don't say it. Don't. But she wasn't thinking straight. The words flew out of her mouth before she could stop herself. "I don't know who your father is. I was raped."

The poor girl looked like she might pass out. "You. Are. Crazy. Get out of here. Now!" She lifted the blue bunny and hurled it at her. Then she tore the door open and ran from the patio.

The stuffed rabbit hit Miranda square in the chest and fell at her feet. Trembling all over, she picked it up, put it back in the bag.

She swiped at her nose wondering how it got so wet. That went well, didn't it? What did she expect? She should have listened to Parker.

Leaving the canvas bag of toys on the floor, somehow she found her way out of the mansion, got into her car and stared up at the crystal blue sky. It was fall now, though the weather was still warm. Bright and sunny. Perfect day to ruin your daughter's life. Mackenzie Chatham would never be the same.

As she turned on the car and rolled down the long drive, Miranda wondered if she'd ever stop shaking.

He wanted to cuss at the sticks and briars poking into his sides, but he didn't dare make a sound. Not a whimper, not a move, not a whisper. So he knelt, hands and knees in the dirt and listened.

He'd seen her turn into the estate's driveway in the fancy red sport car. He spotted the guard sitting along the opposite side of the road, watching over the place.

He'd known.

So he'd backtracked. Turned down a street that ran behind the property. He'd parked the SUV and studied the landscape. Luckily, he knew how to navigate terrain like this from the Van Aarles' place.

A small black spider ran over the back of his hand. With his other, he snatched it up, squeezed it between his fingers. But he didn't make a sound. He listened.

And as he heard the angry words echo over the stone wall where he knelt, he smiled. Emotional, female words. Words that told him exactly what he wanted to know. He'd heard them all—from the very beginning of their conversation.

He'd been right all along, hadn't he? She'd led him straight to the girl. After all this time, all his careful planning, all the disappointment and struggle, he had found her.

The child she'd called Amy. The girl who was now Mackenzie Chatham. A friend of Wendy's.

He could have grabbed her right then and there. But no, *she* was there. She'd fight him and he couldn't risk losing to her again. And then he heard the girl leave.

Excitement pulsed through him so hard, he thought he might ejaculate on the ground.

Not now. He couldn't take her now. But soon. Very soon.

He heard footsteps. He waited and after a while heard a car start in the distance and drive away. It was safe now.

But not for long. Another car was coming up the driveway. The parents? Visitors? He had to get out of here. He crawled away as fast as he could.

An hour later he'd parked the SUV in a lot, had taken MARTA back downtown to the library, and was combing through press releases and back issues of newspapers on the computer. Mackenzie Chatham was quite a talented little girl.

She'd won scads of local figure skating competitions, recently the Atlanta Open and the Regionals. He scanned the photos of her. Pretty, healthy, fit, graceful on the ice. Her neck, he noted, was always covered by a scarf or a turtle neck. She was hiding the dark spot on it.

The sign that marked her as the devil's child. The filthy thing she was.

You must release her.

Yes and soon.

How to get to her? She was surrounded by people all the time. And there was so much preparation. The rope, the ribbon, the cooking oil, the herbs. The ritual had to be done just right for it to work.

You're missing something.

His head jerked back at the voice. What? Missing something? What could he be missing? Hadn't he done it just right before?

No.

No? What am I missing? A searing pain shot through his shoulder the knife in his memory plunged into him again. He bent over as he reached for the spot, forcing himself not to cry out.

That's what's missing.

Pain?

You did not hurt the girls before you released them. Pain is cleansing.

She was right. Mother had cleansed him with pain. She had beaten him with a wire hairbrush when he was bad. So many times. When he cried like a girl, she beat him harder.

Her legs. She loves her legs. They are her life.

And so?

Take what matters to her most. Break her bones. Start with her toes. One by one. Cleanse her well.

Yes, yes. It all made sense now. That was why he had failed before. Why he could never find her. But he had found her now. He would not fail again.

His breath grew ragged with excitement, with joy. This would be the biggest moment of his life. He was about to fulfill his mission, his destiny. He would cleanse the world of this horrible, wicked blemish. People everywhere would know about it. Remember him for it. But would they understand his mission?

His gaze returned to the computer screen.

The story said that right now, Mackenzie Chatham was preparing for the Junior Interstate Championships in Lake Placid next month. It was a big, important event.

A plan began to form in his mind. Could he really pull that off? It would take a lot of planning. Everything had to be done just right. There were so many details. So little time.

He had to be careful. They were looking for him. He had to do this before they found him. Fear began to pound in his chest.

They'd be coming for him soon. Police. Hoards of them. He blinked, looked around at the other patrons sitting in their chairs, reading. Any one of them could recognize him. Panic made his hands shake as he gripped the table to steady himself. He should turn himself in. He should let his daughter live and end this now.

But she isn't your daughter.

No, she wasn't. She was the offspring of that vile whore. She was the source of all his pain. Of everything that had gone wrong in his life. She was the source of evil.

He scratched at his false goatee and his mind began to race again. Plans, plans. He needed a distraction, didn't he? Yes, but that would take more time. So much to do. So much to do. What was he doing loitering here? He had to get back to the abandoned house in the vacant subdivision where he was staying and get busy.

He rose, nearly knocking over the computer chair. Someone glared up at him and he remembered to turn back, close the window and clear the history. Then he fairly ran from the library back to the MARTA station.

Are you going to fail me, again?

He could smile with confidence now. No, Mother. I won't fail you. Not this time.

CHAPTER TWENTY-THREE

It was five in the afternoon by the time Miranda got back home. She'd stopped at Coco's, but no one was home, so on impulse she'd gone over to see Fanuzzi.

She'd never had a friend like Joan Fanuzzi. Miranda knew she would listen, sympathize. The woman was the only person beside Parker and Estavez who knew the sordid details of her past and about her search for her daughter. So far. But for some reason Miranda couldn't bring herself to go in. She just couldn't go through the details again.

She drove around the block three times and finally gave up and went home.

She found Parker in the large upstairs office, with its massive computer monitors, doing research. He turned as she entered the room and she saw nothing in his handsome face but compassion.

"How did your visit with Mackenzie go?" He knew her so well.

Her shoulders slumped and she felt her eyes fill with tears again as she answered. "Not as well as I expected."

"Oh, my darling." He rose and drew her into his strong arms, held her against his muscular chest.

Miranda closed her eyes against the heaving sobs she couldn't hold back. It felt so good here, so comforting in his embrace. She wished she could stay here forever. "I should have listened to you."

He stroked her hair. "You did what you thought was best."

That felt good to hear. A few months ago he would have been angry with her for going off on her own. "Mackenzie really hates me now. She didn't listen to a word I said when I told her about Leon. She thought I was making it up because of Wendy." She took the handkerchief he held out to her.

"Give her some time to take in the news. She's upset. The whole family is upset."

She pulled away and looked into his eyes. So he hadn't read her mind just now. "How did you know I'd gone there?"

"I know you. And," he breathed out a sigh. "I got a call from Oliver Chatham. They aren't happy at all."

She put her head in her hands and sank into one of the desk chairs. "Guess you told me so."

"Actually, I've been thinking you were right. It is best they know Groth could be after Mackenzie, no matter how disturbing and painful it is."

She looked up at him again and realized he had something to say to her. "Why?"

His jaw clenched. "I also just got another call from Hosea."

"And?"

"The police found the Lexus Groth purchased on the side of the road near the Interstate in Five Points."

"Five Points? That's back near the hospital. Not anywhere near where we looked for him last night."

"No, it isn't. But that doesn't mean he's not in Druid Hills."

"Doesn't mean he is, either." That bastard could be anywhere. Anywhere in the six hundred or so square miles of the metropolitan area. "He's zigzagging around, trying to throw us off."

"Yes," Parker said grimly.

She shot up, palms pressed to her temples and paced the room. "I saw an SUV this morning when I left the subdivision. I thought it was following me."

His gray eyes filled with alarm. "Was it Groth?"

"I don't know. It turned off down a side street before I got a tag number." An old tailing trick. Why hadn't she seen it? And she'd even felt that heebie-jeebie feeling she always had when something was off. "It was tan. Light tan, I could hardly see it. An Escape, I think." She paced again as Parker picked up the phone and reported the details to Erskine.

When he clicked off, she stared at him, feeling as if she were going insane. "What are we going to do, Parker?"

"I'll double the guard on the Chatham house. Erskine is going to release the new information about the Lexus and the SUV to the news stations. For now, the only other thing we can do is keep searching."

CHAPTER TWENTY-FOUR

They searched everywhere they could think of.

They talked to the cop who had found the Lexus. They scoured the area on foot, talking to a clerk in a shoe store, a beauty shop operator, people coming out of a nearby apartment building. They didn't learn anything.

The next day, Parker organized search teams in the office and they all spread out, focusing on the downtown and the northeast section of the city, all the way to the Perimeter.

They talked to everyone who might have seen him, they went to abandoned buildings, visited homeless shelters and cruised through local parks, all the while knowing the police were doing the same and making as little progress.

News stories flooded the airwaves. Tips flooded back to the police station. Most of them were bogus. Someone thought he saw a guy with a shaved head at a gas station, but a look at the surveillance videos showed it was an old man from the neighborhood everyone knew. A women called to say her neighbor was hiding Leon. That turned out to be getting back for a long-standing fight over a barking dog. A barber swore Leon had come in for a haircut, even though his picture clearly showed him with a shaved head. Some people were just trying to help. Others just wanted to be in on the thrill. No one had any solid information.

Over the next four days, the Agency guards reported Mackenzie and Wendy were following standard operating procedure, going to classes and the ice rink after school to practice. And Iris seemed to be keeping a closer eye on Wendy. It was a relief to hear they were safe, but Miranda wondered how Mackenzie was and whether the truth had sunk in yet. She wondered whether the girl had talked to Wendy about her visit and how much both of them collectively despised her now.

And then the worst possible news came.

It was past eight on Thursday night when Miranda found herself sitting in Parker's office, staring at the map of the Atlanta area he had projected on the wall. Beside the map were photos of Leon's victims. Madison Taggart, Dr.

Taggart's little girl. Tiffany Todd, the daughter of one of Estavez' co-workers. The middle-aged woman from Philly.

The case had all the earmarks of a serial killer, but Leon was really only after one victim. Mackenzie. The rest were just milestones along the way. Practice.

On the map, little red dots marked each of the places where they knew Leon had been. Brandywine-Summit Memorial Hospital. Uptown Inn near Fifteenth. The house in Druid Hills where the bastard had bought the Lexus. The ice rink in Marietta. The Chatham house off West Paces Ferry. The downtown street near Five Points where they'd found the abandoned Lexus.

But they still didn't have a clue where the sonofabitch was now.

Becker came running into the office, out of breath and waving a piece of paper in his hand. "I've got it." Parker had sent the others home, but Becker had stayed to follow a lead.

Parker got to his feet. "What is it?"

"I just got off the phone with a clerk from Save More Car Rentals. She rented Groth the tan SUV. I've got all the details here."

Miranda shot up, snatched the paper from Becker's hand and scanned it. A cold chill went down her spine. "I was right. It was an Escape. He claimed he was taking it on a trip to Milwaukee. Bull."

Becker nodded. "The clerk said the customer had light brown hair over his ears and wore a ball cap."

"A wig?"

Again Becker nodded. "He had on dark glasses, but he took them off to sign the papers and she saw his eyes. They were the same eyes as the guy in the picture they've been flashing on the news. At least that's what she thought when she caught the afternoon broadcast today. She was going to call the police, but thought she didn't have enough to give them." He poked at the carpet with the toe of his shoe. "I did have to sweet talk her a bit to get that much out of her."

Parker gave him an approving look. "Excellent work, Detective."

Miranda pressed a few keys on the laptop and another little red dot appeared on the map. "That rental office's a mile or so south of I-20. What was he doing down there?"

"Misleading us."

"So he wants us to think he's here," she strode to the wall and pointed to the downtown and southern area of the map. "When he's really somewhere up here." She pointed to the Druid Hills spot. "Maybe we should be looking closer to Mockingbird Hills." Where Wendy was. Where they were.

Parker shook his head. "Too much of a chance of being spotted. He's had to spot the guards by now and he's got to go out and perform routine activities. Buy groceries, gas for all this travel."

"Especially for an SUV," Becker agreed. "And it sounds like he's bought some disguises."

The three of them stood staring at the map, trying to make something click. When the silence in the room was broken by Parker's cell, Miranda jumped.

Parker strode over to the desk and picked up his phone. "Hosea, I was just about to call you. One of our detectives just found where Groth rented the tan SUV." His face went dark. "Just a minute, I'll put you on speaker. I have detectives Becker and Steele here with me." He set the phone down on the table and pressed a button. "Go ahead."

The police lieutenant's grim voice echoed against the wall. "As I was saying, there's been an extremely unfortunate development in the case."

Extremely unfortunate? Miranda's gaze shot to Parker's as panic gripped her. Wendy? Mackenzie? "What happened?"

"We just received a report from Hampton, Georgia. There's been a homicide. Victim is a thirteen-year-old middle school student. She's been missing since Tuesday. Someone walking a dog found her body about an hour ago.

Miranda's head buzzed with pain as she tried to take in Erskine's words. Thirteen-year-old? Middle school student?

Erskine drew in a long breath. "It's the same MO Groth used last spring."

"What do you mean?" Parker asked, though he knew the answer.

"Hands tied together with rope. White ribbon around the neck. Body covered in seasoned cooking oil. But in this case—there was some mutilation involved."

Dear God. Miranda grabbed the back of a chair and put her hand over her mouth to keep herself from crying out. If only she could get her hands on the bastard she'd make sure he never hurt another child.

"COD?" She heard Parker ask. He sounded like he was underwater.

"Same as before. Ligature strangulation. The local police are handling the investigation for now, but the GBI is on the way. I'm heading down there myself."

"And we will as well. We'll see you there." Parker hung up and without a second's hesitation, headed for the door. "Let's go," he said.

But Miranda was already beside him and Becker was at her heels.

CHAPTER TWENTY-FIVE

Police floodlights lit up the wooded area down a long stretch of rural road. As soon as Parker stopped the car, Miranda got out and headed up a hill where officers and investigators were milling about. Parker and Becker weren't far behind her.

Near the edge of the trees, technicians gathered evidence into bags while other officers took notes on clipboards, their faces somber, their movements as silent as the tall Georgia pines that rose overhead into the darkness.

She stopped when she caught sight of the body.

On the ground beside a line of thickets and weeds, underneath a dense grove of trees, a young girl lay just as Erskine had described her. Hands clasped together in a prayer-like pose and bound with rope, a white ribbon tied around her neck in a bow, her face an expression of serenity. Miranda could smell the scent of rosemary in the oil on her.

The scene reminded her of the night she'd found Madison Taggart's body—except for the lower part of the body. The legs and feet were bloody and mangled. It looked like the girl had been beaten. It took all Miranda had to hold it together.

How many more victims would there be before Leon got a chance at his real target?

They had to stop him.

Miranda spotted Lieutenant Erskine's round face and compact form as he crouched over the body to inspect it. He gestured toward the legs as he rose. "That's not a usual part of Groth's ritual."

"No, it isn't," Parker said, a rough edge to his voice.

"Could be a copycat. Or he's turning more violent." A tall, broad-shouldered man in a police uniform approached, a hand extended. "I'm Captain Robert Temple from the Hampton police. You're from the Parker Agency?"

"Yes, I'm Wade Parker." Parker shook the hand then gestured toward Miranda and Becker. "My associates, Miranda Steele and Dave Becker."

Everyone shook hands grimly.

"Lieutenant Erskine said you'd be coming along." Looking at a loss, the captain scratched at a thick, crop of wavy dark hair with his pen. "Normally I'd be in charge of a case like this, but I'm turning this one over to Inspector Whitman here, from the Georgia Bureau of Investigation."

"I'm acquainted with Ms. Steele and Mr. Parker," a gruff-sounding female voice with a slight Southern accent said.

"Yes, I remember." Miranda turned to the petite, stocky woman in her mid-forties with short, choppy dark hair dressed in a blue business suit and low pumps picking her way across the weedy grass. Miranda had worked with the woman over a month ago and recalled the grim expression that told her the inspector had seen a lot of death and gore in her time.

After another round of businesslike handshakes, the inspector looked down at the victim's mangled legs. "Looks like he used a hammer on her."

Leon had always been violent. But the part of the body he'd chosen to disfigure made Miranda think of Mackenzie and her skating. A sickening shudder went through her as she considered the face again. "How could she look so peaceful after he did that to her? He must have drugged her. He used the date rape variety with his other victims."

"Good point."

"We can have our Narc boys see if they can find a recent exchange of GHB," Erskine offered.

"That could be helpful." The inspector consulted her clipboard. "The victim's name is Julie Kimble. According to reports, she was walking home from girls' softball practice after school on Tuesday and never arrived. The parents called the police and a missing child report went out on the airwaves. There was no response until a neighbor was walking his dog and found the body under these trees around five p.m. today."

Rubbing her arms, Miranda looked down at the body again. "Terrible tragedy."

"Awful," Becker murmured beside her. He looked a little pale. He'd never seen a real murder victim before.

Inspector Whitman let out a weary breath. "Yes, it is. We won't be able to keep the press away from this story much longer. I'm about to inform the parents. Would you, Ms. Steele, and Mr. Becker care to go with me, Mr. Parker?"

"If it's just the same, Inspector, I'd like to pursue a different lead."

The inspector eyed Parker a moment the way a law enforcement official eyed a PI who liked to play by his own rules. But she let it drop. "Of course. I'll catch up with you later then."

Parker nodded and turned away.

"Why aren't we talking to the parents?" Miranda wanted to know as they made their way back to the car.

"They're going to be distraught, hysterical."

"Of course, they are." Her own heart ached for them. They'd be going through impossible pain.

"There won't be much information they can provide tonight. We'll see them tomorrow once they've had a chance to absorb the news."

Guess that was the smart thing to do.

Parker sent a disappointed Becker home to get some rest and checked himself and Miranda into a local hotel so they wouldn't have to fight city traffic in the morning. The place was nothing like the fancy ones his father owned in the city, but neither of them was thinking of amenities right now.

In the room, the first thing Parker did was check on the guards watching the Chatham and Van Aarle estates. All was normal there, much to Miranda's relief.

But she saw the deep lines of grief on his face as he wearily took off his coat, hung it on the provided rack, and settled into one of the hotel chairs.

"We'll get something to eat in a bit and get an early start in the morning," he said, rubbing his face. His voice told her he felt as helpless as she did.

She sat down on the edge of the bed. "We'll find him. Sooner or later, we'll get that bastard."

He gave her a sad smile. He was usually the one to say things like that. "I hope it's before any more young girls die."

Parker focused his gaze on Miranda and suddenly saw her in a way he never had before. There she was, long and lean and beautiful, in tank top and jeans, her dark hair as wild as ever. But her exquisite face was full of the very same emotions that tore at his heart this very instant.

He rose, pulled her to her feet and took her into his arms. He ran a hand through that lovely, thick hair. "I've never had anyone to share the grief of working a case like this. Not deeply."

Her face said she understood that as well. Understood it all. She got him like no other woman ever could. "I'm here now," she whispered, her voice full of pain.

He kissed her hard, drinking in all of her, taking in all he could of their connection, their bond, and wanting more. He touched her skin, warm and soft, ran his hands over the fabric of her top.

She yielded to him with a low moan and began to pull his shirt out of his pants. He responded in kind, his hands groping under the cotton of her tank top, searching for the solace of her soft flesh.

It didn't take long before their clothes were pooled on the floor. They stepped out of them and he leaned her back on the bed.

She attacked his mouth with hers. His mouth answered back, drowning their sorrow in their love, willing away the pain, the sorrow, the sense of futility. His hands were all over her now, as hers were on him. Touching breasts and stomach and thighs.

He had to have her now. He couldn't wait another instant. He pulled her thighs apart and thrust himself inside her. He watched her eyes go wide with a fireburst of desire, heard her gasp. More, more.

He pummeled her as she pistoned her hips in a fury and met each stroke. Harder, harder. Deeper, deeper. Until they erupted. Light exploded behind his eyes and flooded his very soul. And as they came together, he felt more at one with her than he ever had. And he knew more surely than he ever had that his life would never be the same if he ever lost her.

CHAPTER TWENTY-SIX

The homeless shelter was full of derelicts, just as he'd expected.

He picked up his tray of food and scanned the tables. No, not that one. Too fat. Not him. Too short. He spied a man about his own build and age sitting alone, digging into the meal like he'd just been rescued from the desert.

That one.

He strolled over to his aisle, scooted down it and laid his tray on the plain, cheap surface. "This seat taken?"

"No, help yourself." The man didn't even look up. He just kept shoveling.

He sat down and eyed his tray. Mashed potatoes, corn, some kind of mystery meat smothered in gravy.

He leaned over to his neighbor and nudged him. "Didn't we used to call this shit on a shingle in the pen?"

The man grinned but shook his head. "It's pretty good for free."

He took a bite of the potatoes. They were real. It was good. Of course, not having a hot meal for over four months might have something to do with the taste. But he started shoveling it in, just like his neighbor though he was careful not to get any on his beard.

The growth on his chin was short but full now. His own. He'd dyed it gray and wore a wig of stringy long hair to match. His clothes were clean, but ragged. He looked like he belonged here.

He'd been very careful. He'd moved and changed his appearance again. He'd done the rest of his shopping well of out the areas where they were looking for him. He'd done everything at night so there'd be less chance of being spotted.

Just a few more details and he could put his plan into motion. He had to hide his excitement as he ate.

The hall was about three-quarters full of men of various ages. Younger ones with Bibles strolled around the room.

He gestured with his roll as he chewed. "So what's this place like?"

"You haven't been here before?"

"First timer."

"It's not so bad. You have to listen to a lot of crap about hope and walking with God and stuff. The counselors talk to you, try to help you with your problems. They give you a suit and get you ready for a job."

He made a face of disgust. "Job?"

The neighbor shrugged again. "It's not so bad."

"Anybody here know where to score some smack?"

The man chuckled. "Don't be talking about that in here. That can get you kicked out on your ass."

"If I had known it was so strict, I might not have come."

"Better than the streets."

"I've got a place. Just no electricity. A man needs a hot meal once in a while."

"Behind on your bills?"

He nodded and kept chewing.

"That's bad, but it could be worse." A sad look came over his face. "I lost my family in a tornado two years ago. Wife. Two kids. Whole house was destroyed. I couldn't face life after that." He sopped up gravy with his roll.

"You had no one else you could turn to?"

"Both our parents were gone. I was an only child. She had an older brother who'd died of cancer three years before."

No family. Perfect. "You know what? I've got beds in my place more comfortable than the ones I saw back there. Why don't we blow this joint and go back there? I'd like to hear more about your story."

The man turned to him, his eyes bright. "Really? You'd take me in?"

"Maybe we can work something out together."

He thought a moment, licking his teeth. "I don't know. I've been here three times. I don't want to lose my spot."

"There's always a spot waiting here. Isn't that what they say?"

His lips pursed and moved to the side as he considered.

He leaned toward him and whispered. "I've got a bottle." He opened his jacket and showed him the flask in his pocket.

A smile broke out on his neighbor's face. "You can't bring that in here."

"I just did," he grinned. "Come on. Let's kick a few back and tell each other our life stories."

His neighbor looked around the room once more and nodded. "Why not?"

They got to their feet, dropped their trays off on the conveyor belt along the wall and headed out the door.

"Anthony," a man with a Bible called after them. "Aren't you staying for the challenge?"

"I'll be back, George. Just talking a little walk."

CHAPTER TWENTY-SEVEN

The next morning, Miranda showered and put on the fresh clothes Parker had had delivered to the room. As she pulled on the slacks and short-sleeved sweater, while he finished in the bathroom, she eyed the pressed suit on the hanger, the hairbrush and cologne on the dresser, and wondered how he pulled such things off. She ought to be used to it by now.

After a quick breakfast in the hotel dining room they drove down a long country road to a middle class subdivision with well-kept lawns and nice brick homes that lined a curving street. The red one at the end of the row was the Kimbles' house.

They may have waited a day, but this still wasn't going to be easy, Miranda thought as she stood on the front stoop with Parker and watched him use the brass knocker on the front door.

Inside a dog barked and there was the shuffling of feet. After several long moments, a man in a bathrobe with bloodshot eyes opened the door.

"Can I help you?"

"Mr. Kimble?"

"Yes."

"I'm very sorry to disturb you, but I'm Wade Parker from the Parker Investigative Agency and this is my associate, Miranda Steele. We're here about the incident with your daughter."

The man closed his eyes and shuddered and Miranda's heart went out to him. "Yes, the investigator last night mentioned you might stop by. Come in."

So Inspector Whitman had guessed what Parker was up to.

They stepped into a short, hardwood hallway with a white staircase leading to the second floor, then Mr. Kimble led them through a set of indoor glass doors to a cozy living room.

A light-colored, comfortable looking couch sat by a bay window. It was bordered by overstuffed chairs and a coffee table littered with cups and sports magazines. A big screen TV was against one wall, a white painted fireplace along the opposite one, with framed pictures and trophies.

Miranda recognized the victim in one photo. In another was an older boy in a high school football uniform.

"Please, have a seat," the man said gesturing to the chairs.

"Who is it, James?" called a pleasant voice through an open door Miranda assumed led to the kitchen. She could smell bacon and coffee.

"People here about Julie, honey. You remember Inspector Whitman said they might want to talk to us?"

"Oh, yes." A pretty woman with thin, dark blond hair that fell past her shoulders appeared in the doorway. She was in light blue cotton slacks and a pink-and-blue checked blouse. Sandals with plastic flowers were on her feet and she carried a dishtowel she was using to wipe her hands. Her face looked drawn and pale.

"We didn't mean to interrupt your breakfast," Parker said, apology in his voice.

"We're just finishing up. We'd be happy to answer any questions." She entered the room, hand extended. "I'm Tamara, Julie's mother. But I guess you know that."

Miranda took the woman's hand between hers. It was cold as ice. "We're so sorry for your loss."

Nodding, the poor woman rubbed at her nose. "Thank you. Please, sit down. Would you like anything to drink?"

"No, thank you, ma'am. We're fine," Parker said. "We just have a few things to go over."

"Certainly," said James.

Parker waited for Miranda to select one of the chairs and took the one beside her while James and Tamara settled onto the couch.

Two pairs of sorrowful, red-rimmed eyes looked at them for direction.

Miranda felt at a loss, though she knew the procedure. She let Parker get started.

He began with his usual tact. "We apologize for disturbing you at this terrible time, but hopefully you can provide us with answers that may lead to the capture of the perpetrator we're looking for."

The woman rubbed her arm and the man put a comforting arm around her. "Yes, we understand."

Parker scanned the mantelpiece. "Looks like your daughter was quite the athlete."

James smiled with a father's pride. "Both Julie and Cameron, her older brother, are active in sports. Or she—was."

"I understand she played on the girls' softball team for the local middle school?"

"Short stop. She was good. The team was heading for the tournament in a few weeks."

"The Red Devils. They're the best," a youthful voice declared. It belonged to the young man in football gear in the photos. He stood in the kitchen doorway in pajamas, his dark red hair tousled.

James patted the couch. "Come here, Cameron. You might as well listen to this."

Head down, the young man shuffled across the room and plopped down next to his father. He was large for his age, tall, big shoulders, long muscular legs. The body of an athlete. Obviously did some weight training. He also turned to them with red-rimmed eyes.

Miranda smiled sadly at the trio. The picture of a once happy family, now destroyed. She took a deep breath and asked the next question. "This past Tuesday night, Julie was walking home from softball practice. Is that correct?"

"Yes," Tamara answered. "She usually walked home if it wasn't raining. We only live a mile and a half from the school and she said it kept her shape. She was a little obsessive about her conditioning. And her figure. You know how girls that age can be."

"Yes, I do. Did she typically walk with friends?"

Tamara turned to Cameron, as if for confirmation. "Usually, yes. She has a lot of friends. She's very popular. Everyone likes her. But her closest friends are on the softball team."

Cameron sat forward on the couch. "Tuesday she stayed late to help Abbey get some extra batting practice in. Abbey Roberts. She's over five hundred and she's working to do better. That's good for softball," he explained.

"How do you know Julie was with Abbey, son?" Parker asked.

"She texted me." He held up his phone, scrolled through messages. "It's right here." He stared down at it as if realizing this was the last text he'd get from his sister.

"May I see it?" Miranda asked as gently as she could.

Nodding, the boy handed her the phone. She read the text. *Batting practice with Abbey. Tell Mom I'll be home late.* The time sent was six oh three.

"How long is practice?"

"Until six," Tamara said. "She's usually home by quarter after. James gets home at seven and that's when we have dinner." She rubbed her hands together. There had been no nice family meal that night. Miranda could imagine the worry the poor woman had to endure.

"Abbey didn't walk home with Julie that night?"

The boy shot a thumb over his shoulder. "She lives in the opposite direction."

"I see. No other texts from Julie after that?"

Cameron shook his head. Miranda handed the phone back to him.

Parker picked up the questioning. "Was Abbey a good friend of Julie's?"

"Yes, she was friends with several girls on the team, as my wife said." James gave a stiff nod to emphasize the point. Good that a father knew his daughter's friends. But he might not know all of them. "Faith O'Donnell and Rebecca Turner in particular."

Parker made a note of the names in his phone. "Anyone else?"

Cameron shot his father a guilty glance. "There's that Zachary girl."

James scowled back at his son. "She's been told she's not allowed to go anywhere with that girl."

Tamara smoothed her slacks with an awkward laugh. "That's Samantha Zachary. She's what you might call one of the bad crowd."

"The kind that hangs around out behind the gym smoking." Cameron rolled his eyes.

Miranda watched James's scowl grow deeper and noted his son didn't mentioned exactly what the kids were smoking.

Parker cleared his throat. "Any boyfriends?"

James shook his head. "We don't allow her to date. She's too young for that."

"Of course." Parker smiled with understanding. "I raised a daughter myself. Do you happen to have the addresses of Julie's friends?"

"Yes, I do. I have them in my address book." Tamara rose to get it.

"I hope you don't mind this question, but," Miranda gestured toward the photos on the mantelpiece. "Julie's hair seems lighter in that picture." The body she'd seen last night had long, jet black hair.

Tamara turned back, touched her lips to hide her displeasure. "Oh, she suddenly decided to dye it dark last month. I don't know why. You know how girls are."

"Yes."

As the mother turned to get the book, Miranda wondered if the Zachary girl had black hair.

James patted his son on the back. "Why don't you help her, son?"

"She can find her address book, Dad."

"Go on."

"Okay." With a look of disappointment, Cameron shuffled out of the room.

"Detectives," James said quietly after the boy was gone.

"What is it, Mr. Kimble?"

"Inspector Whitman said, well she implied this might have been done by that man on the news. The one who escaped from the hospital last week?"

His fists were balled at his side. He looked like he could kill the man who took his daughter's life. Miranda didn't blame him one bit.

Parker nodded sadly. "We don't have conclusive substantiating facts yet, but yes. That seems likely."

Watching the grief trickle over the father's features as he took in those words, a hard, nauseating fist knotted in Miranda's stomach. The loss of a daughter was the worst pain a parent could endure.

As the mother returned and Parker jotted down the information, thanked them for their time, her thoughts began to race and her heart break all over. A popular girl, athletic and successful in sports, with dark hair.

Too much like Mackenzie to be coincidence.

CHAPTER TWENTY-EIGHT

Four hours later they had talked to the parents of each of Julie Kimble's friends, visited the middle school and spoken to the girls individually, and questioned Julie's teachers.

The parents were desperately worried about their daughters, the girls were jittery and afraid of the crazy killer on the loose, the teachers defaulted to the grief counselors to deal with the tragedy, but everyone's narrative was essentially the same as the one the Kimble family had given them.

When Parker showed them the photo of Leon that had been on the news, no one recognized him. And no one had seen a tan SUV in the area.

The school was closing early due to the tragedy and the halls were empty. Miranda and Parker were following Julie's homeroom teacher down one of them to examine the victim's belongings when they spotted a kid at Julie's locker holding a backpack.

He was tall and gangly, dressed in the baggy-pants style of the day and a really ugly tank top. And what was that red thing on his head?

"Jake Sullivan," the teacher called out. "What are you doing there?"

The kid turned, did a double-take and when he saw three adults coming at him down the hall, he dropped the backpack, turned tail and ran.

"Hey!" Miranda shot after him with Parker right behind.

"We're investigators," Parker called out. "We need to speak to you about Julie."

He ignored them and shot through a pair of double-doors at the end of the hall. In two seconds Miranda reached the spot and plunged through the doors.

Stairs.

She could see the red mop bobbing up and down below her. She heard Parker behind her and the frazzled teacher trying to keep up as she scrambled down the concrete steps two at a time. She couldn't catch up to the boy. Frustration chewing at her, she watched him shoot through another set of doors at the bottom of the stairs.

She jumped over the railing, pushed through the doors, kept running. A long, cream-colored hall stretched before them. Their fast-paced footsteps echoed against the walls as they passed posters announcing school events and empty rooms. The kid looked back over his shoulder and sped up.

She sped up.

She had almost reached him when he pressed through another door. Right behind him, she shoved it open before it shut all the way and found herself in a large room with long rows of tables and chairs stacked against the far wall.

Cafeteria.

The kid was scrambling across it, but the floor must have just been waxed. He was having trouble with his footing.

She made one last sprint, and when she was within two feet of him, she leapt up and snatched him by the shoulders. Down they went, skin smacking on the linoleum and skidding about a foot as they landed.

Ouch, that hurt.

"What's your problem, kid?" Miranda gasped once he was still.

He leaned up on an elbow. "What's yours, bitch?"

"I'll thank you not to call my associate names." Parker had just reached them and was barely winded.

"Jake," the teacher cried, her heels clicking in quick mincing steps across the shiny floor. "I have a good mind to suspend you."

"I wasn't doing nothing."

The teacher opened her mouth as if she were about to correct his English, then shut it again.

Parker turned to her. "Is it all right if we talk here? Alone?"

She hesitated a moment, then nodded. "Of course. Behave yourself, Jake," she said to the boy. Then she clicked back across the floor with only a tad of doubt in the last look she gave them over her shoulder.

Miranda hoped she wasn't getting the principal. She got to her feet and dusted off her clothes. Parker yanked the kid up by the scruff of the neck, retrieved a cafeteria chair, placed it at the end of a table and shoved him into it. "Have a seat, Mr. Sullivan."

The boy scowled as he rubbed a shoulder and pulled down his top that had rolled up when they landed. "Taz. My name's Taz."

Cute nickname. Miranda strolled around the table and leaned over to sneer at him. "I think I'll call you Jim Bob."

He curled a rebellious teen-aged lip at her. Hah, he didn't know how used to that she was.

"I didn't do anything wrong."

"Then you don't have anything to worry about, Jim Bob."

His eyes flared, but he didn't say anything this time.

Miranda looked the kid over. The mop on his head was a burnt red Mohawk. To go with his baggy, torn up jeans, he wore a nose ring, a puke green tank top and a bright orange sunburst tattoo on his left shoulder.

The tat really clashed with the do. "Your color coordination is a bit off there, Taz."

"Huh?"

"Never mind."

Parker stepped before the kid and spoke in the dark, threatening tone he usually reserved for hardened criminals. "Did you know Julie Kimble?"

"What's it to you?"

"We're from the Parker Investigative Agency. We're trying to find out who killed Julie. Your silence indicates you must be involved in the murder."

"You gotta be jokin'." The kid's voice went up two octaves. "The last thing in the world I'd do is hurt Julie." He put his chin on his chest and folded his arms as he stared down at the table. "I loved her."

Miranda looked at Parker, a brow raised. Boyfriend? The father hadn't thought there was one.

Parker rested a thigh on the table and softened his voice. "Was Julie your girlfriend, Taz?"

He swiped at his nose with his arm. "Yeah. We'd been dating for two months."

So much for parental supervision. "How old are you, Taz?" Miranda wanted to know.

His bony shoulders went up and down. "I'll be sixteen in three weeks. I'm going to get my learners permit. I thought we could go on a real date then."

She just bet. "Do you know Samantha Zachary?"

Again the shoulders bounced. "She's a friend. Julie and Samantha and I hung out."

Parker gave her a sad look. "Do you know what happened to Julie?"

"Somebody killed her. They found her last night." His voice broke. He put a thin hand over his mouth to stifle a sob.

Patiently Parker drew out the photo of Leon and laid it on the table.

Taz leaned forward to study it. "That's the photo of that creep who escaped from that hospital in the city."

"Did you ever see Julie with this man?"

"No," he said slowly, his eyes growing wide.

Miranda leaned in again. "Did you ever see a tan SUV around the area."

"Tan SUV?"

"When was the last time you saw Julie?"

The kid looked at her, then at Parker, then swallowed. "We'd stayed after school. After softball practice, you know—to talk."

Sure they knew. So she wasn't helping Abbey Roberts with her batting. "Go on."

"I was walking her home. Well, I usually only took her to the corner. And we got in a fight." He hugged himself and shivered.

"What was the fight about?"

He rolled his eyes. "I wanted her to tell her parents about us and she didn't want to. She got mad and stormed off."

"And what did you do?"

"I said some things I shouldn't and then I took off in the other direction. Toward my house. Then I realized I had her books and ran back." He stared off into space and began to rock, arms tight around his torso.

"What did you see, son?"

"I—I saw her get in a car. I thought it was another guy. I was so mad I couldn't see straight."

"What kind of a car was it?"

"I don't know. Was it an SUV? Maybe. Yeah, I remember thinking that's probably Kyle Adams. What's he driving his mother's car for? Yeah, it was an SUV."

"The color?"

He blinked several times as if he were reliving the scene. "It was under some trees. Then it pulled out." Slowly he nodded. "Yeah, it was tan. I remember now." His face took on a look of panic as his eyes filled with tears. "Is it my fault? Am I the reason she's dead?"

"No, son. You're not the reason."

"I didn't say anything to anybody. I didn't want to get her in trouble. And then they said she was missing and—I don't know. I just didn't see the connection. I thought she went home and maybe tried to run away. I didn't want to rat on her. That's why I was at her locker just now. I was trying to put her backpack in it." He laid his arms on the table, put his head down and sobbed. "It's my fault. It's my fault she's dead."

Gently Parker reached over and patted the kid's arm. "It's not your fault, son. It's the killer's."

Miranda watched the poor kid, waiting for him to get the worst of it out of his system. But she knew it wouldn't be the end for him. It might have helped if the kid had reported what he'd seen, but probably not much. Not with a psycho like Leon.

What she wouldn't give for fifteen minutes alone with the bastard. She'd finish the job she started in that wine cellar four months ago when he took Wendy. That wasn't going to happen. She'd never get that chance. But she'd see the sonofabitch put away.

Now that he'd killed again, the search would intensify. They'd get him sooner or later. And once they found him, she'd get to watch as an army of cops and investigators closed in on him. Maybe she'd be in the lead. Maybe she'd be the one to put the cuffs on him. She wanted to watch his face when she did.

He'd get life, or worse, for killing Julie Kimble and Tiffany Todd and Madison Taggart and the woman in Philly. And child killers didn't do well in prison.

She'd see him dead in due time.

CHAPTER TWENTY-NINE

They reported their findings to Inspector Whitman, had a quick bite in the local diner, and joined the police and the GBI in the search for the SUV. Down the main road to the speedway to Highway 20, through the catacombs of subdivisions and neighborhoods, past long stretches of farmland and grassy fields, around to Highway 81.

"How can it be so hard to spot an SUV in an area this small?" Miranda groaned, chewing the ends of her hair as she peered out the window at a dilapidated white frame house surrounded by pine trees.

Parker slowed the car and pulled into the gravel lane that served as a driveway far enough to scrutinize the area behind the house.

Nothing there.

"Groth could be hiding in one of the neighboring towns."

"Or he could be back in Atlanta. Or in Florida for all we know."

Parker let out a breath that betrayed his frustration. "Erskine has released the information about the tan SUV and the tag number Becker found to the news stations. The police in every area around Atlanta have been informed. It's the best we can do."

So she had to be satisfied with this detail for now, she guessed.

They kept driving and searching until the sun went down and for several hours after that. But the darker it got, the more Miranda felt like they were chasing their own tails. And Leon was somewhere else. Laughing at them.

It was well past midnight when they reconvened at the police station with a disheartened Inspector Whitman and Captain Temple in his office.

As the captain studied the results of the search, their collective discouragement hung in the air like a dark cloud.

He slapped the file shut and blew out a breath. "Goose egg. This sucker's harder to find than my granddaddy's brand of snuff."

"He's crafty and he knows what he's doing," Parker said darkly.

"He used to be in law enforcement so he knows the procedure," Miranda added.

Inspector Whitman gave her a sorrowful look and got to her feet. "Sad to say, the GBI may have exhausted the possibilities here."

The Captain looked even more dismayed. "Oh?"

Parker extended a hand to the captain. "I'm not sure there's any more we can do here, either."

The captain looked bewildered. "You're going?"

Parker gave his hand a brief shake. "It's likely Groth is no longer in the area. We'll be returning to Atlanta in the morning and continuing the search there."

Miranda was relieved to hear that. She didn't see a reason for Leon to stick around here when his real target was in Buckhead. It was one explanation why nobody could find him in this vicinity.

The large man nodded solemnly. "I suppose the best hope for our town is that Groth has lost interest in the area. That doesn't help you out, though. I'm sorry we couldn't do more."

"As are we."

"Yes." Miranda took in the sorrow in the lines of the captain's face as she shook hands with him. She didn't know what else to say. As much as she wanted to get back to Atlanta, she hated going home in defeat. And with no answers for Julie Kimble's poor family.

The inspector moved to the office door. "If anything turns up in this case, don't hesitate to call."

"I won't." The captain rose, his big frame towering over the desk. "Let me walk you out."

He was only halfway across the small room when his phone rang. "Excuse me." He crossed back, reached for it, listened.

Miranda watched his wide brow crease, his face fill with alarm. "Are you sure?" He jotted something down on a pad. "We'll be right there." He hung up and stared at them with glazed eyes. "Anonymous caller just reported a barn fire at the old abandoned Anderson farm on 81. The caller said he saw our SUV there."

Miranda's heart raced in time to the screaming sirens and they sped down the dark country road following the flashing lights of the police cars ahead of them. Her mind flooded with questions. Would they find Leon at this farm? Would there be a shoot out? A chase through the woods?

Whatever happened, she would do all she could to bring that bastard in tonight and turn him over to the fate he so richly deserved.

"There." Parker pointed to a bright blaze lighting up the sky as they zoomed over a hill.

"Good Lord," Miranda said. She hadn't realized the site would be such a disaster.

At the bottom of the hill, Parker pulled the Mazda to the side of the road behind one of the fire trucks and stopped. They both got out and dashed up the street to where the commotion was.

When they reached the farm's front yard, firefighters shouted at them to stay back.

All Miranda could do was stare open-mouthed at the ball of white flame consuming the barn, illuminating the silhouette of surrounding trees, a shadowy billow of thick, black smoke pouring into the dark sky overhead.

Across the road behind them, neighbors began to arrive in pickups and cars. Women with worried faces in housecoats and robes. Bare-chested men in quickly pulled-on jeans. Stunned children in pajamas. Her training made her turn and scan the faces, but she didn't see the glee of an arsonist on any of them.

All she saw was shock.

In the yard, firefighters shouted directions to each other as they surrounded the building and wielded hoses at the blaze like machine guns. Thick streams of water snaked high into the air, dousing the structure in a zigzagging motion.

The fire raged on. Flames crackled and dripped from the eaves like rain. Along the building's side, she could see part of the wall. Or what was left of it. Dark boards between the glow and the outline of the rafters against the white blaze. A fighter off to one side shouted something. Another one answered. Miranda couldn't understand them.

Minutes passed. Gallon after gallon poured onto the flames. The air became saturated with a sickening wet char smell. At last the fire died a little. The fighters seemed to have it contained to the inside now, but it still had life. They kept their hoses trained on the blaze.

"Look out," someone shouted and part of the roof caved in and thudded to the barn's floor. The char smell grew thicker.

It seemed to take another hour before at last the bright flame turned to a deep red glow and the last embers began to flicker and go out. Then inside the barn, all went black.

Personnel began moving about the area, the sloshing sound of their footsteps echoing in the dark. Floodlights were set up for examination. Billowing gray smoke filled the inside of what was left of the structure.

Gradually Miranda became aware of Parker's arm around her, stroking, comforting. She was too much in shock to respond.

She realized Captain Temple was on her other side. "No owner. No live stock, thank the good Lord," he murmured. "This structure is almost a hundred years old. Rotten and dilapidated as hell. I'm surprised it hasn't fallen down on its own."

Shouts came from the far side of the demolished barn. "We got it."

"C'mon."

She and Parker and the captain hurried across the grass in the direction of the cries. It was some of Temple's officers. Inspector Whitman approached from the opposite way.

"What do you have, Johnson?" the captain called.

"The SUV, sir."

Heart thumping, Miranda followed the group with Parker behind a shed that was well away from the barn, hidden by a tall row of weeds.

"We scanned this area five times today," one of the men said.

She and Parker had been past this farm, too.

"But we didn't look back here."

Someone shined a light over the vehicle.

Miranda stared at it. "The color's right. So's the model. Is this the one?"

"We'll confirm that with fingerprints," said one of the men, pulling open the back door, gloves already on his hands. "Whoa, look what we have here."

Everyone rushed around to the back of the vehicle and peered inside as the officer swept his flashlight over the contents. Miranda didn't know whether she was thrilled or sick at the sight.

A coil of thick rope. A large spool of white ribbon. A bottle of oil. She could see the herbs floating in it. Could this car have been back here the whole time they were searching the area? Or had Leon just driven it here, stopping in that barn for the night?

Another cry came from one of the firefighters near the barn. "We've got a DOS."

Her muscles went rigid. A Death on Scene?

"There's a body in here." The man gestured back to the inside of the structure.

Miranda stared at Parker. Could it be? No, that was too much to hope for. But they both took off toward the barn.

One of the firefighters in his gear and helmet held his arms out as they approached. "You can't go in there. Too dangerous."

"We're investigators," Parker told him. "We need to see the body."

Whitman made her way to the front. "I'm Inspector Whitman from the GBI, requesting access. There may be evidence vital to an ongoing investigation."

"She's right, George," Captain Temple told him.

Indecision on his face, the man signaled to his superior and after a protracted discussion, Miranda and Parker and a select group of officers were given slickers, protective hats and masks and allowed into the barn.

"If anything goes, you'll have to vacate the premises immediately."

"Understood." Nobody wanted to be crushed under falling debris.

Gingerly, Miranda stepped under the charred doorway and onto the pile of wet ashes that used to be the barn floor.

It was a large, open area. The smoke had mostly cleared, but still lingered in the burnt out rafters overhead.

"The body's over here." The fireman named George escorted them as they sloshed across the ash-covered floor to a charred mound. "He must have come in here for shelter. From the burn pattern on the barn floor and the walls, it looks like he started a fire for warmth and it got out of control."

Captain Temple picked his way to a spot along the wall. "There's a gas can here. Melted."

George nodded. "We saw that. Once the fire reached the gas can, the flames would have spread too fast to contain it. His only chance was to leave the structure. Apparently, he was asleep."

"We found an empty liquor bottle over there." Another man pointed to a corner.

"Right. He might have been too intoxicated to wake up."

Miranda approached the dark mound on the floor where the officers were standing and felt Parker reach for her arm to steady her. Good thing he did. She felt pretty shaky when she looked down.

The clothes had disintegrated and the naked body was covered with black and bloody char. The face was gone. The groin area looked like an over grilled steak. So did the legs and arms. There were a few spots where the flesh had escaped being seared. Part of a shoulder, the back of a hand. Not that it had saved him.

Someone bent down, picked at the scalp with a pair of tweezers until a matted piece of something that looked like fried hair came up. A faint odor of sulfur was in the air. "Looks like he was wearing a wig."

A disguise.

"There's a patch of fabric there."

Parker walked over and leaned down to examine it. "It looks like a match to the shirt the rental agent described Groth was wearing."

That had been on the news, along with all the other details.

"Got a hammer over here." Across the floor another technician crouched near a support beam. "Handle's gone, but it looks like there's blood on it."

"Bag it," Captain Temple told him.

"Hey, here's a charred bit of rope."

The tools Leon used to mutilate Julie Kimble's legs. So this was where he did it. Where he killed her and performed his stupid ritual. She put a hand over her mouth.

Hands on hips, Inspector Whitman surveyed the scene. "Collect all you can. We'll have an arson specialist go over the scene and the evidence as soon as possible."

"Yes, ma'am."

Miranda rubbed her arms and stared at the woman. "Can you get a positive ID from that body? The face and fingerprints are gone."

"We'll have to use dental records and hope we can get a match."

"How long will that take?"

The inspectors face was grim. "Could be a few weeks."

Miranda tugged at her hair. How could they go that long without being sure? She had to know.

"I think I've got something, Inspector."

Miranda moved to where an officer was still going over the body. His tweezers were working a spot at the end of the blackened arm, along the equally blackened fingers. The air was foul here, but she wasn't about to turn away.

"Well, lookie here." He pulled away the scorched fragments to reveal something shiny. After a minute or two, he had it pried off the singed finger. He held it up with the tweezers. "Does this mean anything?"

Miranda bent down. It was a ring. A shiny gold ring. A wedding ring. One that looked vaguely familiar. She began to shiver as if she had the flu. Her eyes started to water, but it wasn't from the smoke. Stubbornly she brushed at her eyes and looked hard at the ring.

Her heart stopped.

Inside was an inscription. She read it aloud, her voice quivering. "*Miranda and Leon. Love is forever.*" She'd forgotten she'd given that ring to him all those years ago. And he'd kept it?

Air. She had to have air. She rose, stumbled through the ashy shards until she was outside. She bent over, hands on her knees, gasping, inhaling deeply, trying not to throw up.

She felt Parker's hands on her back. "Miranda, are you all right?"

"It's him, Parker." She drank in air between words, waved an arm at the building. "That horrible charred body in that barn is Leon."

"Yes, I know." He took her arms, pulled her up, held her face in his strong hands. "It's him. It's over. He's gone."

Over. Leon gone. Burnt to death in an accidental fire. Could it really be possible? She thought she'd feel more joy, but she just felt sick. Closing her eyes, she leaned her face against Parker's chest and sobbed.

It was over. At long last it was over. But right now, she only had one thought.

"Take me home."

CHAPTER THIRTY

Miranda opened her eyes and squinted at the sunlight streaming in the tall bedroom windows. Her head felt like she had a migraine. "I don't think I can make it to work today," she groaned without rolling over.

Parker's low, soothing voice came over her shoulder. "It's Saturday."

"Oh." Now she remembered. And she remembered the fire last night. The smell of smoke was still in her nose.

Leon was dead. Gone forever. She rubbed her eyes. It was Saturday? Wendy and Mackenzie would be at the ice rink. A wave of sheer relief washed over her. Now Mackenzie can go there and practice and Wendy can watch and nothing bad will happen to them.

It was over.

But then she thought of her talk with Mackenzie and the toy bunny she'd thrown at her and the relief was replaced by a dull ache. Her search for Amy was over, too.

For good.

She tried to pull the covers up, but her whole body felt like lead. Her muscles were as sore as if she'd tried to climb Mount Everest. "I think I might be coming down with something. I'm going to stay in bed."

"It was a long night. You're exhausted."

She remembered the long, silent ride home and that she couldn't stop shivering. She remembered Parker helping her shower and putting her to bed.

She laid a hand against her temple. It ached. "What time is it?"

"Almost ten." Parker came to the side of the bed and leaned over to kiss her on the forehead. He was dressed in one of his fancy suits. A dark charcoal that made his eyes deliciously vivid. He was so handsome. Tenderly, he stroked her hair. "Just rest today. I'll have Sarah make you something to eat when you get up."

"'kay." She almost had the energy to nod.

"I have to see a client this afternoon, but it shouldn't take long."

"Sure." She closed her eyes and barely heard him leave before she drifted off again.

"Wade, I'm so happy you stopped by again."

Parker was sitting on the hummingbird couch with Patricia in the small sitting room next to her bedchamber. "You texted me six times over the past few days."

"Oh, I know. I hope I wasn't being a pest," she said in her low, aristocratic Southern voice. "I just thought you might have forgotten about li'l ole me." She laughed and casually touched his hand with her long, graceful fingers.

This afternoon she wore a low-cut but elegant late summer dress. He eyed the silky flower print that accented her breasts, set off her thick red hair and made her flirtatious green eyes come ablaze.

He drew back and hid the action by reaching for the glass of sweet tea she'd insisted on serving him this time. He took a sip. Too sugary for his taste. "I've been rather busy."

"Oh, that's right. You've been chasing that horrid man they've been talking about on the news. Every day something new about him. It must have been awful."

"It's my job."

"I don't know how you do it. But now the news says he's, well—dead. In a fire."

"Yes." He didn't like discussing his cases with people outside the business.

"Well, you're a hero, aren't you? But then you made a name for yourself as a hero a long time ago." She took both of his hands so that he couldn't reach for the tea.

"Thank you, Patricia. But this time I didn't do much."

"Oh, nonsense. You've always been so modest about your accomplishments. I'm proud of you, Wade." She smiled that winning, full-lipped smile at him.

She was an attractive woman. Sylvia used to tell him she was proud of him. He gazed about the quiet room. After a trying case, he used to cherish coming home to a peaceful place like this and being with his lovely, understanding wife who didn't know a thing about the danger or the gore or the evil he'd faced. She didn't care to know. Instead she made another world for him that was safe and far from the turmoil.

She was one of his class and they'd understood each other on that level. Perhaps it would be easier if he had married someone like her the second time. Someone like Patricia. Gen would certainly have been happier.

But instead he had married Miranda. A woman who could share his deepest purpose. The sorrows as well as the triumphs. He had no regrets.

He cleared his throat. "Now, Patricia. About your surveillance."

"What about it?"

"We haven't found anything."

"What do you mean you haven't found anything?"

"I had my men go over the videos and there's no unusual activity on them whatsoever."

"Well, I haven't been missing any pieces lately. Maybe it was a fluke."

"Are you sure you didn't misplace the diamond earrings you thought one of the staff had taken."

Her eyes went round, blinked several times. She looked down and smoothed her skirt. A tell-tale signal. "Yes, Wade. I'm very sure."

"Let's do this then. I'll remove the equipment."

"Oh?"

"And make it somewhat apparent that I'm doing so. That way, if someone did figure out that there are cameras watching the area, that person will let his or her guard down."

"And if another piece goes missing?"

"Then we'll have more evidence and can try a different approach."

She chewed on her lip as she thought it over. "It sounds reasonable. Very well."

"I'll take care of it right now."

In the large, feminine bedroom, he made a deliberate show of taking each camera out and shutting it down. The one in the desk lamp, the one behind a photo. But when he came to the third one, the one in the smoke detector, he feigned disabling it and putting it in his pocket. Actually he left it in place. It would either prove or disprove his theory.

As he descended one of the curving twin staircases to the mural-lined entrance, Parker made casual conversation. "That's that, then. I'm so sorry we didn't find anything, Patricia."

Patricia grinned at him with a sly wink. "That's all right, Wade. It was good to see you. Do you have everything you brought with you?"

"Yes, right here." He held up his kit and watched her face. He saw exactly what he expected in her eyes.

As they reached the front door, she touched his arm in a friendly squeeze. "Now, you haven't forgotten about my fundraiser at the Town Club, have you, Wade? It's this coming Wednesday."

He had forgotten. Wednesday was only a few days away. He wasn't sure Miranda would be up to it.

Her face filled with genuine disappointment. "You're not going to tell me you won't be there, are you?"

He didn't want to hurt her. He still considered her an old friend, even if all this about the jewelry was a ruse. He shook her hand as he stepped out the door. "I'll give you an answer soon."

Then he turned away, eager to get back home to his wife.

CHAPTER THIRTY-ONE

The fire burned with a fervent heat. It swept around her, its flames licking her arms and legs. Her lungs filled with smoke.

She had to keep going. She had to save the girl.

She stumbled down the long, dark hall, trying to escape the roaring flames, trying to find her. At last she reached the end of the passage. It opened into a large cavity with sooty stone walls covered in eerie dark tapestry.

And there near the front was the girl—lying on a funeral pyre.

She was completely still and covered in a black cloth. Her face was hidden, but somehow she knew her. Or thought she did.

She heard the soft echo of a child's cry. *Mama, Mama.*

She started toward the girl, but the flames swept across the floor and pooled near the platform where she lay. It cracked and flickered and leapt, growing higher, stronger.

And out of the midst of it arose a body. A man.

His flesh was charred and bloody, half his face burned off. His jaw fell open and words boomed out of his gaping mouth. "Did you really think you could get away from me?"

She screamed and the sound echoed against the dark stone walls. "You're dead. I saw you."

He only laughed. "*Love is forever.* You're bound to me eternally. You can never escape me."

No!

She turned and ran. Back under the archway. Back down the long hall. If he followed her, she'd save the girl from him. The flames lashed out at her, searing her flesh. She smelled her own skin burning. She ran faster. The flames became a whip, beating her. A belt. Leon's belt. Striking her over and over.

Not anymore. She could fight now. She turned, kicking high in the air. The blow should have landed square against his jawbone. Instead it only went through air.

And then that bloody, charred body appeared again.

He shoved her down. Her bones smacked against the hard concrete.

He watched her, hovered over her—and smiled as he unzipped his pants.

The grotesque thing was going to rape her.

No. No. Her hands groped over the stony floor, searching for a weapon. Anything. She found the knife. She picked it up.

It was already dripping with blood. Soon there would be more. She scrambled to feet, turned and stabbed at him. She didn't hit air this time. This time the knife pierced through flesh and muscle.

But he only laughed.

She stabbed him again. Blood spurted out of the wound.

He kept on laughing. The ugly sound of it echoed in her eardrums, in her head. "You can't kill me. I'm already dead. You'll never get away from me. Never."

"Yes. Yes, I will!" And she stabbed him again. Again and again and again. "You bastard. I'll kill you. I'll kill you."

"Wake up, Miranda."

Her eyes shot open.

She was on her stomach, pounding her pillow mercilessly with her fist. Parker's hand was on her wrist trying to stop her. She opened her hand. It was empty.

She turned to him. "Oh, my God."

"You had a nightmare," he told her in a reassuring tone, as if he wasn't sure she knew that.

But she did. She'd had another one. Maybe the worst one yet.

She buried her forehead in the pillow. "I saw him."

"Groth?"

"Yes. He was bloody and charred like that body in the barn. He said I'd never get away from him."

He took her in his arms and pressed her to his chest as he kissed her hair. "Oh, my darling. It was just a dream. A bad one, but just a dream."

Yeah, just a dream. She laid her hand on his chest. It was bare. She frowned. "You're in bed. What time is it?"

He turned to look at the clock on the nightstand. "A little past one in the morning."

"What day is it?"

"Sunday now. You slept through Saturday."

"I did?" She laid her head down on the pillow, feeling disoriented. "I don't know if I can go back to sleep." Or dare to.

"Do you want to get up?"

"No, I think I'll just lay here awhile."

Parker studied her face, saw the lines under her eyes and thought of the sheer terror he'd seen in them when she awoke just now. If only he could take away her bad dreams. Wounds that bastard of a husband had left her with, even in death. Parker had had nightmares himself after a particularly gruesome assignment. He knew what it felt like to be haunted by a case.

She should see Dr. Wingate as soon as possible, but he wouldn't push her into it. Right now, he had to find something to take her mind off the ordeal she'd been through. With what? Sex? That would be pleasant but fleeting.

He thought of Patricia's fundraiser at the Town Club. That would give her something to look forward to. Or to dread. A better choice than a nightmare. Perhaps they could have rousing fight over it.

He threaded his fingers through hers, brushed his lips over her knuckles. "How would you like to go to a party with me?"

Miranda raised her head and looked into those cagey gray eyes. He was trying to get her mind off the nightmare. "A party? Now?"

He chuckled. "Not now. This Wednesday. A friend of mine is having a fundraiser at the Town Club."

"Town Club?"

"It's a country club here in Buckhead."

"Right up my alley," she grimaced.

"There will be dinner, dancing, champagne. Oh, and a silent auction."

"A silent auction? Goodie," she sneered.

"We can go shopping for a new dress for you."

She raised a brow. "Because you know I love clothes shopping about as much as I love parties?"

"Exactly." He smiled at her, sly and sexy and proud of himself. Then he bent his head and kissed her.

A slow, sensuous kiss that had her skin tingling with arousal. Especially when he ran the tip of his tongue lightly over her lips. He was trying to make her forget her dream. And doing a darn fine job of it.

She came up for air and poked a finger in his hard, naked pectoral muscle. "It's you who wants to go to this shindig, isn't it?"

As if considering her question, he ran his fingers up her arm, sending delicious shivers up to her head, down her spine to her groin. He wasn't playing fair. "I'm obligated in a way. And I haven't been to a social event in quite a while. It's expected."

"You have to go."

"More or less." He turned her over, unbuttoned her cotton sleep shirt and began to nibble the side of her neck.

Was he trying to seduce her or piss her off? She'd show him. She'd give in on both counts. "I'll do it, but let's don't pretend a silly party is supposed to cheer me up after that bad dream." She slid her hand down his side, found his manhood, stroked and cupped him and watched his eyes flame.

"Very well," he said, his breath growing ragged as he ran his thumbs over her to pay her back for her last move. "We'll say it's a sobering social obligation. A dour duty that will distract us from everything else."

Yeah, everything else. She opened her legs, reached around him and pulled him into her. "Okay, I'll go to the party."

"As bravely as you'd go to your own execution."

"Right." She pushed against him, smiling in spite of herself, letting herself drown in the sensation.

He worked her hard, his delicious breath panting over her face, his fingers still tormenting her. She let her mind go. She was safe now. Safe. No matter how dark her dreams, this wonderful man would always be there to bring her back from the edge. She needed him more than ever now. And for once, that thought didn't terrify her.

When they came together, she cried out and held onto his neck as if for dear life. He was her rock, her anchor. And just now, she didn't care if that made her vulnerable.

CHAPTER THIRTY-TWO

Despite the quiet rest she'd had after Parker's skillful and tantalizing lovemaking, Miranda couldn't find the energy to do anything but mope around the house on Sunday. She flipped through boring magazines, nibbled at the food he had prepared, watched an old movie on TV with him, and went to bed early.

The next day she went to work and stared at the stack of background checks to be done.

"I told Washington to take over those cases."

Miranda looked up and into the dark eyes and sharply angled face of Detective Tan. "I thought I was on probation."

"Not anymore. We've got another subpoena to serve."

She looked down at the folder in her lap. She was still embarrassed over the last incident with that deadbeat dad. What if she lost control again? Besides, for some reason, she didn't feel like it. "Okay if I pass today?"

Tan's expression grew sympathetic. "I know what it can be like after a tough case."

"Yeah?"

"It can get to you. You must be worn out after all you've been through, Steele."

Miranda shrugged. "Guess I am." Hard to believe Tan could be so empathetic. But she'd had some rough cases herself over the years.

"Why don't you take the day off."

"Really?"

"Sure. Go home, get some rest, get it straightened out on the inside. Then you can report back here tomorrow as good as new."

Yeah, maybe she should. She wasn't doing any good around here and sooner or later, she'd just screw up again. "Thanks."

She grabbed her things and left.

Back home in the Parker estate, Miranda lay on the soft leather couch in the living room flipping channels on the big screen television.

The news about the barn fire in Hampton was all over the TV. Everyone was talking about the murderer who'd escaped from the hospital and had been burned to death in the blaze he'd started himself by accident. Of course, further investigation was pending from the GBI but in everyone's mind, the case was closed.

So why wasn't it closed for her? Why couldn't she move on?

She turned off the TV and closed her eyes.

She didn't dare go to sleep. She didn't want to have another nightmare alone in this big house. She smirked at herself. What a basket case she was. What the hell was wrong with her? Was she going crazy?

Today was the first time since she'd started at the Parker Agency that she hadn't wanted to go out on a job. She used to fight tooth and nail to be assigned to field work. She was losing it.

Maybe she should call Dr. Wingate and see if she could fit her in this afternoon. But she'd been going to the shrink for months and it hadn't helped.

She thought about the cases she'd solved. Each time, she'd had that same creepy feeling. Like ants crawling over her skin. Maybe that's what had led her to the right conclusion. Maybe it wasn't skill or her "highly tuned instincts," as Parker had once called them. But in Hampton, she hadn't felt anything like that. Maybe she was losing that, too.

Maybe she didn't have what it took to be a private investigator any more. Maybe she never did. Maybe she was a fraud.

What if her destiny or whatever you wanted to call it had been to put an end to Leon and to save Mackenzie? She'd done that, so the job was over.

And maybe, so was her career as a PI.

With a groan, she got up and plodded into the kitchen. She wasn't really hungry. The cook was off today. Maybe she'd make herself some soup. If she could find a can. Or maybe she'd find a bottle of Parker's good Irish whiskey and get rip-roaring drunk.

She almost jumped at the scratching at the back door. She turned around and heard meowing.

Rolling her eyes, she got down a saucer from the cupboard, found some milk in the fridge and poured a bit into it.

Then she opened the sliding glass door and stepped out onto the hardwood deck.

The black cat meowed louder and wound around her feet. "Okay, okay. I've got it right here." She set down the saucer and watched the greedy little thing start lapping it up with her pink tongue.

She bent over and rubbed the creature as it ate. "Hi ya, Inky. How've you been?"

Still crouched, she scanned the tall oaks and pines that hemmed in the lush backyard. Her gazed focused on the latticework fence with its climbing vines that divided the Parker lawn from the neighbor's.

It wasn't too long before she heard a rustle, watched the vines started to move, and the fence part.

Wendy slipped through the opening.

She had on black jeans and a red top accented with black buttons. Her dark hair hung to her shoulders.

Miranda rose and folded her arms. "Mighty neighborly of you to stop by."

"Hi, Miranda." The kid just smiled at her as she crossed the yard and bounced up the stairs to the deck. "Inky got out again."

"So I see."

She crossed the deck and plopped down on the red wood bench that bordered the space. "So, how have you been?"

"Just fine. Why aren't you in school?"

"Fall break."

"I see."

Still smiling Wendy bobbed her foot up and down. "I, uh. I was wondering what you were doing this weekend?"

"This weekend?"

"Uh huh."

"No plans. What's this weekend?"

The kid rolled her eyes. "What planet have you been on?"

"I've been a little busy and that's not something you should say to someone you're about to ask for a favor." Kids never would appreciate what you went through for them.

The foot went still and her expression turned to annoyance at being discovered. "How do you know I was going to ask you for a favor?"

"Just a wild guess. What do you want?"

"Well, since you don't know, this weekend is the Junior Interstate Championship in Lake Placid."

Now all this made sense. "Ah. Mackenzie's competition."

"She's really on her form, Miranda. She's going to do so well. I just know she's going to win."

"And what does this have to do with me?"

Now the kid looked down and poked at the deck floor with the toe of her sneaker. "I just have to see her. I just have to be there."

"And?"

She looked up and her big brown eyes were watery. Miranda knew that was real. "My mother can't take me. She said she would before and now she says she can't. She says she's got an important conference call coming in that she can't miss." Her lower lip quivered and she bit down on it, turned her face away.

Miranda's heart went out to her. How could Iris break the kid's heart like this? She had a good mind to go over there right now and bitch slap the woman. "Does your mother have tickets?"

Wendy shook her head. "She forgot to get them. And it's supposed to be sold out."

"What about Jordan's mother?"

She rolled her eyes. "Jordan's not going. She's staying home and reading. Can you believe it? Everyone else has already left." Then her expression turned to a plea and her dark eyes glistened with girlish hope. "Can you take me, Miranda? Can you get us tickets?"

"I don't know—"

"Please, please, please?" She clasped her hands together in supplication.

Take Wendy to Lake Placid and watch Mackenzie win that championship? It would be the thrill of a lifetime. Maybe she'd never have a relationship with her daughter. Maybe the girl would never speak to her again. But for that single moment, she could pretend everything was all right.

Tickets. Parker ought to be able to do something about that. She nodded. "Okay, Wendy. I can't promise I can pull it off, but I'll see what I can do."

"You will?"

She lifted her palms. "What are neighbors for?"

"Oh, Miranda. You're the bomb." Wendy jumped up and threw her arms around her, grinning the biggest grin she'd ever seen on her.

A flood of emotion rippled through Miranda. She had two daughters, didn't she? Two young girls that at special, fleeting moments she could pretend belonged to her. She hugged the girl back and grinned pretty big herself.

As soon as Wendy had taken Inky and gone back home, Miranda ran inside, grabbed her cell off the island in the kitchen and dialed Parker.

He picked up right away, alarm in his voice. "Miranda, is everything all right? Detective Tan said you left work."

"Yeah, I did. I was wondering, would it be okay if I took a few days off? Maybe 'til next Tuesday?"

"Certainly," he said, caution in his tone. "I was going to recommend it. I thought we might go somewhere, but—"

"Oh, really? Maybe another time. Look, I need a favor."

She could feel him doing a double-take. "What is it? Do I need to come home?"

"No," she laughed. The first time she'd laughed in days. "Wendy just stopped by. Mackenzie's championship in Lake Placid is this weekend and Iris can't take her. She wants me to go with her." Did she really sound as breathless and excited as the thirteen-year-old had?

"Oh, do you think that's a good idea?"

"I've thought about. I'll stay out of the way, of course. But I'd really like to see her perform. She might win and I—I'd just be so proud." She started hunting through the kitchen cabinets. She felt so maternal. Maybe she should bake a cake. Or some brownies.

"Yes, I understand."

"We need two tickets and the place is supposed to be sold out." She opened the fridge. No brownie mix in there. What was she doing? She needed to start packing. She'd be gone for five days. And it was cold up there. She'd need a coat and warm clothes.

"I see."

"Do you think you can get them?" Her breath caught. He could, couldn't he?

"And airfare, I suppose? As well as lodging?"

She exhaled on a smile. "Well, yeah."

"When do you want to leave?"

She thought a minute. They'd need time to get settled. "Thursday, I guess."

"I'll see what I can do."

Hot dog. She knew he would come through. "Cool. Oh, and maybe we can go shopping for that dress for your party tonight? I need to pick up some things for the trip."

Now he chuckled, relieved that she'd come out of her funk. "I'll be looking forward to it. I'll take you to dinner afterwards."

"That sounds good. See you tonight."

"Miranda?"

"Yes?"

"I love you."

The sweet words made her giggle. "I love you, too." She hung up and threw a fist of victory into the air.

She was going to Lake Placid with Wendy to see Mackenzie skate. She better get on the Internet and bone up on figure skating. She'd use Parker's computers.

She fairly danced up the stairs to the office.

CHAPTER THIRTY-THREE

How did she ever let Parker talk her into going to a party at a members-only country club? Miranda thought, fighting the sharp-spiked nerves attacking her stomach as they rolled up the long drive to a sprawling gray slate estate with massive, ultra-manicured grounds that made the Parker mansion look like a little country cottage.

Unless she was hunting a murderer among the wealthy set, the horsey set, or whatever other set might show up at a bash like this, she didn't have much to say to anyone.

But dutifully, she let the valet open her door and stepped out in a shimmering midnight blue sheath that matched Parker's Lamborghini and sparkled as brightly as the diamond necklace and earrings he'd bought her on a whim last night during their shopping spree.

Parker came around, offered his arm and they made their way into a sun-drenched entrance hall that extended three stories overhead.

She leaned over and whispered. "I didn't know we'd been slumming it at your place."

He laughed and patted her hand. Then he led her into another large open hall where everyone was drinking champagne and chatting about whatever rich people chatted about. They were doing the silent auction in here and tables were set up around the room's perimeter displaying the offerings.

Miranda's stomach went into an Irish jig as she surveyed the crowd of well-dressed men and women in tuxedos and glittery gowns and expensive jewels. When Parker handed her a champagne flute from a server and started introducing her to the hostess and his other peers, the jig in her gut became a jitterbug.

Everyone who was anyone in Atlanta was there. Legislators, judges, lawyers, doctors, business people.

She knew some of them. The Taggarts, whom she liked. The Ingrams, whom she didn't. Wilhelmina Todd, a coworker of Estavez', who was standing beside Mr. P and Tatiana while the elderly gentlemen entertained a group of listeners with some far-fetched story of his real estate conquests.

The Chathams were a no show, of course. Colby and Oliver were already in Lake Placid with Mackenzie. Iris wasn't here either. A country club probably reminded her too much of her absentee, golf pro husband.

Miranda thought she recognized a woman studying one of the baskets being auctioned. A finger against her chin she cocked her head thoughtfully. Sure enough, it was Coco. At last, someone she could talk to.

"Excuse me," she said to Parker and the couple he was chatting with and made her way across the floor to her friend.

Coco's baby blue eyes went wide when she caught sight of Miranda coming toward her. "Oh, hi there," she grinned shyly.

Her pretty blond hair was styled and she was wearing a silky pale pink gown that gave her that angelic look she often had.

"Are you playing tonight?"

"What? Oh, no." She shook her head. "I'm here with Antonio."

Miranda followed her gaze and caught sight of Estavez. He had just found Parker and was pulling him off to the side for what looked like a serious private chat. Uh oh. This evening could get more heated than Parker expected.

She turned back to Coco. "Anyway, I've been trying to get a hold of you. I want to talk you about you and Estavez."

"Miranda—"

She held up a hand. Now that she had the opportunity, she was going to say what she had to say. "I know it's none of my business. I know I'm no one to judge. But we're friends, aren't we? And I care about you."

"That's very nice, but—"

"So what I have to say is that I think it's too soon. You and Estavez haven't known each other that long and you met under duress. And we just went through that awful thing with your ex and—what?"

The girl had a very weird expression on her face and was chewing her bottom lip like a squirrel with a fresh nut. "Um, there's something I need to tell you."

"You did what?"

"Papa, keep your voice down."

Parker pressed his hand to his head, feeling as if it might explode. He couldn't believe the words that had just come out of his son's mouth. "Do you mean to tell me you ran off and got married?"

"'Eloped' is the term for it."

"After I told you my reservations about this decision? Why, Antonio?"

The handsome Latin features that had helped this young man win countless cases in the courtroom took a more pensive expression than Parker had ever seen on him. "We saw the news about Groth on television. An escaped murderer. A killer. I knew you and Miranda would go after him. I thought about the things he did last time." Antonio put his hands in the pockets of his tuxedo and sighed. "And so I said to Coco, 'life is too short to wait. How long do any of us have, anyway?' And she agreed with me."

Parker stared at him tongue-tied. "I don't know what to say to that, son." It wasn't as if he'd never had the same thoughts. Or taken a rash action because of them. Though he'd never regret his decision to marry Miranda, and he hadn't moved as quickly as Antonio, he certainly had wasted no time.

"How about 'Congratulations'?"

Parker ran a hand over his face and forced down the wave of temper he'd been fighting. "It's going to take me some time to get used to this, Antonio."

"I understand."

But he wanted more from him. If only he'd—what? Told him first? He only would have argued. It wouldn't have changed anything. He let out a sigh. "The best I can do for now is simply wish you both well." And hope his fears about their union wouldn't come to fruition.

Antonio gave him a wry smile. "That's all I wanted from you, Papa."

CHAPTER THIRTY-FOUR

Miranda took one look at Parker's face as he seated her at one of the thirty or so tables in the elegant dining room and knew Estavez had let the cat out of the bag.

"Shocker, isn't it?" she murmured in his ear.

"Quite," he said after settling into his seat and greeting the person next to him.

"You want to go home early?"

He shook his head, dashing her hopes for a short evening. "I have something to take care of before we leave."

She gave him a suspicious look as a server laid a salad plate in front of her. "Don't you usually go to these events to get the goods on a suspect?" she whispered.

"Sometimes." He picked up his fork, waited for her to start eating.

"Will you be doing that tonight?"

He almost smiled. "You never know."

Okay, Mr. Tight-Lips. Miranda dug into her salad and while Parker chatted to his neighbor, listened to the stately-looking woman next to her inform her she was one of the founding members of the club and her family had been prominent in Atlanta since before the Civil War.

Managing to eat at the same time, the woman kept on talking. She was about up to 1890 when the main dish was served. Some sort of shelled scallop and lobster deal in a buttery sauce. It tasted rich, though a little bland without a good douse of hot sauce. Several more dishes were served and the woman moved on to gardening and her prize begonias. During dessert, while munching on a creamy raspberry cheesecake, Miranda learned the difference between annuals and perennials.

She was glad when the meal ended and everyone moved back into the other hall for the silent auction and dancing.

Parker went off to hobnob or whatever it was he was doing while she looked over the donated items up for bid and hoped he would finish his business here soon.

There was a beach lovers' basket, a wine lovers' basket, a spa day, a new BMW, and even a trip to Brazil. Some of these sponsors were really generous.

She was eyeing the chocolate-lovers' basket when someone came up beside her. "I have my eye on those Godiva Truffles."

Miranda turned around and grinned. Finally. The second person here she knew and liked. "Wilhelmina. How are you?"

The tall, lean, elegant-looking woman nodded solemnly. Tonight she was in a deep green gown and wore her dark brown hair to her shoulders. "Fine, in general. Felicia and I have our good days and bad days."

"I can imagine." As well as being a top defense attorney at Chatham, Grayson and McFee, Wilhelmina was the mother of Tiffany Todd, one of Leon's victims last spring. Felicia was Tiffany's older sister.

The woman took her hand. "I want to thank you for what you did."

Miranda was surprised at her gesture. "What do you mean?"

"You finally put an end to Leon Groth."

She shrugged. "I didn't really do much, Wilhelmina. Lieutenant Erskine did more to solve the case coordinating press releases."

She gave her a knowing smile. "And you're modest as well as a fine investigator."

Miranda stared down at her high heels. She hadn't felt like a fine investigator the past few days. But she was glad for Wilhelmina. "I'm happy you have some closure now. I just wish we could have stopped him sooner."

"You did your best, I'm sure." She looked over the room, a sad anxiety in her gaze. "I don't think I'll be staying much longer. Felicia's with her father tonight and I have a big case to work on."

"I see." Miranda didn't want to talk about Wilhelmina's philandering ex. For all she knew, he'd been in Iris Van Aarle's bed doing the hoochie coochie all week.

Wilhelmina sighed. "He says he's getting married again."

Oh, dear Lord. What would that do to Wendy? She opened her mouth, but nothing intelligible came out.

Wilhelmina squeezed her hand. "I'm fine. It's over for us. He can do what he wants." She straightened her shoulders. "Well, I've bent your ear long enough. Where is that husband of yours? I want to thank him as well."

"He's around somewhere."

"I'll find him. Call me sometime." And she strolled gracefully away.

Where was Parker? she wondered.

A server passed by with more champagne. She took a flute and was about to take a sip when she caught sight of her debonair husband ducking into an alcove across the floor with a buxom red-head in a gold dress.

Now what was that about?

"Oh, Wade. You are such a flirt. I'm so glad you're enjoying my party."

"You look like you're enjoying it yourself, Patricia."

"I think I might be about to enjoy it even more." Her low laugh echoed in his ears as her green eyes fixed on him with a look that was decidedly seductive. "Now what did you want to talk to me about?" She took his hand in a gesture far more adult than any hand-holding they'd done as children.

Parker studied the woman. Her expertly applied makeup. The deep red that accented her full lips. Her thick hair caught up in an intricate braided sweep. Her golden, low-cut dress pouring over her breasts like a fountain of champagne. Her flowery perfume filled his nostrils and at the moment, made him just a bit nauseous.

He hadn't wanted to do this now at her event. But her callous flaunting had provoked his ire. "I see they're back," he said ambiguously.

She frowned, tilted her head coyly. "Who's back?"

"Not who. What." He touched the lobe of his own ear. "The jewels that were stolen?"

Her mouth opened as she blinked at him and touched one of the diamond-and-emerald antiques on her ear. "Oh, you mean these?"

"Yes, that's precisely what I mean."

"Oh, well. The uh, perpetrator must have put them back. I opened my jewel box this afternoon and there they were." She lifted her hands with a laugh.

"Really?"

"Yes." She gave him that full-lipped smile.

"But I saw you putting them back in the jewel box earlier today myself."

Now her blinking grew rapid. "You—what?"

"When I took down the surveillance cameras I didn't tell you that I left one up."

"You—you did what?"

"It captured you putting those very earrings you have on back in your jewelry box. At 1:12 p.m. this afternoon to be precise."

She made a little gasp, looked around as though searching for an explanation. "Oh, well. That's right. I didn't find them in the box." She smoothed her hair. "One of the staff returned them to me personally."

"Who?"

"Who? Well, I wouldn't want to say."

He clucked his tongue. "Really, Patricia. Blaming your staff for what you did yourself?"

"I—" she suddenly went speechless.

"Why would you do such a thing?" His voice was tender now. He wanted her to know how disappointed he was in her.

She read the signal incorrectly and slipped both arms around his neck. "Oh, Wade. I'm so sorry. I just wanted a chance to talk. To rekindle things between us."

He grabbed her wrists and pulled her arms away from him. "We were children together. There was never anything between us."

"Oh, Wade. I used to lie awake at night and dream about you after your visits. And then you grew up into such an enigmatic man."

Now she was making him angry. "I'm married, Patricia. It would be best if you remembered that."

"But are you happily married, Wade?" She reached for him again.

Again he pushed her away. "Your case is closed, Patricia. I'll be sending a bill to your house."

And he stepped out of the alcove to escape, despising that he'd lost an old friendship. Straightening his coat and tie, he looked around the room. Where was Miranda? It was time to go home.

Near the hall's far corner Miranda considered the mannequin with a lavender gown worn by the governor's wife to the White House. Parker might like to win that for her, but she had so many dresses. Besides it might be too much of a conversation piece and she hated being the center of attention.

She turned away taking the last sip from her flute and nearly choked on the champagne.

Eyeing her from a few feet away was Tanya Terrance.

The tall, model-thin, long-haired beauty was in a gown of bold red with a cowl neckline that hung to just under her boobs. Pricey bracelets snaked around both arms and ruby red lipstick gave her a blood-thirsty look as she smiled and raised her flute.

As if on the spur of the moment, she turned and sidled toward her, the hem of her dress flaring. "Well, well, well. If it isn't the latest subject of my show. I'm surprised to see you here, tonight, Miranda."

"I do get out once in awhile. Who let you out of your cage?"

"Oh, what a sense of humor you have." She waved a hand as she reached her. "No, really. I'd like you to be a guest on my show."

On the *Talk of the Town*? She'd sooner jump into a snake pit. She forced a smile to hide her smirk. "I don't think so."

"Oh, come on, Miranda," Tanya crooned in her smooth radio show voice. "We all want to hear from the woman who took down Leon Groth."

"Except I didn't take him down."

Tanya shrugged. "Technicality. Saying you did makes better press."

Miranda felt her lip twitch. She didn't want to talk about what she'd seen in that barn to anyone let alone broadcast it over the airwaves. "Gee, that's so sweet of you to ask, Tanya. But I think I'll pass."

The woman gave her a how-dare-you-say-no-to-me glare and took a sip off the top of her full champagne glass. "And here I'd thought someone like you would be lapping up the limelight." Her voice was loud and getting louder. People nearby turned around to gawk.

Walk away. Just smile and say good night and walk away. Instead she put her hand on her hip and curled a lip at the bitch. "And why would you think that?"

"Well, someone with your background? You are after all you can get, aren't you?"

Miranda couldn't help baring her teeth. A circle of guests gathered around them. She wondered if someone was placing bets.

Tanya's red lips slowly parted in a vicious grin. "What I really what to know, Miranda, is how you feel now that your husband's dead."

A murmur went through the crowd. Anyone in the upper crust who hadn't heard Tanya's broadcast or who'd forgotten about it knew about it now. She wanted to kick that grin right off that bitch's face.

Instead, she set her empty flute down on a nearby table, raised her chin and spoke just as loudly. "I seem to recall my *husband* paid a visit to your station manager to complain about the show you did a few days ago."

Laughing, she batted the air with her hand again. "Oh, people complain about the things I say all the time. Charles doesn't pay any attention to them. And I've dug up some new information about you, Miranda. About a certain incident involving a courthouse in Chicago? And a cherry bomb in the men's room?"

Miranda felt her face go as red as Terrance's dress. That was about Amy. She'd done a little vandalism years ago when a judge denied her first petition to open her daughter's adoption records. Did Tanya know everything? Did she know who Amy was?

"You'd better be careful, Tanya or you might find yourself with a hefty lawsuit."

Again she laughed and shook her head. "Par for the course in my business. They never stick. My lawyers are too sharp."

Not if Parker went after her. Not if the Chathams got involved.

Now she leaned in, her voice low. "I'm going to make you pay for stealing the best catch in the city. I'm going to tell the world what a lowlife he married. Face it, Miranda. There's nothing you can do to stop me."

Rage pulsed through her. Miranda stood shivering with it, glaring at this audacious excuse for a human being. It took all she had not to bloody her nose. But she wouldn't start a brawl here and embarrass Parker. Besides she'd learned to control her temper. Most of the time. And yet, once in awhile, things just got out of hand. Like right now.

With a quick move, she snatched the drink out of Terrance's hand, pulled open her cowl neckline and poured the chilled liquid over her boobs.

"What?" Tanya gasped. "What do you think you're doing?"

"Paying you back for being a bitch." She handed the flute back to her.

And as the famous talk show host stood there dripping on the floor with all the important people in Atlanta staring at her, Miranda waltzed away with a smile.

When she was almost at the door, she thought she heard someone start to applaud.

CHAPTER THIRTY-FIVE

"That was a hell of an evening." Miranda had just stepped out of her midnight blue dress and was hanging it up in the huge walk-in closet.

"You provided an entertaining end to it." Parker gave her a sly smile as he removed his bow tie and unfastened his cummerbund.

"Not as entertaining as it could have been. You should be glad I know how to behave myself."

He chuckled and gave her a kiss on the cheek. "I'm very proud of you. But I might have paid money to watch you go after that shrew."

"Next time, I'll check with you first." She pulled on her night shirt, plodded into the bathroom to brush her teeth.

When she returned, Parker was in bed, his hard, muscled chest exposed, his handsome face pensive. He was the best catch in town. Tanya Terrance's words still stung her. Maybe he would have been better off with someone from his own kind.

With a sigh, she climbed into bed next to him. She hadn't thought that way in a while. "I'm sorry I ruined the event for you."

He looked up, coming out of his reverie. "You didn't ruin it. I was thinking of Antonio."

"Oh." She sank down into the covers, not feeling much better at that thought. "I wish I could have gotten to Coco before they jumped the gun."

"I don't think you could have stopped them." He turned off the light and lay down, slipping an arm around her.

"Guess not." She laid her head on his chest, reached for his hand and tucked it under her chin.

She felt him exhale wearily. "There's nothing we can do about it now. They're married."

"Except say 'I told you so' when—"

"It all falls apart."

"I was going to say when they have their first fight." She turned and studied his face in the moonlight from the window. Antonio's marriage to Coco really bothered him. Did he think the girl wasn't good enough for his son? Except for her bad marriage, Coco's background was a heap of a lot better than her own.

She thought about how awkward she'd felt tonight and how comfortable Parker had been in that setting. "I'm sorry I don't fit in."

"Fit in?"

"With your social set."

"You fit in just fine."

No, she didn't. And it was hard to believe it didn't bother him just a little.

She scrutinized his face. His eyes were open. Through the dark, he was staring at the ceiling.

"What is it?"

Parker ran his hand over her hair, took in her lovely features. If he had known Tanya Terrance would be at the fundraiser, he never would have taken Miranda there tonight. He knew she could handle herself. She was a tower of strength when she had to be. But even the mightiest tower could tumble if enough force were hurled against it. And she'd had some bitter blows lately.

He wasn't about to stand back and let that shrew get away with attacking the woman he loved. He'd contact Antonio tomorrow and begin proceedings against the radio station. He'd see Tanya Terrance fired before she uttered another word about his wife.

In the meantime, it was best if he could get Miranda away. Work was the thing. The only thing he could count on to bring her out of a funk. The sooner the better.

"Do you remember the proposal I mentioned a few days ago?"

Miranda cocked her head at him. Yeah, she remembered. "About branching out the Agency and offering services to a lot of different organizations?"

"Yes, filling a need when they're short on manpower."

"You and me going off and doing that, you mean."

"Yes. I think now is a good time to start."

She sucked in her breath. Had he been so humiliated about what happened at the party tonight he wanted to leave town? He'd never admit it. When he'd first mentioned the idea, she'd been thrilled. But now?

She thought of the weird way she'd been feeling the past few days. She hadn't even been able to bring herself to go to work. She didn't have her investigator mojo back. What if she couldn't get it back? What if she'd never really had it in the first place? She couldn't commit to a plan like this. She couldn't let him risk blowing important cases because of her.

She pulled at her hair. "Uh, I don't know. I'm not sure."

She saw the worry lines in his face crease. "I thought you were excited about the idea."

"I was. I am. It's just that—I'm going to Lake Placid tomorrow. How about I think about it while I'm there and we talk when I get back?"

"All right." In the dark, she felt him study her a long moment and knew he was reading her mind. "I'm going to put the wheels in motion at work tomorrow. I want a plan in place so we can leave as soon as you're ready."

If she would ever be ready. But she nodded.

Parker picked up his phone and consulted his calendar. "I have meetings all afternoon tomorrow. I might not make it home in time to see you before you leave." Was she reading in a subtle chill in his tone?

She shrugged. "That's okay. I was going to leave a little early, anyway. Spend some extra time with Wendy."

He smiled tenderly. "I'll say good-bye now then." He kissed her. But it wasn't as fervent a kiss as his usual. "I'll miss you, Miranda. Take care of yourself."

"I will. I'll miss you, too."

She settled down on the pillow and watched him close his eyes. Uneasy, she made herself relax and closed her eyes as well. Big day tomorrow. But as she drifted off, she had the distinct feeling something very precious was slipping away from her.

CHAPTER THIRTY-SIX

Miranda grinned down at the tickets on the marble kitchen counter. Two first-class seats on a flight to Lake Placid and two tickets to the Junior Interstate Championship. Parker had given them to her when he came home from work yesterday before they went to the country club.

Actually, the flight wasn't straight to Lake Placid. There wasn't a direct flight there so Parker had booked a chartered plane from a nearby town and the two vouchers were tucked behind the other tickets. Man, he was classy.

She'd texted Wendy right away with the terrific news and the time of the flight but hadn't heard a word from the kid. She was probably busy getting ready. Or chatting with her friends about it on Twitter.

She smiled as she thought about Parker apologizing that he couldn't get an earlier flight. Silly man. Didn't he know how amazing he was? She missed him already.

She'd slept late and hadn't caught him before he left for the Agency this morning though he'd left instructions with Sarah to make her a breakfast burrito with extra hot sauce when she woke up. Their housekeeper could make almost as tasty an egg wrap as Parker could.

He was so darn thoughtful.

She picked up the tickets, pressed them to her chest, then shoved them into her carry-on.

Let's see. Did she have everything? She'd carry her black leather coat. It was too warm to wear here and too big to fit in the duffle bag. Underwear, sweaters, a knit cap. Jeans and T's. Oh, candy.

She rummaged in the drawer for the bags she'd bought this week. Wendy liked chocolate, didn't she? If not, she'd get something else when they got to the hotel. She imagined sitting up all night and talking. Of course, it would be all about Mackenzie, but that's just who she wanted to hear about.

Sarah came in from the pantry and laid some jars on the counter. "Will you be taking off soon, Miss Miranda?"

"Yeah, I've got to get going. Pays to get to the airport early."

"Oh, yes. The lines can be long. Is there anything else I can do for you?"

Miranda zipped up her bag, slung it over her shoulder. "No, I think I've got it all."

"Have a good trip then."

"Thanks. See you in a few days." She bounced down the hall and out the mansion door. As she tossed the bag in the backseat, climbed into her Corvette and took off, she felt as if she were already flying.

The temperature was a nice comfortable seventy-two and the sun hadn't quite gone down yet when Miranda pulled around to the Van Aarle estate and stopped along the curb.

She scanned the sky. Not a cloud in the deep blue expanse. Great flying weather. She glanced at the door, half-expecting Wendy to come bounding out with a servant carrying her luggage behind her, but everything was still.

She hoped the kid was ready. She hoped she'd seen her text.

She got out of the car and climbed the drive past the landscaped lawn to the front door.

She knocked. Nothing. She glanced at her watch. They had to get going. She rang the bell and waited. No answer.

Finally she heard something that sounded like a small elephant bounding down the staircase. Wendy flung the door open, her hair in a towel. "Miranda."

"You're not ready. Did you get my text?"

"Uh, yeah. Did you get mine?"

Miranda pulled out her phone. She hadn't missed any messages. "No, I didn't."

"Uh, I guess I forgot to send it."

Miranda noticed now there was an edge to the kid's voice. "What's the matter?"

Her dark eyes flaming, she opened the door and stepped out onto the stoop. She was in shorts and a light T-shirt. Not ready to get on a plane at all. Hugging herself, she fairly shivered as she glared at Miranda.

"What's wrong with you?"

"I can't believe what you did."

"What are you talking about?"

"I talked to Mackenzie on the phone last night. She's so nervous about the championship."

"She'll be okay. She's a pro." As much as a girl her age could be.

"She said she can't stop thinking about what you told her."

Uh oh. "What did she say I told her?"

"That you're her real mother. That she's adopted and you don't even know who her father is. I can't believe you lied like that."

Miranda opened her mouth, but she didn't say anything. Maybe it would be better if everyone thought it was a lie.

"Why did you do that? It could throw off her performance. She could lose just because she's upset."

Miranda closed her eyes and shuddered. She wished she hadn't gone to see Mackenzie that day. "I made a mistake. I'll explain it to you on the plane. But we have to get going or we'll miss the plane."

"I'm not going with you," she sneered. "My mother's taking me."

"What?"

"Who's that at the door, Wendy?" Iris appeared in the open space wearing a chic business suit and slipping a demure earring through a lobe. "Well. Hello, Miranda." She didn't sound at all friendly. Wendy must have spilled the beans to her.

Miranda met her patronizing gaze. "Is what Wendy said true? You're taking her to Lake Placid?"

"Why, yes. I managed to get a late flight and ticket to the championship." Must be easy if you had bucks.

"Are you sure another meeting won't come up?"

Iris scowled. "No, I don't think so."

"Are you sure there won't be another *business* meeting?" She said it with enough sarcasm to make sure Iris understood what she meant.

Her scowl deepened telling Miranda she caught the drift. "No, I don't have a business meeting." She turned to Wendy. "We have to get going, dear. Run along now."

With another hateful glare, Wendy went inside and headed up the stairs.

"If you want to change your mind, Iris, feel free. I'll take Wendy to the Lake Placid."

Iris stiffened, and straightening her shoulders put on a phonier air than even Miranda thought she was capable of.

"Thank you very much for offering, Miranda. But we won't be needing your help." And with that, Iris shut the door in Miranda's face.

CHAPTER THIRTY-SEVEN

Miranda stood staring at the ornate door, fighting the tears without success. She couldn't feel worse if the kid had kicked her in the gut. Shakily she turned, somehow made her way down the driveway.

She got back in the Corvette and started to drive. She was halfway to the airport when she realized where she was heading and pulled off an exit and onto the side of a road.

She wasn't going to Lake Placid. She wasn't going anywhere. Wendy hated her. Mackenzie hated her. And now even Iris thought she was the scum of the earth. That woman had a lot of nerve. She could never explain herself. Wendy would never believe her. Or forgive her. She'd never have any kind of relationship with either her or Mackenzie now.

So where was she heading?

Home. To Parker. She had to talk to Parker.

His kind understanding always made everything better. Didn't he mention going off somewhere with him? Maybe that was just what she needed.

It was after dark when Parker pulled the Mazda into the driveway and hit the remote to the garage, barely noticing the unfamiliar car parked on the other side of the street.

He stopped the vehicle and gazed over at the spot where Miranda's Corvette usually sat. He missed her already. He hadn't heard from her, but her plane hadn't landed yet. She might get busy with Wendy and forget to contact him for awhile. He hoped she could lose herself in the activities. That everything would go well and she'd have a good time. She needed something good to happen.

With a weary sigh he reached for his briefcase and made his way to the kitchen entrance. A pleasant odor greeted him. Sarah had something warming in the oven, but he didn't see his housekeeper anywhere just now. The place seemed empty without Miranda here.

He went up the back way to his office, laid down his briefcase and took off his coat.

Details flooded his mind. At the Agency today, he'd met with the accountants and gone over the financials and the structure of the new contracts. Then he'd had a long meeting with Judd and Tan to divide responsibilities that would need to be taken care of in his absence.

Gen wasn't pleased with his decision and tried to talk him out of it, but his mind was made up. And he was certain Miranda would be open to the idea once she got back.

He intended to finish a little more work before bed, but he wanted a shower first. He picked up his coat and headed for the bedroom.

As he neared the end of the long hall, he was surprised to find the door closed and light streaming out from under it.

Was something wrong? He reached for the knob, turned it, stepped inside. And froze.

She lay on the bed wearing a crimson dress with a zipper along the front. It was pulled down halfway to her navel, revealing most of her ample bosom. Her thick red hair fell around her face sensually. Two full wine glasses sat next to a bottle of Riesling on the night stand.

She gave him that flirtatious, full-lipped smile as she slid one leg over the other. "Good evening, Wade."

At first he couldn't find his voice. When he did his words came out in a gruff growl. "Patricia. What are you doing here?"

"I heard the little woman was out of town. I thought you might want some company."

The room reeked of her flowery perfume. At the moment, it made him sick. "How did you get in here?"

She bit her little finger thoughtfully. "Oh, Sarah let me in. I told her we had a little unfinished business to take care of." She laughed, low and sensual.

His jaw tensed. "Sarah did not put you in this room." And how did she know Miranda was out of town? Was she watching the house? That was her car he'd seen parked across the street.

"No, she put me in a sitting room downstairs. But I found my way up here. I remember this was where the master bedroom was when I came here as a child." She smiled again and wiggled a finger at him. "Come over here, Wade. Don't you want to relax after your long, hard day?"

He took a few steady breaths to quell his anger then as reasonably as he could he told her, "You'll have to leave now, Patricia. As I told you I'm a married man."

She clucked her tongue at him. "I know you are, but I understand. At our age you can get a little desperate. But darlin', you deserve so much better. Let me show you."

Old family friend or not, he was at the end of his patience with Patricia. He'd remove her bodily if that's what it took. Laying his coat on the valet rack, he moved toward the bed.

Miranda opened the front door, dropped her backpack on the marble floor and stared up at the grand mahogany staircase. She'd left the Corvette in the drive, too exhausted to even bother pulling into the garage.

Parker was home, though. She saw the light in the window upstairs.

She couldn't wait to feel his arms around her, to hear his low, soothing voice telling her everything would be all right. She wanted him to make love to her. To take her away somewhere. Maybe to the north Georgia mountains where they'd spent time before.

Not knowing where she found the strength to move, she trudged across the hall and up the stairs.

It was on the landing that she heard voices. Was he on speaker phone? Did he have someone over for a business meeting? She hoped not. She didn't want to wait until he finished a meeting to pour out her heart to him.

She headed down the hall and realized the voices were coming from the bedroom. Parker and a woman. A woman with a thick Southern accent. A rich accent. What the hell?

She hurried to door and shoved it open.

Did she cry out in shock? If she did, she hadn't heard herself. It seemed as if the earth had opened and suddenly swallowed her up and she was in some cavernous hole where nothing was real.

What she saw before her couldn't be real. It was impossible. Ridiculous.

In his dress shirt and slacks Parker was bent over their bed. Beneath him some woman lay on the comforter. She had on a red dress. Sort of the color Tanya Terrance had worn last night. The fundraiser. That's where she'd seen that woman before. In a gold dress—ducking into an alcove with Parker.

Right now, her long bare legs were around Parker's waist. Her long bare arms were draped around his neck. She was—kissing him?

Her jaw started to work but it seemed like several minutes before she could hear herself. "Parker? Parker?"

He turned, alarm in his eyes. And something else she never thought she'd see in them—guilt.

He winced. "Miranda. I know it sounds very clichéd, but this isn't what it looks like."

"Iris is taking Wendy to Lake Placid," she murmured, barely hearing him. Her vision blurred and she couldn't see him, either.

All she could see was the look of triumph on that woman's face.

Trembling from head to foot, she turned and tried to make her way down the hall, though the floor seemed to be bobbing like waves on an ocean. Somehow she managed to stumble down the hall to the stairs.

"Miranda, please. Listen to me," she heard him call over the landing.

She kept going.

Parker hurried down the stairs reaching the bottom just in time to see her pick up her duffle bag and go out the front door with a slam.

He stared at it unable to move. Before he could get his car keys and go after her, he felt a bare arm slink around his shoulder. "Let her go, Wade. She doesn't deserve you."

He spun around and knocked the embrace away. "What the hell do you think you're doing, Patricia?"

She dared to give him that coy smile. "To paraphrase Rhett Butler, I'm tired of waiting to catch you between wives."

He turned, fire in his eyes. He grabbed her wrist.

"Oh, you want to get a little kinky?"

He'd never hit a woman in his life. It took all he had not to do that now. "Get out, Patricia."

"Of course, you're upset but can't we talk about it? Really, I can't believe you'd choose that gutter snipe over me, Wade. Have you forgotten your breeding?"

"I'm through talking with you. Get out."

"Wade, what are you saying?"

"Do I have to pick you up and throw you out? Get out of my home. I never want to see you again."

He spied her jeweled pocketbook on the table. He picked it up and shoved it into her hands. Then he muscled her out the door and slammed it in her aristocratic face.

CHAPTER THIRTY-EIGHT

Miranda sped down Georgia 400 wondering how fast this baby could go. She pressed the Corvette's accelerator to find out and the tires swerved. She gripped the steering wheel tight, fighting for control of the car as hard as she was fighting for control of her raging emotions.

What if she lost control and hit the wall? Go out in a blaze of glory. That would be a fitting ending to her miserable life, wouldn't it?

But hey, she'd been bitten off, chewed up, and spat on the side of the road before. What was one more time?

And she'd *known*. She'd always known this would happen. That was why she never wanted to get involved with Wade Russell Parker the Third. He was a rich man, worlds apart from her.

But she never thought he would do this.

For a second she took a hand off the steering wheel and swiped it under her nose. It was wet. Her cheeks were wet, too. How did that happen? She wasn't crying. She didn't cry over cheating bastard husbands.

He'd been so good to her. She was so sure he loved her. Maybe he did, but wasn't that what rich men did? Love your faithful wife but have a little something on the side.

And who had he chose for the side dish? Someone who was like him. She thought back to meeting that woman at the fundraiser last night. Didn't she say she and Parker had grown up together?

She was his kind.

And Miranda wasn't. No matter how many fancy dresses and jewels he bought her, she was still a lowlife from Chicago who'd been married to a wife beater who turned out to be a psychotic serial killer. She'd been raped. Broken in just about every way possible.

No wonder his infatuation for her had died so fast.

She was a real prize, wasn't she? Most of her adult life, she'd roamed the country taking construction jobs here and there. Listless, hopeless, meaningless. All she'd cared about was finding Amy.

And now that she had—?

Maybe she should go back to that life. She certainly wasn't a detective any more. She certainly wasn't going to show up at the office bright and chipper tomorrow morning.

What was she going to do now?

She looked up and saw she was moving south on I-85. Where the hell was she going? She took the Peachtree exit and headed north, her heart feeling like it had been raked over with a meat cleaver.

Her head buzzed, anger pounded her temples, misery pummeled her heart. She drove a little farther and saw a familiar sign.

The Gecko Club.

A place where she could get completely smashed and maybe get in a good bar fight or two. If Coco wasn't playing there tonight, she'd stop in. She couldn't face her now.

But she did have one friend she could talk to.

She found a parking spot down a side road and pulled over. She took out her cell and dialed Fanuzzi.

"What is it, Miranda?" Fanuzzi sounded concerned.

"Just wondered if you'd like a girls' night out."

"Now? It's after eleven."

"Remember the blast we had last time?"

"I—guess you could call it that."

Okay, Miranda had wound up in jail that night. "I—I just need someone to talk to. I'm at the Gecko Club."

"Sure. I don't have to get up early tomorrow and I can get Dave to watch the kids. Be there in twenty."

She forced herself to sound chipper. "See ya then."

"What the hell is wrong, Murray?"

At the sound of the familiar Brooklyn accent, Miranda looked up from her second beer to see her short, dark-haired friend dressed in jeans and a denim top standing at her booth, hands on her hips. It reminded Miranda of the pose she used to take when she bossed big men around on the road crew.

Miranda gave her a half-hearted grin. "Why should anything be wrong? Have a seat."

Fanuzzi slid onto the cream-colored bench. "Because you look like hell, that's why. What are you doing here?"

"Having a beer. Anything wrong with that?" She took a swallow to hide her tear-stained face from further scrutiny and hailed a waiter.

Fanuzzi ordered a Bud. After the waiter left she drummed her fingers on the granite table in time to the jazzy background music and eyed her friend. She was calculating how much she could say without setting Miranda off. "Did you hear about Coco and Antonio?"

Miranda smirked. Marriage. Nice topic to pick. "Yeah, I heard."

"Well, what do you think?"

She studied her beer. Why had Parker been so against his son and Coco getting hitched? Just another signal he was having second thoughts about marrying beneath him. There must have been a lot of signals she missed.

In reply, she shrugged. "To each his own."

The waiter brought Fanuzzi's beer, set it down on a coaster and left them alone. "I thought you'd be happy about it. Or mad."

Again Miranda shrugged and slurped down more beer, ignoring her friend's look of alarm. "Drink up."

Rolling her eyes, Fanuzzi took a small sip. "Anyway, I was thinking of throwing them a reception. Something kind of fancy. What do you think?"

"That would be nice."

Miranda scanned the crowd around the salmon-colored bar. The place was still as hip as ever. She remembered the night she'd met Coco in here. She'd had a hell of a good fight with a jerk that was bothering her. Maybe she could get into another one tonight.

"Well, will you help me plan it?"

"Plan what?"

Fanuzzi let out a huff of exasperation. "The reception for Coco and Antonio."

Miranda turned and eyed her friend. While she'd waited for her, she'd been thinking over her next move and had made her decision. "I won't be here," she told Fanuzzi flatly.

Fanuzzi looked like she was about to choke on her beer. "What?"

"I'm leaving town."

"You and Parker going on a trip?" she asked cautiously.

"Nope. Just me."

Fanuzzi reached for her arm. "What happened, Murray? You two have a fight?"

She laughed, pulled out of her friend's grasp and ran her fingers over the condensation on her beer glass. If only it were that simple.

"I just decided I need to get away."

"Get away? For how long?"

Miranda let out a weary breath. "Forever."

"What?" The Brooklyn accent turned into a screech. "What about Parker? What about your job?"

"I'm quitting my job."

She'd never seen such alarm in Fanuzzi's dark brown eyes. "Quitting? You can't quit. You're a terrific detective. Dave tells me so all the time."

She really had everybody fooled, didn't she? "I'm thinking of escalator maintenance."

"What?" she squeaked.

"You know. Wiping down the railings, keeping the grating and the stairs clean. With a job like that you could really move up in the world."

Fanuzzi didn't laugh. The alarm on her squarish face had turned to terror. "Murray, will you please tell me what the hell is wrong?"

When she didn't answer, Fanuzzi reached across the table and snatched her beer away. "Out with it."

"I'm going away, Fanuzzi. To wherever my fancy takes me. Just like before I came to Atlanta."

"You're what?"

"I'll get a job in construction or something." Maybe she could go back to work for that demolition company in Pittsburgh. "Hey, will you give me a reference?"

Fanuzzi's brown eyes turned hard. "Not unless you tell me what's going on. I'm sick of this run around."

Now it was Miranda's turn to drum the table. There was no beer and no way out. Might as well tell her.

She blew out a breath. "Parker's cheating on me."

Fanuzzi made a sound like a leaky fire hose. For several minutes she stared at her, wide-eyed. Then she started to shake her head. Back and forth. Back and forth. "No way. That can't be true. I don't believe it."

Miranda reached across the table, took her beer back, swallowed another mouthful. "Why not? I should have known it would happen sooner or later."

"How can you say that?"

She smirked and shook her head. "Because Parker's the most sought-after man in Atlanta. He belongs with someone who's like him."

"You're like him. Dave tells me all the time how good you two are together."

"Becker worships the ground he walks on. He sees what he wants to see. Parker was married to a socialite for twenty-two years, for Pete's sake. So he had a craving for something different for awhile. There's no way it could have lasted. He's gotten tired of me and gone back to his own kind." Not that he'd ever looked down his nose at her or think less of her as a person. He was too classy for that. He just needed to be with someone on his social level.

"That can't be right."

"Fanuzzi. I caught him with another woman."

"What?"

"I walked right in on them. He thought I'd be away for a while."

Tears glistened in Fanuzzi's eyes. "There's got to be some mistake, Murray."

Miranda leaned over the table and lowered her voice, the anger pounding against her temples again. "She was in my bed. He was kissing her."

"Oh, my God."

While she waited for that to sink in, Miranda looked down at her own hands and saw the diamond-and-sapphire ring. Ought to bring enough for a couple months' rent in a pawn shop.

Fanuzzi took a tissue out of her purse and blew her longish nose. "This awful, Murray. Just awful."

"You can't tell anyone."

"No, I won't. But you really don't have to leave town, do you?"

"How can I stay in a place Parker's father just about owns? Where everyone knows who Parker is?" Everyone would be talking about the break up for months. Tanya Terrance would have a field day on her show.

"Okay, okay. I know nobody can change your mind when it's made up. And I guess I can't blame you for leaving. But—will you keep in touch?"

"Sure." For as long as she could anyway. She'd never had long-term friendships.

"You've got my number. You want my address?"

She had it in her phone. Phone. She pulled it out of her pocket and stared at it. It was a company cell. Parker bought it for her and she probably wouldn't be able to keep up the bills on it. She reached for a napkin. "Write everything down here."

Then she slid the phone over to Fanuzzi.

"What's this for?"

"Give it back to Parker."

Fanuzzi looked dumbfounded but nodded and reluctantly put the phone in her purse. She scribbled down the information on the napkin and handed it back to her. "Where will you go first? Do you know?"

With the first real smile she'd had tonight, Miranda nodded, thinking of the tickets in her backpack. There was no reason not to use them. "Lake Placid."

Fanuzzi frowned. "What's there?"

"The Junior Interstate Championship."

She looked blank for a minute and then said, "Oh, yeah. Isn't some local girl skating in that?"

"Mackenzie Chatham."

"She's pretty good, I heard. But I didn't know you were a figure skating fan." Confusion riddled her brow.

Miranda took in another breath. Fanuzzi was the best friend she had. She couldn't keep this from her. "I guess I never told you. I found my daughter."

Her eyes went wide and her mouth dropped open. She grabbed her beer and took another swig as if she needed fortification after Miranda had unloaded so much on her. "You mean the baby your crazy ex stole from you?"

"Yep."

"Your crazy ex who got burned up in that barn in Hampton?"

"Yep."

"Are you saying—?"

Miranda smiled with a mother's pride, her eyes glowing with tears. "Yeah, I am. That's my daughter. Mackenzie Chatham. And I'm going to Lake Placid and watch her win that championship."

They chatted a little more, finished their drinks and said goodbye with tearful girl hugs. Then Miranda took off for the airport, exchanged the two tickets for a single seat on a redeye and boarded the plane to a nearby airport where she'd catch the chartered flight Parker had arranged to take her to Lake

Placid. She'd catch a few hours sleep in the fancy Alpine motel he'd booked on the lake, then head for the arena where the championship was being held.

She'd left the Corvette in the airport parking garage in Atlanta and told Fanuzzi to tell Parker to come pick it up. She'd get a cheap ride somewhere. She'd saved a good bit of dough in her checking account, but she'd have to budget carefully. Maybe she'd hitchhike to Maine and look up her old boss on that fishing boat.

As the plane took off, she looked down on the shimmering lights of Atlanta for the last time. Wherever she was going, she was never coming back here.

Parker could track her down, of course. But she had a feeling he wasn't going to bother. She tightened her jaw, fighting back the mountain of emotion inside that she hadn't let go of. She wasn't going to do that yet. She didn't want to think about Parker now. She didn't want to think about what she'd just walked away from. She didn't want to think of what heartache lay ahead in the coming weeks and months.

All she wanted to think about was Mackenzie.

CHAPTER THIRTY-NINE

"Man, am I ever glad to see you." The uniformed man behind the wooden counter was rotund and round-faced. He wore a friendly, unassuming smile.

He extended a hand. "Thanks for calling me. I was beginning to worry. I sent in my application two days ago."

"Sorry we didn't get back to you sooner. And with such short notice. Had to run a quick background check. The usual thing."

"Of course." He pulled his jacket around him. It was in the low forties up here in Lake Placid and he wasn't used to the change in temperature.

"Gotta tell ya, I'm really relieved everything checked out. I've got three men down with the flu and this big ice skating event coming up. That's where you'll be assigned to, by the way."

He smiled. It had been worth it keeping his firearms license up-to-date since he'd been here years ago when he'd followed her here. "That's what I was hoping for."

The man's round cheeks grew rounder with a friendly grin. "You a figure skating fan?"

"I have a niece who's into it," he lied. "You know how young girls are."

"Sure do. My daughter's beside herself. So what are you? A thirty-six?" he asked, reaching for one of the shelves piled high with neatly pressed clothes.

"Thirty-four." He hadn't gained back all his weight after his stay in the hospital.

The round man took down a uniform. "This ought to fit. You can try it on back there." He pointed toward a dressing room. "We like our men to look shipshape."

"Of course."

"And here," he unlocked a drawer and drew out a black leather holster, "is your weapon." The man slid it across the counter to him. "I can see from your application you've had a lot of experience with firearms."

He eyed the gun greedily. Exactly what he needed for his plan. It was finally all coming together. "Used to be in law enforcement."

"Good qualifications. Security has to be tight around these sort of events. You know, there's been so much trouble over the past few years."

"I understand."

"Okay, here's the schedule. Be there at five p.m. tomorrow night. You'll work through the last set then stay until eleven or the crowd is gone. You can pick up your check the next day. That sound good?"

He smiled his most eager smile. And meant it. "It sounds just perfect."

CHAPTER FORTY

Parker raised his head from the living room couch where he'd ended up last night and squinted at the morning sunlight flowing in from the windows. He rubbed his chin and found stubble. And the smell of liquor. The bottle of bourbon was still on the floor next to him.

He sat up and put his head in his hands.

He'd known better than to go after Miranda when she was in a state like the one last night. She'd never listen to him when she was so upset. But he thought, believed, hoped she would come home after she calmed down.

She could stay angry a long time, though. And this time, he couldn't blame her one bit. Why hadn't he seen through Patricia's scheme? He had, he supposed, on a certain level. And it had flattered him. And because he was so flattered, because she was an old family friend, he hadn't set her straight when she first walked into his office.

He should have handed her case off to someone at the Agency. He never should have let her talk her into taking it on himself.

And now, because of that foolish mistake, he had wounded his wife.

A voice came from the hallway. "Mr. Parker? Where are you, Mr. Parker?" It was their housekeeper.

"I'm in here, Sarah."

The woman stepped into the room and her eyes went wide. "Mr. Parker, are you all right?"

"Well enough. What is it?"

"There's someone here to see you. The Beckers."

His heart leapt. Of course Miranda would have confided in Joan Fanuzzi. She and Dave would know where Miranda was and what state of mind she was in. And most important, if she was ready for him to reach out to her. To try to explain what had happened last night.

"They're in the sitting room," Sarah told him.

"Thank you." He rose and lumbered down the hall to the room, not caring that he was unshaved and still in the shirt and slacks he'd slept in.

He found the couple on one of the settees.

Dave shot to his feet as he entered. "Sir."

Joan remained seated. She eyed him with a cold, suspicious glare. Miranda had told her.

"Excuse my appearance," he said. "Please, sit down." He took a seat across from them. "I take it you have news about Miranda?"

Joan rubbed her folded hands and glanced at her husband before she spoke. "She wanted me to give you this." She reached into her pocket and drew out a cell phone. Rising, she handed it to him and sat back down.

Parker looked down at it, feeling as if he'd been stabbed in the heart. Miranda's cell phone. So she was still murderously angry. "Where did she go, Joan?"

The woman's lips pressed together in a line as thin as a dagger's edge. "She also said to tell you her Corvette is at the airport."

He inhaled sharply. Hadn't she said Iris was taking Wendy to Lake Placid? He'd thought so. He'd never had a chance to find out why there'd been a change of plans. She'd been so excited about going. Wendy or Iris must have dealt her another devastating blow before the one he'd given her last night.

He put his hand to his chin and stared blankly out the window. She may never forgive him this time. "Did she go to Lake Placid?"

"I promised not to tell."

Dave patted her hand. "Aw, c'mon, honey. The man has a right to know."

She shook her head. "I don't think so."

Parker closed his eyes. Time to confess. "I've made a very serious mistake."

Joan squinted at him with a you-bet-your-life-you-have look. Dave's mouth opened.

He continued. "I made an error in judgment. But I can assure you both no indiscretion was involved."

Dave put out his palm. "Sir, Joan hasn't told me everything Miranda said to her last night. Ouch." Joan had just punched him in the ribs. "Honey, he already knows that."

She huffed and folded her arms.

"If you'd like me to leave the room—"

Parker leaned forward, appreciating Joan's loyalty to Miranda and Dave's to him. "As you are obviously aware this matter is of a personal nature so you'll forgive me if I don't divulge the details. However, I will say that I have never cheated on my wife and I don't intend to start. I love her more than the day I married her. And I want her to come home."

Joan's expression seemed to soften at that.

"I'm going to find her sooner or later, with or without your help. Though the information you have could save me some time."

Dave gave his wife a pleading look. She didn't say anything.

Parker got to his feet. "So if you won't tell me where she is, I'll have to take my leave of you so I can start looking for her. I'll start by calling the motel I booked for her in Lake Placid." He started for the door.

"You're right. That's where she is. Lake Placid." Joan's shoulders sank as she hung her head. "She said she was going to see her daughter win that ice skating championship."

Dave turned to her. "Miranda has a daughter?"

Joan shot him a warning glare. "You're not supposed to know that."

He raised his hands. "Okay. I won't say anything to anybody."

Parker returned to the settee where the couple sat. "Thank you, Joan. Very much."

The poor woman rolled her eyes. "She'll kill me if she finds out I told you."

"I'll make sure she doesn't. Now if you'll excuse me, I need to get busy."

Parker left the Beckers in Sarah's hands while he ran upstairs to clean up and make phone calls. Within ten minutes, he had confirmed Miranda was at the alpine lodge. The flights were all full but within another hour, he had cajoled, bribed, and offer twice the rate with an airport attendant and finally managed to book a ticket to the town near Lake Placid. He booked a rental car for when he arrived as well.

He should invest in a Lear jet, he thought as he hurried out the door with a hastily packed suitcase. With the connecting flights, he wouldn't arrive until nightfall. Still, he would be in Lake Placid before the championship was over tonight. With any luck, he'd have his wife in his arms and something of a second honeymoon in that alpine lodge before midnight.

CHAPTER FORTY-ONE

Miranda had butterflies in her stomach as she settled into the shiny blue seat in Elysian Stadium in Lake Placid and gazed down at the rink below.

She'd come a little early and the Zambonis—the machines with the name that sounded like an Italian sandwich—were still moving around the ice, polishing its surface until it shined like glass. She'd read the ice had to be kept around twenty-five degrees for figure skating so it was soft and gripped the blades just right.

A variety of advertisements were plastered along the boards. Car companies, phone companies, credit cards, aspirin. So many things for a thirteen-year-old to choose from.

She could see the painted designs on the floor beneath and the letters spelling out "Junior Interstate Championship." The auditorium got noisy as people came and took their seats. She'd heard the turnout was expected to be around seven thousand. Television cameras were dotted around the arena, the crew setting up and doing sound checks and what-not.

A thrill went through her. Soon, Mackenzie would be on that surface going through her routine.

Parker had gotten them good seats, she thought, pulling the new angora scarf around her neck. It had shown up in her room in the alpine lodge along with the earmuffs and gloves, and a matching set for Wendy. Along with two passes to the spa. She didn't go to the spa and wouldn't have worn the things if it hadn't been so freaking cold. She'd forgotten how chilly this part of the country could get.

She was sure he'd arranged for the personal amenities when he got the tickets. Before the incident last night. She closed her eyes as pain washed over her and the vision of their bedroom came to her.

Who was that woman in her bed? Someone he'd dated before she met him, no doubt.

He'd gone through a boatload of high-society chicks after his wife passed away. She usually got cold stares from them at the social events she attended with him. Tanya Terrance had been one of the ones he'd dumped. And like so many others, she was spinach-green with jealousy that Miranda had ended up with the best catch in town. That was the reason she'd attacked her and had focused on her on her talk show.

Was that woman in her bed like Terrance? Just without a talk show? Had she been chasing Parker and taken a different tack?

That didn't excuse him kissing her. She didn't want to think about that anyway. The event was about to start. People were taking their seats and an announcer was making preliminary remarks on the loudspeaker.

She focused on the rink below.

The head honcho of the figure skating association talked about the history of the event, the contestants who'd gone on to the Olympics, and introduced the judges. After the obligatory applause at the end of the speech, the lights went down and the show began. Excited young girls bounced up and down in the row in front of her and Miranda smiled with pride when she heard one of them mention Mackenzie's name.

Music flowed out of the speakers overhead and the first skater appeared. Miranda held her breath. There would be ten young girls performing tonight and she knew the competition would be stiff. Mackenzie was last.

The first girl began to swirl across the ice and Miranda caught her breath. After her afternoon of research, she knew her swizzles from her spins, her twizzles from her toe jumps. Still it was hard to judge technique. The girl seemed nervous and a little stilted. Nowhere as smooth as Mackenzie had been back in Atlanta. Though Miranda might be a tad biased.

As the girl glided over the ice to the opposite side of the rink, a cold sensation shot up Miranda's spine.

She shivered.

That didn't feel like nerves or excitement. Was she catching a cold from the change in temperature? She was always pretty healthy. She pulled the scarf around her and turned her attention back to the ice.

The first girl finished and everyone applauded as she skated over to the side and disappeared into an opening in the boards.

There was a pause for the judges to make their decisions then the second contestant appeared and a new musical number came from the speakers.

This girl was Asian and dressed in a sparkling, deep red outfit. She had the energy of a jack rabbit and her moves were quick and decisive. Not as graceful as Mackenzie, Miranda thought, watching her do a spinning jump that got the crowd's applause.

Okay, she was pretty good.

The next few performances were just so-so in her opinion. But Miranda knew there were two girls who were the ones to beat and they were up next.

Alexis Jones from Minnesota was first. The lights came up and girl appeared crouched, arms out, watching her coach and waited for the music to queue her. Her light blond hair was caught up in a ponytail and she had on a white skating dress with gold sequins in a swirl pattern that shimmered under the lights.

As Miranda watched the girl, another frosty chill came over her. This one so intense, her whole body shivered for several long seconds. She must be getting a cold. Crap.

She rubbed her arms, pulled her scarf around her and managed to warm herself up as Russian-sounding music came over the speakers.

Alexis began to move over the surface like a swan gliding over water. She did a double spin, stretched out her arms and skated the other way as the crowd cheered. She was good and Miranda started to worry for Mackenzie.

Alexis did a one-foot turn and went the other way. She executed several more fancy moves and ended, one leg bent behind her, in a fast standing spin.

The music stopped and the audience applauded loudly.

Wow. Mackenzie better bring her A-game tonight.

The next performer was even better. In a sparkling silver dress, redheaded Gabrielle Thomas from California scissored across the ice with dance-like strides to a peppy tune that matched her quick, precise moves. Man, she was good.

A big girl for her age, her spins were strong, her jumps high and steady. But she lacked grace, in Miranda's opinion. Still, she garnered hoots and cheers from her fans. And a huge round of applause when her routine ended.

She would score well. Could Mackenzie beat her?

Time to find out.

Miranda held her breath. Her heart began to pound when Mackenzie appeared.

She stood on the ice in a dramatic pose, head down, one arm behind her back. She was so beautiful. Her dark hair was caught up in a silvery band. Her dress was a shimmering teal, accented in colorful sequins. Her neck was bare tonight, but the dark mark on it must have been covered with makeup. She couldn't see it at all. Maybe that meant her confidence was growing. She hoped so.

Miranda put her hand to her lips in anticipation and an icy pain shot up her spine and into her head. Her temples started to throb. She bent over wondering if she were about to heave. Was she getting the flu? Not now. Please, not now.

And then it passed as quickly as it came.

A lovely violin solo began to play. So sweet, it was heartbreaking. Miranda lifted her head and saw Mackenzie start to move across the ice, slowly swaying her arms as she skated backward, twisting one way then the other, as graceful as a little angel.

At the edge of the rink, she did a sudden turn, jumped and spun. She seemed to hang in the air suspended for several minutes. When she landed, she glided forward confidently, without breaking form, and the crowd broke into another round of applause. Miranda thought it sounded more enthusiastic than for the others.

She skated over the full length of the ice, her sheer skirt flaring as she moved, enhancing her skill. Forward, backward, turning. She reached the middle and her arms flew out like bird's wings behind her.

Balancing on one foot she went into a slow spin. She bent backward as she twirled, her neck extended, her head behind her, she reached down for one foot, pulled it up as she came erect into a perfect Biellman, as Miranda had learned it was called from Wendy. Gorgeous.

The crowd cheered and Miranda thought her heart might break in two with pride.

The music became choppy and Mackenzie fairly flew to the opposite side of the rink. She began to move in slow circles, Miranda put her hand over her mouth. She was going to do a sit spin. The one that gave her so much trouble back home.

Don't fall. You can't fall. Not tonight.

She turned did a short spiral, one leg extended behind.

She began to turn again, this time one leg in front. She bent her knees and began to spin fast. As she reached the sitting position and her body became a silvery teal haze on the ice, she didn't wobble one bit. She spun at lightning speed for what felt like a full minute. Then grabbed her foot and keeping the leg straight, came up into a standing position, still spinning. At last, as the music crescendoed, she lowered the leg, came to a blazing halt, and threw her arms up in triumph.

The crowd went into a frenzied applause and cheers. Miranda found herself on her feet, hopping up and down, tears in her eyes. Surely she would win after that.

Mackenzie was at the far end of the rink, near an open gap in the boards. As the girl posed, drinking in the victory, Miranda saw a figure approach the opening in the darkness. At first, she thought it was a cameraman. Then she saw he wore a uniform. It was a security guard—with his weapon drawn.

Her head began to pound, her heart hammering along with it.

Her mouth opened. "Look out!" she cried. But nobody heard in time.

She saw the flash, the barrel. Heard the crack of gunshot ring through the cold air. Watched in frozen terror as Mackenzie went down. The bullet hit her in the upper leg. Blood oozed from her thigh and onto the ice. Her lovely face filled with confusion and horror.

A second shot rang out from the same place.

The crowd screamed. The girls in front of her shrieked and went berserk, but Miranda couldn't move.

All she could do was stare at the man, the one dressed as the security guard, as he came crawling out onto the ice. "Get away! Get away from him, Mackenzie."

But the girl couldn't hear. Miranda watched him grab the boot of her skate, pull her off the ice. Sick with fear, she saw Mackenzie cry out in pain.

He turned to scan the crowd and she caught a glimpse of his face. He had a moustache and brown hair that had grown out on the top. But she knew who he was. She knew that cruel face. Those hollow cheeks. Those dark, evil eyes.

That's what those chills she'd had been. Not a cold. Not the flu. A premonition.

The man below was Leon.

But the barn in Hampton. They'd found his charred and bloody body. They found her wedding ring. Her dream. The fiery body in her dream. That was what it meant. She didn't know how he'd done it, but somehow he was alive. And putting the plan he'd had all along into action.

Not if she could help it.

She shoved her way down the aisle, grabbed the railing and jumped it. Then she scrambled down the bleacher steps.

She had to get to Mackenzie.

CHAPTER FORTY-TWO

Her heart feeling like it had been sliced up with skate blades, Miranda reached the bottom step and started down the aisle that ran along the backside of the boards.

People were screaming and crying and yelling to each other—and going every which way. As she shoved her way through the crowd, trying desperately to get to the spot where Leon had grabbed Mackenzie, a harsh, mechanical voice came over the loudspeakers.

An emergency has occurred in the stadium. Stay calm and proceed to the exits in an orderly manner. Repeat. An emergency has occurred in the stadium—

That was supposed to keep people calm? But they did seem to be moving out of the building now. And she was going upstream.

Stubbornly she fought through the women, the men, the boys, the young girls. She had to get to Mackenzie. She had to find her.

At last she came to a clear section and broke into a run, but just as she rounded a curve she ran smack into a group of mothers and skaters.

Everyone here was panic-stricken. Crying and screaming and trying to figure out what to do while two security guards struggled to get them all outside.

A woman grabbed her by the shoulders. "Miranda. What are you doing here?" It was Colby Chatham. The tall, stately woman in cream-colored winter clothes and perfectly coiffed graying hair wore a wild look.

"I—I came to see Mackenzie perform," Miranda stammered. "You need to get out of here."

She shook her head with one quick motion. "I can't leave. I have to find my daughter. Didn't you see? That madman has her." Miranda could tell she was hysterical. And didn't blame her.

"I know. I'll take care of it."

Her grip on Miranda went tight. "I'll go with you."

"No. You're unarmed. Untrained. Besides, I know how he operates."

Her eyes glowed hot with shock and pain. "You mean that's the man—who escaped from the hospital? I thought he was dead."

"I did, too. But he isn't."

She let go of Miranda and put her arms around her waist as if her stomach was convulsing. It probably was. "And he went after Mackenzie, just as you told her."

"Yes."

"You were right. We should have listened to you."

Miranda dared to put a hand on her shoulder. "I'm sorry I couldn't put him away before now."

Colby grabbed her wrist, her eyes going more wild and desperate. "You've got to get her away from him, Miranda. You've got to save her."

"I will." Or die trying. It was all the reassurance she could give the poor woman right now. "Now let me go so I can do that."

As the words sunk in, Colby nodded, stepped aside and with a reluctant, sorrowful look let the security guard lead her out.

The other guard was still trying to herd up the rest of the group. Miranda started around them again and hadn't gone more than a few more steps when a girl in a pink jacket with a fake fur collar barreled into her.

Holding onto her, Miranda lifted the kid's chin. It was Wendy. One good thing in this nightmare. "Thank God you're safe."

"Miranda? You came?" Her face was drawn, her eyes red and swollen, her youthful brow creased with panic.

"Of course, I did."

"There you are. I've been looking everywhere for you." Iris's frantic voice rang in Miranda's ears.

She turned and saw the frazzled woman fighting her way toward them. "Iris, you have to take Wendy and get out of here now."

"No!" Wendy shrieked. "We have to find Mackenzie. That man's got her."

A look of sheer alarm came over Iris's impeccably made-up face. Her blush-covered cheeks turned pale. "What man? Are you talking about the same man that kidnapped you?"

"Yes. It's him. I saw him."

"I saw him, too, Wendy." Miranda bent down, put her head close to the girl's. "Remember last time? I took care of him, didn't I?"

"Yes, but—"

"I'm going to do that this time, too. Do you believe me?"

"Yes, I do. But—"

"Do you trust me?"

She hesitated a second, then nodded, tears streaming down her cheeks.

"Listen to me, Wendy. You've got to take care of your mother. You've got to go with this guard and leave the stadium so you'll be safe."

"But what about Mackenzie?"

"She'll be okay. I promise."

"Okay. Okay." With a reluctant nod, the girl took her mother's hand.

"Please get that bastard," Iris muttered to her over her shoulder. And they turned and hurried away.

The path was almost clear now. Only a few stragglers other guards were escorting out. One of the guards gave her a wary look, as if he were going to stop her, but the panicky people he was herding distracted him and she slipped around him.

At last, she came to the spot where she'd seen Leon.

No one was here now. A blood trail ran from the ice over the concrete, leading somewhere down a long hall. As she passed the opening, she saw a body on the ground. One of the other guards. He was lying in a pool of blood. That was the second shot.

His drawn weapon was still in his hand. Reaching him, Miranda crouched down, laid two fingers along his neck. He was gone. Damn that bastard. He didn't care who he killed.

Gritting her teeth, she scooped up the gun. Glock. Nine millimeter. Reminded her of Parker's weapon. Not as comfortable as her Beretta, but she could handle it.

She checked the chamber. Fully loaded.

No time to lose now. Forcing back the pain, the sick feeling, the dread for Mackenzie that threatened to drown her, Miranda stepped over the body and followed the blood trail down the hall.

CHAPTER FORTY-THREE

Parker drove down the country road through the Adirondacks to Lake Placid in the deep blue Camaro he'd rented at the airport. He'd chosen the sporty car hoping to lure Miranda with it, even though she'd left the Corvette he'd given her as a wedding present at the airport in Atlanta.

He gripped the wheel and stared out the windshield at the dark road. The drive to Lake Placid was short. He'd be at the stadium in half an hour or so.

What would he do when he saw her? What could he say to her? He blew out a breath. Never had he doubted his ability to win her over, win her back when she'd left him in a fit of anger. But this time?

Once again he wondered how he could have been so thoughtless with Patricia. So careless when Miranda had needed him most. She'd been so different lately.

Since they'd found Groth in that barn, instead of being relieved, she'd been as tense and depressed as if he'd gotten away. She hadn't wanted to go to work. Something he'd never know her to do. She'd loved working at the Agency. From the moment he'd hired her and she got her first taste of what investigation was like, he hadn't been able to hold her back.

But now?

It was almost as if she'd become another person. He never should have submitted her to that fundraiser. Tanya Terrance. He would sue that woman and have that radio station shut down.

He ran a hand over his face. What if Miranda had had enough of being a detective? What if she wanted to do something else? He couldn't imagine her staying home and baking cookies. But there were any number of things she could do. She a talented woman.

That would certainly put an end to his plans for consulting work. His proposal she'd been avoiding these past days. What if she didn't want that?

He'd wanted a partner. He felt closer to Miranda when they worked a case together than to any other person he'd ever known. If she didn't want to be at his side any longer?

No, it wouldn't matter. Not to him. He loved her for her tenacity and strength of will and fiery spirit. But if she chose not to work with him—he could live with that. As long as he had her.

He didn't love her merely as a fellow investigator. He loved her as a woman, a human being. A delightful, tantalizing mystery he'd never grow tired of trying to solve. Whatever problems she had were his problems. He wanted to share her life no matter what that meant.

Whatever she wanted, it would be all right with him. Whatever she needed, he would give to her. If only. If only she would come back to him.

His cell buzzed in his pocket.

Was she trying to contact him? Hope banged in his chest as he reached for the phone. No. It was a message from Inspector Whitman at the GBI. He found a patch of gravel near a country store on the side of the road and pulled over.

He put the car in park and read the message. Dental records of the body in the Hampton barn had been processed. Good. Time to put a final lid on the case. Something to break the ice with Miranda when he found her.

But he frowned as he read the rest of the text. Evidence of arson had been discovered. The dental impressions matched a thirty-seven year old man from Marietta who'd lost his wife and two children in that dreadful tornado two years ago. He'd been unemployed and in and out of homeless shelters ever since.

Parker's heart went as cold and dark as the frozen mountains surrounding him. How could that be? There had been the SUV, the fingerprints. But the inspector had attached all the documents. Quickly he opened and scanned them.

The result was conclusive.

The man who'd been burned to death in that barn was a stranger. And that meant Leon Groth—was still out there. Parker scrolled down to view the end of the message. The inspector said the search for the killer would be reopened. She would contact Hosea.

He returned his phone to his pocket and sat back.

What had it taken to plan and execute such a scheme? Intelligence. Skill. He'd underestimated the enemy. He'd been so eager to be done with the scourge on Miranda's life, he'd let his desire cloud his objectivity. Groth wasn't the disoriented weakling recovering from a four-month coma Parker had thought him to be. He was a man possessed with a demonic will.

Parker had hunted serial killers before. He knew their insanity and drive grew as they killed over and over. Suddenly it all made sense.

The murder of Julie Kimble hadn't been a random act, to satisfy a sick urge to kill. It had been planned. Calculated to make the authorities think Groth was heading away from Atlanta. And the barn fire? A way to make them stop looking for him. So he could focus on his real target.

Miranda thought he'd discovered who Mackenzie was. Perhaps he had followed her to the Chathams' house the day she'd spotted the SUV.

She may very well have been right.

And if she was? If Groth knew who his daughter was? He could be heading straight for that stadium.

Or he was already there.

There was no time to waste. He put the Camaro in drive and spun back onto the highway.

CHAPTER FORTY-FOUR

The elongated drops of blood along the concrete floor of the hall were like exclamation points crying out for help. They weren't big enough to be arterial, Miranda knew. Still, Mackenzie might be in shock by now.

She followed the stains and the occasional scrape mark of a skate down a dark corridor, through a long empty locker room full of abandoned clothes and backpacks. She hurried past empty offices full of computers and papers and advertising placards, everything that had been quickly deserted by coaches and marketing people when the shots rang out.

The police would be gathering outside by now. Controlling the crowd, helping people find each other and preparing to deal with a hostage situation. In a town this size it was unlikely any officer had much experience with that. It would take them forever to figure out what to do. By then it would be too late.

It was all up to her.

She stepped through an open door and into another dark hall. The bloodstains were smaller here, about to disappear. She felt a pang of hope that the bleeding had stopped. But it was mixed with mortal fear that she'd lost her way to find them.

But they had to have gone down this way. Quickly and quietly, she hurried over the surface, weapon drawn. Where was he taking her? Somewhere he could perform that damn ritual of his. But where would that be? He couldn't leave the building, could he?

Someone would see him for sure.

And then she heard breathing. Panting. It took a lot of effort to haul a thirteen-year-old this distance. A shadow up ahead.

She spotted him.

He was dragging Mackenzie along under one arm as he hobbled down the empty corridor. Just before he reached a corner, he turned his head and saw her.

They stared at each other for a long moment, reading each other's minds or trying to. He raised his hand. The one with the gun in it.

Miranda leapt behind an open door to an office just as the bullet hit the wall where she'd been standing a second ago.

As the shot rang in her ears along with her pounding heart, she stood, gasping for breath. She forced herself to calm down. "Come over here and face me, Leon," she shouted through the doorway. "Or are you the same spineless coward you always were?"

Nothing.

She steadied herself and with the Glock in both hands, dared to peek around the door. He was gone.

Gun aimed, she ran from her hiding place and sprinted around the corner.

CHAPTER FORTY-FIVE

Iris Van Aarle followed the crowd down the sidewalk outside the stadium, hugging her weeping daughter close to her side. Her vision was blurred. She was crying herself and she had no idea how to comfort Wendy.

"He's going to kill them. He's going to kill them both."

"You can't think like that, honey. We've got to have hope." She caught sight of a policeman getting out of a squad car and forced her way through the moving crowd to get to him. "Officer?"

"You need to keep moving, ma'am. We've got things under control."

"No, you don't."

His scowl told her he wasn't used to being contradicted by civilians. She didn't care.

"There's a madman in there. An escaped criminal from Georgia."

"And how do you know that?"

"Because that's where we're from. My daughter and myself."

Wendy latched onto the poor man's arm. "Please help. Mackenzie Chatham. He's got her and Miranda went after them. But he's got a gun. He's going to kill them. You've got to help."

Gingerly, he patted Wendy on the head and glanced around at the crowd in frustration. "Get inside the squad and tell my man about it." He stuck his head through the passenger window. "Frank, take care of these two and get a statement from them. Radio me with any pertinent details."

The officer inside nodded. "Will do, Sergeant."

The sergeant opened the door to the back, ushered them inside and ran off to inform the other officers the situation was worse than reported. At least Iris hoped that was what he was doing.

Holding her sobbing daughter against her in the backseat, she gave her statement to the officer, while Wendy punctuated the report with emotional particulars. When she finished the officer relayed the information to his superior.

Then he turned to them and handed Iris a box of tissues. He must be used to tears. "I have to go join my sergeant, ma'am. You're welcome to stay here as long as you need. Once this settles down, we can take you to your hotel. You have a room already?"

"Yes," she nodded. "Thank you very much."

"I don't know how long this will take, but I'll come back and check on you as soon as I can."

"Thank you," she said again and watched him get out of the car and trot down the sidewalk where people were still milling about.

Iris stroked her daughter's head, kissed her hair. She wished she could comfort her somehow. She had so wanted this evening to be a happy one for her. If Mackenzie had won the championship, she would have taken the girls and Colby out to celebrate. And then later on, she would have broken the news she'd been waiting to tell her.

This wasn't at all the way she'd wanted to do it. But maybe it would take her mind off this horrible tragedy.

She took a deep breath and started. "Wendy, dear. I have something to tell you."

"What?" Wendy lifted her head and blinked at her. The poor little girl. Her cheeks were soaked, her nose was runny and her eyes were nearly swollen shut from crying. Iris took a tissue and dabbed it over her face, recalling when they used to do each other's makeup.

Iris took her daughter's face in both hands. "Oh, sweetheart. I know I've been a crappy mother to you."

Wendy pulled out of her mother's embrace and glared at her like she was a space alien.

"You're not contradicting me, are you?"

She pressed her lips together and looked away without a word.

"Well, you shouldn't contradict me. I've been selfish and stupid."

Wendy let out a scoff. "You're not stupid."

Iris was glad Wendy had that much respect for her. "But I am selfish." She looked down at her deep green cashmere coat, stroked the soft material. "I just never had anything I could call my own. Your father has his golf. He's always away. So I wanted my own business."

"I know. You started it in your kitchen and now you're a big successful CEO of your own cosmetics company." She rolled her eyes. "Why are we talking about this now?"

This was so hard to say. "Because I was stupid about that, too."

Wendy gave her as cautious look. "You mean with Mr. Todd?"

Iris brushed her hair away from her face and shook her head. "You always were too smart for your own good."

"What's that supposed to mean?"

"Oh, sweetheart." She sighed from the bottom of her soul. Confession was supposed to be good for that part of you, wasn't it? "Why does it always take a life and death situation to make people realize what's important in life?"

"Mama, I don't know what you're talking about." Her gaze drifted out the window.

Iris didn't want her attention there. She took her hand. "I'm telling you I'm sorry for being such a bad mother. For not paying attention to you. For neglecting you for my business. And I promise from now on, things will be different."

Wendy pursed her lips and shrugged. She'd promised things like that before.

This time it was different. "Someone's made me an offer. I've been thinking it over for weeks now. Tonight I made my decision."

Wendy's eyes widened with apprehension. Her lip began to quiver, her eyes to tear up again. "Are you going to divorce Daddy and marry Mr. Todd?"

Iris stared at her little girl. How perceptive she was. She should have known she couldn't hide anything from her. Especially the impetuous affair she'd had with that man. But she was glad she could shake her head and laugh. No need to hide the truth now. "No. We broke up weeks ago. Since then—I've been talking to your father."

"Daddy? Don't you always talk to him?"

"We've been talking more than usual. He's had some disappointments on his last tour."

"That's too bad." She turned her head away again, already bored with the subject.

Iris forced herself to be patient and continue. "In his last three tournaments, he's finished nine, six, and eleven over par."

Wendy shrugged without looking back at her. "He's been in slumps before."

"He's feeling it more. He says his body's not what it used to be."

"Okay. Whatever."

"I saw him last night."

Now she turned around. "What?"

"Your father's playing in a tournament a about a hundred miles away. That's why I changed my plans to take you to the championship. He flew up here and we met at a hotel in the next town while you were with Mackenzie." One of the reason she'd let Wendy spend the night in Mackenzie's room. "It was—romantic."

Wendy stared at her, a flicker of hope in her eyes. "No lie?"

Iris made an X over her the breast pocket of her coat. "No lie."

She smiled fearfully. "Really?"

"Really. I had to make a choice, Wendy. I thought about it long and hard for weeks. I thought about all that your father and I used to have together. The good times. I wasn't sure we could have that again. It would have to work both ways, you know."

She nodded solemnly. Wendy was also aware of the affair her father had had with a neighbor. "So—" she said, caution in her tone. "What's going to happen?"

Iris smiled for the first time since they'd left the stadium. "Your father's tournament will be over tomorrow. And after that, he'll call for a press conference."

Wendy frowned. "Press conference? About what?"

Just say it. The bubble wouldn't burst if she said it out loud. "To announce his retirement."

"From golf?"

"You're father's coming home."

"Really? No lie?"

"Really."

"Daddy's coming home? We're going to be a real family again?"

"Yes, that's right, sweetheart."

And then Wendy threw her arms around her and became a little girl again. "Oh, Mama. That's the best news ever."

"Isn't it wonderful?"

"I just hope—"

"What?"

"I hope Mackenzie can meet him."

"I do, too."

Hugging her daughter, Iris watched the crowd out of the window and thought of the woman inside that stadium fighting that killer. She owed Miranda Steele a deep debt of gratitude. The bold woman had made her see how wrong she'd been. Had made her start to reconsider her life and the choices she'd made.

She only hoped she'd have a chance to thank her.

CHAPTER FORTY-SIX

He wasn't there.

The Glock still drawn, Miranda sprang around the dark concrete-block corner and found herself staring into another empty hallway. Where had the bastard gone? She had to find him. She couldn't let him get away.

She tiptoed down the passage, staying alert but glancing down at the floor as she went. No more blood drops. That told her Mackenzie's leg had stopped bleeding, but it didn't mean she didn't have internal damage.

Up ahead she saw a light pouring into the dim corridor from a side opening. She headed for it and when she reached the spot, came to a halt. She had a decision to make.

Go forward or turn down this way.

It looked like the short passage led back to the stadium. Would Leon have gone that way? Back out into the open? She doubted it but studied the intersection anyway. The cheerful blue paint on the walls. The radiator pouring out its warmth. If she made the wrong choice she could lose him for good.

As she stood there considering, icy fingers began to dance up and down her neck. She could feel the hairs stand on end. That familiar sensation. But this time she didn't dismiss it. She wasn't alarmed or sickened by it. This time she welcomed it. She had no explanation for this feeling, but whatever it was, she knew she could trust it.

Right now it told her to go down that short passage.

Okay. She stepped into the side hall, hurrying as she went. Sure enough, it led back into the stadium. But as she reached the open area and looked around, she was hit by a sharp punch of disappointment.

Lights on the rafters high overhead shined down on an empty rink and ten thousand empty seats. There was no one here. No one in the whole gigantic space. Where the hell were the police?

Panic welled up in her. She'd lost him. She'd lost Mackenzie. God, no.

And then she heard it echoing behind her. Scrape. Scrape. Scrape. Grunting. Heavy breathing.

She spun around and saw Leon. He was climbing up the bleacher steps backwards, dragging Mackenzie with him. Relief and vicious fury hit her at the same time. Keep your head, she told herself.

Where in the hell was he taking her? She didn't know, but he was out in the open now. She glanced around. No way to get behind him and surprise him. Nowhere else to go but up—and face him head on.

She turned and scrambled up the stairs.

Halfway there he looked up and saw her. He waved his gun at her. "Go back down, Miranda. You have no business here."

She stopped, her breath ragged. "And you do?"

"Of course, I do. It's my destiny. I have a mission to fulfill."

Mission, hell. The sick bastard. She took another step.

He raised his gun, pointed it at Mackenzie. "Don't come any closer or I'll shoot her."

She stopped cold now, studied him carefully.

He was sweating through the blue shirt of his uniform. The patch on one arm had been ripped. It flapped as he moved. Mackenzie had fought him. But not anymore.

He had her thin body under the chest in one arm. Her limbs were limp, her head hung down, her eyes closed. Her hair had come loose and it dangled over the seats along the aisle as he pulled her up another stair. If only she could reach out and snatch her from his grasp.

The police had to get here any minute now. She had to buy some time. Piss him off, she thought. Get him distracted. Make him point the gun at her instead.

She sneered at him. "You know it's a felony to impersonate a security guard, Leon."

"I'm not impersonating anyone. I was once a police officer."

"Oh, yeah? What's the name on your badge?" He didn't dare go by his real name.

He glared at her but didn't reply.

She put a hand on one hip and took as cocky a pose as she could muster. "So, long time no see, Leon. Looks like you recovered from those stab wounds I gave you in that wine cellar."

He stopped, lowered himself to the stair he'd just left. His lips twitched as he fixed her with a scowl. "Likewise. But whores like you are resilient. "

His barb didn't even sting. "And anyway, aren't you supposed to be dead?"

His lips twitched up the other way as he laughed. "But I'm not."

No, he wasn't. Even though she'd seen him dead with her very own eyes. Or had she? She'd make him tell her. "Who was that man in that barn in Hampton?"

He laughed again. "Why do you care?"

"Oh, I'm just curious."

He smirked. "He was some homeless pile of dung who'd lost his family, a worthless piece of humanity who's better off now that he's dead. Nobody cared about him."

Another victim. Leon's body count was rising.

"I did a good job, didn't I? I even had your smart investigator husband fooled. I even fooled the GBI. Oh, that was a good one."

He knew she was married. He'd done some research. Where were those police? Keep him talking. "You staged it all?"

"Every bit of it. I lured that poor SOB into the house where I was staying, plied him wine laced with rat poison. I had some around to keep them out of the abandoned place."

They'd hunted for him in abandoned buildings, but they couldn't search them all. "Then what?"

"I put the clothes I'd been seen in on him and carried him to the back of the SUV I'd rented. I drove him to that barn in Hampton. I laid him down in the hay as if he'd fallen asleep. I left all sorts of clues for you people to find. A liquor bottle. The hammer and rope I'd used on that worthless girl. She hadn't deserved to be released, but it was necessary."

Miranda's skin started to crawl. He'd killed that poor young girl and brought pain and misery to her whole family, the whole community. And he thought he was doing something good.

"I set the fire and once it was going, I ran out into the street, flagged down a car and told the driver to call 911. He took off and I hid in the woods. I watched it all. What fools you all were."

He had a point on that one. She should have known better.

"I knew you'd find all that evidence and think the body was me. I even put the wig I'd been wearing on him. Oh, and the best part of all was the little gift I left for you to find. Were you surprised, Miranda?"

The wedding ring she'd given him. Anger roiled in her gut. Keep your head, she reminded herself and let out a smirk. "Nice of you to return it after all these years. But I'll let you in on a secret. I didn't pay that much for it."

This time he ignored her and started up the stairs again.

"C'mon, Leon. What do you think you're doing with that skater?"

"I told you. I have a mission to fulfill. I don't expect you to understand."

"At the top of these stairs? Where the hell are you going?"

"You have no intelligence at all, do you? But you never did. There's a room up there. Up at the top. Under the dome of the building. I've got everything set up there. The rope. The ribbon. The oil. The hammer."

Hammer. He was going to mutilate Mackenzie's legs the way he did Julie Kimble's.

"That's what I did wrong last time, you see. I didn't use pain to cleanse them." His neck twitched and, still pointing the gun at Mackenzie, he half turned his head. "Yes, Mother. There will be plenty of pain. I'll do it right this time. I promise you."

Mother? Revulsion pulsed through her. Insane. The man was certifiably insane.

"I've got a camera. I'm going to record my greatest triumph. Everyone will see it. Everyone will know. That's why it had to be tonight. I'm already on the news. Everyone will know who I am and the great thing I've done. Oh, most won't understand it right away, but they will in time."

Humor him, she thought. "Okay, Leon. But wouldn't they understand better if you explained it to everyone? How else are they going to know?"

Glassy-eyed he glared at her, shook his head. "Don't trust. Don't trust a female."

"C'mon, Leon. Let her go. Let me have her and I'll tell the police all about your mission."

He seemed to snap out of it then. "You can't deceive me. I know who she is. I was hiding in the bushes outside the patio of that estate when you told her you were her mother. And she didn't even believe you. Hah! But I did."

He was there when she went to see Mackenzie? Hiding in the bushes? She'd led him right to her. Dear God. But she couldn't think about that now. Couldn't let it throw her.

If only she could shoot him right now. If only she could get her hands around that ugly neck. Slowly, she raised her gun. "Let her go."

"I'll take her from you now just as I did when she was a baby, Miranda. And there's nothing you can do about it."

"Do you think I'm going to stand by and let you perform your stupid ritual? You made it up, Leon. It's meaningless." She dared to a step up a stair.

Mackenzie groaned in his arms. Oh, God. Was she waking up? Not now, honey.

"It's my destiny. Stay back, Miranda." Leon's eyes glowed as he bared his yellowed teeth at her. "You never understood me. That's why I had to beat you to make you comprehend. You were never capable of following directions."

Her breath was a slow, raging pant now, but she had control of herself. His words couldn't touch her.

Once this man had had the power to fill her with fear and shame and self-loathing. Not anymore. Not now. Now she knew exactly who she was. She knew it in every cell of her body. How could she ever have doubted herself?

He was just another sicko. A bad guy. The kind she was born to stop. This wasn't his destiny.

It was hers.

She heard a door bang open down below. "Do you hear that? It's the police. They're coming for you, Leon."

"They'll never take me. Stay back or I'll shoot her."

Mackenzie began to move her head. She had to work fast. He wouldn't shoot her. If he did, he couldn't perform his ritual.

She aimed the Glock straight at his head. "Let her go, Leon."

"Go to hell, Miranda." He jerked the girl up another step. They were near the top of the stadium now.

Mackenzie opened her eyes. She raised her head, saw where she was. With a look of glazed horror she focused on Miranda. "Mama, save me!"

Her heart broke in two at the words. But there was no time to relish them.

"I warned you!" Leon's arm swung toward her, the gun barrel aimed right at her.

Long ago words of some forgotten sensei came to her. A fight was lost by near misses. She couldn't afford to miss this time. She fired.

Only a second later, his gun went off.

In slow motion, she watched his head explode, watched his bullet zigzag through the air toward her.

Searing pain shot through her shoulder as the bullet hit near her heart. She watched him drop, watched him let go of Mackenzie. The girl tumbled down on top of him, just as she fell back.

She felt herself fly through the air, felt her head hit the concrete, her body break as she bounced over the hard edges. As she closed her eyes, she heard the running footsteps of cops' feet.

She'd got him. She knew she'd got him. And at last her daughter was safe.

CHAPTER FORTY-SEVEN

Parker pulled the rented Camaro up the hill, past the twinkling lights of the Alpine-style shops and hotels that lined the street to the stadium, and cursed the traffic. Why was there so much in this size of a town at this hour?

Then he neared the entrance and saw a crowd of people milling about. They looked like they were in shock. He turned down a street and tried to make his way to the front of the building, but soon he couldn't move.

Heart pounding, he abandoned the car and set out on foot. He ran past the flagpoles, under the pines, the decorative scaffolds along the building's exterior. Long before he reached the entrance, he found he couldn't go any farther for the crowd.

There were police cars up ahead. And uniforms on the street. One of them was marking off a spot with crime scene tape.

Terror ripping his heart, Parker made his way to him.

"What's going on?" he demanded.

"You haven't heard? There's been a shooting inside."

My God. He waved a hand at the building. "My wife is in there. You have to let me pass. I have to get in there."

"I'm sorry, sir. I'm not authorized to let anyone beyond this line."

"You have to. I have to find her." He fumbled for cards in his pocket. "I'm a private investigator. Owner of the Parker Investigative Agency in Atlanta. My wife is an investigator at my firm. She's on assignment." He didn't think some fudging of the facts would matter now.

The guard shook his head.

Parker gritted his teeth. "Then I'll need to speak to your superior."

"I can't move from my post, sir. Again, I'm sorry." He sounded genuinely pained, but Parker didn't care.

He was about to ram his foot up the officer's backside. "You don't seem to understand. I have reason to believe an escaped serial killer—" His voice trailed off as he caught sight of the ambulance.

Not one ambulance. Two. And a coroner's van. All backed up to the building's huge entrance doors.

Dear Lord, what had happened?

Slowly the doors opened and EMTs appeared. They wheeled out a covered stretcher, put it in the van. A second stretcher was rolled out next. Parker saw the form of a young girl lying on it. Mackenzie.

As the second ambulance's doors closed, a third stretcher rolled out. How many injured were there?

Parker's heart stopped. Instantly he recognized the dark, wild hair. Miranda. Dear, God. It was Miranda. What had happened to her?

He grabbed the officer's shoulders with iron fists. "That's my wife." Before the man could say, "Sorry, sir," again, Parker shook him. "Where are they taking her?"

"Take it easy, sir. They're going to Mercy Hospital. I'll get someone to take you there."

"The hell you will. I'm riding in that ambulance." And ignoring the man's protests, he broke through the tape and ran, shouting to the EMTs.

CHAPTER FORTY-EIGHT

The brief ride to the hospital in the screaming ambulance was the most agonizing of Parker's life. His jaw tight, his gut wrenched, he sat in front next to the driver and watched four EMTs work furiously on his unconscious wife.

With deft skill, they checked her airway, took her vitals, hooked up an IV, applied hemostats to her shoulder. His jaw clenched tighter when he saw the gunshot wound. It looked like fairly close range. A .22 perhaps. If it had hit her heart, she wouldn't be alive and he was thankful it hadn't. But there was so much blood.

He felt sick when he heard them discover she had a large gash in the back of her head from falling down the concrete steps in the stadium bleachers after she'd been shot. All he could do was sit here and watch as they treated the bloody wound.

It took all the strength he had to keep quiet, to keep from peppering them with questions. That would only distract them from their work. There'd be time enough to ask later.

There was time but few answers.

As soon as they reached the hospital, Miranda was whisked away into surgery and Parker was ushered into a waiting room. On the way, he caught a glimpse of Mackenzie being brought in from the other ambulance. She was going into surgery as well.

None of the staff knew the details of what had happened at the stadium, but Parker was sure the body going to the morgue was Groth. He dialed the police station and found the place in chaos. It took ten minutes to speak to someone in charge. The sergeant refused to give details but confirmed a deceased male was found at the scene.

Miranda must have killed him.

Next he dialed Jackson Taggart, his best friend, and poured his heart out to him. Jackson reassured him the trauma center at Mercy Hospital was excellent.

Nonetheless he'd make some calls, rearrange his schedule, and be on the next flight to make sure and lend support.

Grateful for that, Parker had just hung up when Colby Chatham rushed into the waiting room followed by Wendy and Iris Van Aarle, all in coats and red-eyed.

The tall, handsome woman who was Mackenzie's adopted mother glanced around with a bewildered look before she saw him. "There you are. Someone said you were here."

"Oh, Mr. Parker!" Wendy ran up and threw her arms around Parker's waist. "They said Miranda shot that horrible man. Is that true?"

Tenderly, Parker took her by the shoulders. "I don't know, sweetheart. I think so. Where did you hear that?"

Iris stepped forward and took her daughter's hand. "One of the officers at the scene told us weapons had been fired."

Colby paced toward him. "They told me Mackenzie's in surgery. I saw the ambulance, saw them put her in there and I tried to run after it, but I was too late. A police officer found me and brought me here in his squad car."

"The car we were sitting in," Iris supplied.

"Please, all of you. Sit down." Parker gestured to the fabric-covered chairs lined up along the window. "Tell me what happened."

Iris and Wendy sat down quickly. Parker remained standing until Colby decided to join them. Nothing better to do at the moment.

Wendy waved her hands in the air. "It was all so surreal. Mackenzie was out on the ice. Her performance was the bomb. The absolute bomb. I just knew she was going to win. And then all of a sudden—" Her dark eyes went wild with fear. "He just came out of nowhere."

"Groth," Parker said.

Wendy nodded vigorously. "Yes. I recognized him. But he was dressed like one of the security guards. And he had a gun drawn." She put her hands over her face.

Dear Lord. Hadn't this poor child had enough trauma in her young life?

Colby's fingers held tight to the wooden arms of her chair. "He shot her in the leg. He shot my daughter in the leg. And then he crawled out onto the ice and grabbed her and pulled her away."

Wendy patted the distraught woman's hand looking very mature for her age. "It's all right, Mrs. Chatham. I just know she's going to be all right now. She's got to be." She turned back to Parker. "He took her away, but Miranda went after him. She told us to leave the building and went after him."

Iris picked up the narrative. "The police officer who brought us all here was one of the first on the scene. He said Miranda had Groth on the bleacher steps. He was still holding onto Mackenzie and she was trying to talk him down. Apparently it didn't work. He said two gunshots were fired at the same time. Miranda hit the man square in the forehead. As soon as the police got to him they pronounced him dead."

Fierce pride rippled through him. Along with a fierce jab of terror at what Miranda had sacrificed. What an amazing woman she was. "And my wife?"

Iris's lips went taut. She glanced down at Wendy and apparently decided her daughter could handle the grim details. "The officer said the impact of the shot knocked her off balance. She fell backward and hit the back of her skull against the stairs."

Wendy's mouth flew open. "Oh, my God, Mama. I didn't hear that. Oh, my God. Is she going to be all right?"

"I don't know," Parker said grimly.

"She's got to be. She's just got to be. She saved Mackenzie. She saved us all." The girl began to cry.

Colby straightened her shoulders, put a comforting arm around Wendy. "She will be all right, honey. I know she will."

"How do you know?"

The woman gave Parker a steady, knowing look. "Because we all have to tell her how much we have to thank her for."

Two hours later, a doctor came down a hall and informed Colby Chatham that her daughter would be fine. Groth's bullet missed the femoral artery. However, the right femur suffered significant damage. She wouldn't be able to skate at her current ability for at least a year. But with time and physical therapy she'd be back to normal.

Relieved and worried at how Mackenzie would take the news, Colby hurried off to her daughter's room. Iris and Wendy went with her leaving Parker alone.

After another hour a different physician appeared. "Are you Miranda Steele's next of kin?"

Parker's heart stopped at the sound of that phrase. He shot to his feet. "I'm her husband. Is she all right?"

"I'm Dr. Ngai." He held out a hand for Parker to shake. He was young, Asian, slight of build, with serious, chiseled features. Parker hoped he was as skilled and intelligent as he appeared.

"She's lost a lot of blood due to her injuries," he said.

Parker knew that already.

"The bullet hit in the brachial plexus and nicked an artery. We had to repair the damage and do a nerve graft. She has a large gash in the back of cranium from her fall. That means danger of subdural hematoma. We'll have to watch for that."

Parker nodded slowly, trying to take in the impossible words. But the physician hadn't said what he needed to know. "Doctor. Will she live?"

Closing his eyes, the man seemed to steady himself. Like police and detective work, in his profession delivering bad news to a family member was part of the job, but no one ever got used to it. "I can't tell you that," he said at last. "She's still unconscious right now. If she responds well to the surgery, she has a good chance. For now, we'll just have to wait and see how it goes." He paused a moment and put a hand on Parker's shoulder. "I'm sorry I can't tell you more than that. Now if you'll excuse me." And he hurried away to another patient.

Parker stared at the waiting room floor, unable to move. Nicked an artery. Danger of subdural hematoma. Still unconscious. See how it goes. He'd heard similar words before. When Sylvia was diagnosed with cancer.

Was he going to lose her? Was he going to lose the love of his life?

Exhausted, his heart tearing to bits, he sank into a chair and lost all control. He put his head in his hands and wept.

CHAPTER FORTY-NINE

When they put Miranda in a room in intensive care, Parker went inside and sat in a chair beside the bed, holding her hand, watching her breathe, listening to the steady beeping of the monitors.

He fell asleep there and woke up in the morning with a stiff neck but didn't give it a second thought. He stared at his wife, his heart breaking anew.

She was still unconscious.

When a nurse came and shooed him out of the room, he found his way downstairs to the cafeteria and had a bit of breakfast, though he couldn't eat much of it. He spoke briefly to Colby, who was just arriving at the hospital and related Miranda's condition. Then he called the rental company and arranged to retrieve the Camaro.

When it was brought round to the hospital, he found a hotel room for a quick shower, a shave and a change of clothes. Then drove to the Lake Placid police station and identified Leon Groth's body. He contacted Hosea and put him in touch with the sergeant.

Groth may have faked his demise in Hampton, Georgia. But in Lake Placid, he was truly dead. The bullet wound in the middle of his forehead was positive proof this time.

Excellent shot.

That part of the ordeal, at least, was over. Mackenzie and Wendy and any other young girls the killer may have targeted were safe.

When he stepped onto Miranda's floor in the hospital, Parker found Jackson waiting for him, along with Joan and Dave Becker, who'd flown up as soon as they'd heard the news. And his daughter, Gen.

"I asked Detective Tan to run the office and gave Dave a few days off," she said, giving him a kiss on the cheek. "I hope that was okay, Daddy."

"Of course. That was thoughtful of you."

Gen had despised Miranda when she first came to the Agency, but now she looked as worried as he was about her. "She's going to pull through. I know she will."

He patted her hand, but couldn't reply.

She took his arm. "I'd like to talk to you about something. Can we take a walk?"

"Certainly."

They strolled down a long corridor where the hospital staff pushed trays of medicine or equipment, moving efficiently in and out of rooms. Gen studied the floor as she walked and Parker couldn't guess what she had to tell him.

"This isn't the time or place for this," she said at last. "But I have to get it off my chest."

They came to a halt at a large window overlooking the mountains. Gen's dark eyes glistened as she hugged herself tightly.

"Just say it, sweetheart."

She nodded, ran a hand through her short blond hair. "I was the one who gave the information about Miranda to Tanya Terrance."

He blinked at her, stunned. "The things she said on her talk show?"

"Yes. It was before your wedding. About a week or so after Miranda started at the Agency and you started to get serious about her. I was so angry with you. I called her, met her for lunch and told her what I'd read in Miranda's file. I told myself I was giving you a choice." She bit her lip, tears in her eyes. "It was so stupid. I never would have done it if I had really known her then. What she means to you. What a hero she is."

He took her hands in his. The least of his worries now was Tanya Terrance. "It's all right, Gen. What's done is done."

"Oh, Daddy." She squeezed his fingers the way she used to when she was a little girl. Tears began to stream down her cheeks. "What if I never get a chance to tell her how sorry I am?"

He took her in her arms, stroked her hair. "Oh, sweetheart. She would forgive you. I do and I know she will, as well." And he hoped with all his heart they would get that chance.

Three days later Parker sat in the hospital chapel, staring at the simple table and the plain golden cross at the front shimmering under the dim light. As he listened to the muted music that was supposed to be soothing, he felt little comfort.

Miranda was still unconscious.

His father and Tatiana had arrived at the hospital yesterday, the elderly gentleman looking graver than he'd ever seen him. Antonio and Coco came with them and as soon as he saw them, Parker had given the young woman a fatherly hug and a belated welcome to the family. He'd been such a fool to doubt his son's relationship with the singer. It had been his pride that had made him so condescending. Later, he'd told Antonio so and apologized. But his noble son dismissed it as a misunderstanding. His only concern now was Miranda.

Dr. Ngai told him this morning if she didn't wake up soon, the hospital would start making arrangements to transfer her to long term care in Atlanta. He knew that could drag out for months or longer. Until she was—gone.

Parker drew in a ragged breath, ran his hands across his face. What would he do if he lost her? How could he go on without her? He loved her more than his own life.

She always surprised him, amused him. She was never—boring. After Sylvia passed, he'd dated a myriad of socialites like Patricia. If he had ended up married to one of them, how dull his life would have been.

Miranda always said she was so unlike his first wife. But she was more like her than she knew. Quick witted, sharp-tongued. Though Sylvia always cloaked her barbs in good manners. To hell with that. Miranda was real and raw and alive. He loved her now more than he ever thought possible. And he'd almost let all they'd had together be destroyed by the likes of Patricia Pendleton.

His heart in agony, he put his head in his hands.

If he never felt her lips against his again? If he never got the chance to say he was sorry? To beg her forgiveness? Oh, Lord. How could he bear that?

Tears burned in his eyes. He felt them drip down his cheeks and onto the pew. He bowed his head. "Dear, God. I can't lose her. Let her live. Please, let her live."

He heard a door open behind him. He didn't want company, but quickly wiped his face and turned his head. He saw a wheelchair rolling slowly down the aisle toward him.

Mackenzie.

"They told me you were in here, Mr. Parker. I didn't mean to interrupt."

The sight of Miranda's child lifted his heart. "It's all right, dear. What do you need?"

With a grave look on her pretty face, she rolled up beside him. Her leg was in a cast. Her dark hair was pulled back and she wore a pale blue robe her mother must have brought for her. "I need to talk."

"Very well. Are you feeling better today?"

She nodded. "The doctor says I'm mending well already. Probably because I was in such good shape before—" She shook off the bad memory. "He said I might be able to skate again sooner than he first thought." She sighed. "Skating used to be my whole world—and now?"

"You'll come back. Better than ever."

She shook her head. "That's not what I meant. It just doesn't seem so important anymore."

"Oh?"

She played with the sash of her robe. "Lying in my hospital bed, I've had a lot of time to think. And I've realized—I don't like the person I've become."

Parker smiled tenderly. The girl seemed older than her years.

"Miranda told me I should take care of my own skates. I was making Wendy dry them after practice because she was so obsessive about me. I was so mean to her. I don't even know why. She's been such a good friend."

"Things are different now," he said gently.

Again she shook her head. "That's not what I wanted to say, either."

"Go ahead then."

Her thin shoulders lifted as she took in a fortifying breath and continued. "Miranda came to see me a few weeks ago. She told me—she told me she was my mother. My real mother."

"I know she did."

"You did? Oh." She looked down at her hands. In her lap, her delicate fingers still wound around her sash. "I didn't believe her. I got so mad at her. I was just—awful to her."

So that's what this confession was about. Parker waited for her to go on.

"My mother told me what Miranda said was the truth. She and Daddy were getting older and couldn't have children and so they decided to adopt. They went to an agency in Chicago to get me when I was a month old and brought me home to Atlanta. I still didn't want to believe it. I threw something of a hissy fit." She half laughed and wiped the tears from her cheek.

Parker reached into his pocket and handed her a handkerchief, remembering that he'd done that for Miranda the first night he met her. She'd been crying over her daughter.

Mackenzie took it and daubed her eyes. "But then that awful man shot me and grabbed me and took me off the ice. I was so terrified. I knew I was going to die. He was going to kill me. I passed out. I was in a lot of pain. I'd never felt pain like that."

She bit her lip again. Parker's heart went out to her.

"He was dragging me up those stairs in the stadium. He kept muttering about 'releasing' me. And that I was soiled and it was the only way to cleanse me." She hugged herself and shuddered.

"You don't have to talk about it, Mackenzie." She would later, but Parker felt it was too soon.

Stubbornly, she shook him off. She was so like Miranda. "And then all of sudden Miranda was there. She talked to him. I was still out, but somehow I could hear them. And then I opened my eyes and saw she had a gun."

"Don't, Mackenzie. It's best to say these things to a therapist."

"No, you're not listening, Mr. Parker. I opened my eyes and I saw her face and I knew. I knew she really was my mother. And she was there to save me. And I really wanted her to be." She started to sob. "Oh, Mr. Parker. Is she going to live? Am I going to have a chance to tell her I want to get to know her?"

He held her hand. If only Miranda could hear this. It was what she'd always wanted. "I don't know, dear. But we all have to keep hoping."

CHAPTER FIFTY

She was floating somewhere. Through water? Through the air? She couldn't tell. She only knew she felt lighter than she ever had on earth. It was like skating. Whirling and turning and spinning.

She wore a thin pale gown. It's skirt billowed and swelled as she turned. She was so happy.

And then she saw she was in a meadow. A meadow so green it almost hurt her eyes. It was filled with fragrant wildflowers. Beautiful trees lined its border. She danced through the meadow until she came to the edge of the forest.

In a small glade under the trees, she saw a little girl dancing in a pretty pink dress. She was dancing with an older man. A big man with a round stomach who was laughing. The girl's father.

The girl was herself.

"There are only happy memories here."

She turned and saw a glowing shape beside her. It looked like a man. Her brother? The one she couldn't save?

"Who are you?" she asked.

He only shook his head and took her hand. Together they flew over the forest, through the air, until they came to a house in the suburbs.

She looked down at the porch and saw herself playing with paper dolls. She tensed, remembering how her mother had snatched them away. "I thought there were only happy memories here."

"And so there are."

She watched as a neighbor called to the girl and she ran across the street for milk and cookies. "I loved that woman."

"And she loved you."

The glowing man touched her hand again and suddenly they were over another suburban house. She recognized it and tried to pull away from him. "No. Don't want to go there. Not there."

"It's all right. There was happiness there."

The roof fell back and she looked down at a small crib that held a tiny baby. A little girl. Her baby.

"Amy," she whispered.

"She brought you joy."

She nodded. "So much joy. I didn't have much with anyone else."

"You searched for her."

"For years."

"And ended your search here."

He swept his shimmering arm across the sky and the scene became the Parker Agency. She saw herself laughing and eating sandwiches with Becker and Holloway in the lunch room. She saw herself digging into a case at her computer. She saw Parker coming out of his office in one of his expensive suits, handsome and debonair as ever.

Then her heart sank. She knew what this was. Didn't they say your life passed before you? "I'm dead, aren't I?" Or about to slip away.

The glowing man laughed. "Are you?"

She scowled at him and put a hand on her hip. "You tell me. Aren't you the spirit guide here?"

He laughed again and shook his head. It sure sounded like an angel's laugh to her. "Don't you have a destiny to fulfill?"

She cocked a brow. "I thought I already fulfilled it. Didn't I shoot—"

He raised a hand. "We don't speak of such things here. You've fulfilled part of it. But there's more."

"More?" She felt a spike of hope.

"You have a gift. It is not wise to neglect it. You must use it."

Use her gift? Could she really go back and do that? "Can't very well do that if I'm dead."

"No." He smiled and as he did his face seemed to evaporate into a cloud.

She felt herself falling. Down, down. She swung her arms and legs, but she couldn't float anymore. Now she was running. Running desperately down a narrow hall.

"Amy!" she called out. "Amy, where are you?" She had to find her. She had to find her daughter.

She heard her calling out to her. "Mother. Mother."

She was here. Right here. If only she could get to her.

"Mother, wake up. Please, wake up."

She opened her eyes and saw Mackenzie holding her hand, her eyes full of tears. "Please, please wake up. We all love you. Come back to us."

"Don't cry." Miranda lifted her head and tried to touch her. "Ouch." She laid her head back down.

Mackenzie squealed. "She's awake! Look, everyone. She's awake!"

Blinking, Miranda looked around her. She seemed to be in a hospital room. Somebody must really be sick. There were flowers everywhere.

"She's awake," Mackenzie cried again.

And suddenly Wendy was at the other side of the bed, holding her other hand. Her eyes were teary, too. "Oh, Miranda. You've come back to us. We've all been so worried."

"Worried?" About what?

Behind the girl, Iris appeared. "Oh, Miranda. How can we ever thank you for what you've done for us?"

Thank her?

Iris put her hand on Wendy's shoulder and a man stepped up beside her. "I want to thank you, too." It was Shelby Van Aarle. What was he doing here?

Wendy bounced up and down. "Oh, Miranda. Daddy announced it yesterday. He's retiring from golf. We're going to be a family again."

"Really?" Miranda lifted her head again. It didn't hurt as much this time.

"That's right," Iris beamed. "Thanks to you."

To her?

"And because of you, Mackenzie's alive." The voice belonged to Colby Chatham. She stood beside Shelby with her husband at her side. "We can never thank you enough for that. But from now on, Mackenzie and Oliver and I want you to share her life with us. Please? Without you, we wouldn't have ever had her."

Miranda lifted her hand, touched her daughter's cheek. It was real. It wasn't a dream. At long last, she had her Amy.

She gazed around the hospital room and saw it was crowded with people. Estavez and Coco. Fanuzzi and Becker. Mr. P and Tatiana. Jackson Taggart. Gen. Everyone was smiling and holding tissues to their noses.

"Hey, are you guys throwing another surprise party?"

As they all laughed, Parker stepped up behind Mackenzie and her heart stood still. Man, it was good to see him. "Where have you been?"

He grinned at her, laugh lines creasing his outrageously handsome face. "I've been right here, Miranda." He took her hand and she felt his strong fingers slip around hers. "I've been here all the while, waiting for you. I love you, my darling, and I always will."

CHAPTER FIFTY-ONE

Two days later, Miranda was hobbling down the hospital hallway with a hefty nurse on one side and Parker on the other. She made it to the corner today but couldn't go any farther.

"I give," she said and sank into the wheelchair Parker rolled up behind her. "But tomorrow, the hundred yard dash."

Parker smiled but not for long. "We'll go back to your room. There's something I want to discuss with you."

"Oh, do we have to? I'm a little tired of the scenery. Isn't there somewhere else we can go?" She looked at him hopefully, then at the nurse.

After a moment's consideration, she nodded.

The nurse led them down another hall to a corner spot with floor-to-ceiling windows overlooking the Adirondack peaks and left them alone.

"Nice place to recover."

Parker didn't answer. He moved to the window and stood staring out of it.

He'd showered and changed after a good night's rest in a nearby hotel room where she'd insisted he sleep instead of in the chair in her room. He was in a deep blue-gray suit, so dark and classy it reminded her a little of the tuxedo he'd worn the first night she met him—in jail.

"I have something I need to say to you, Miranda." His low Southern voice sounded ominous.

Her shoulders tensed. "What is it?"

"The night you left Atlanta—"

Oh. That night suddenly came back to her. What she'd seen in their bedroom. Going to the Gecko Club with Fanuzzi. Heading for the airport in the Corvette. Leaving it there for him to find.

So he wanted to have it out about that now? She was a little shaky from the walk, but she was game. And she'd go first. "What the hell were you doing with that woman, Parker?"

He sighed in angry resignation. "Being a damn fool. I didn't invite her to our home. She let herself in. She was chasing me. She told me she'd had a crush on me since we were children together. I never pursued her. You have to believe me. She threw herself at me that night."

Miranda blew out a breath as the tension drained out of her like a balloon. "I thought it might be something like that."

"What?" He spun around frowning.

She lifted her hands, let them drop into her lap again. "You're a hot guy, Parker. A girl's got to get used to women pawing over you."

His mouth dropped open and she laughed. She'd never seen him so stunned.

"You forgive me?"

"Didn't you just say you didn't do anything with that bitch?"

"That's exactly what I said."

"Then what do I have to forgive you for?"

Parker gazed at his wife. Even with her dark wild hair sticking out over the bandage on her head, her lean body encased in a hospital gown and an IV in her arm, she was the most beautiful creature he'd ever laid eyes on. He didn't know how it was possible, but right now he felt even more love for her than he had a moment ago. What an amazing woman she was.

But there was another item on his agenda. "There's something else."

Her smile disappeared. "There's more?"

"Just one thing." He steadied himself again. "I've realized I pushed you too hard after we came back from Hampton."

She cocked a brow. "Pushed me?"

"I pressed you for an answer about my proposal."

"Your plan for us to go out as investigative consultants?"

He clasped his hands behind his back, soldier-like. "Yes. I've had a lot of time to think these past few days."

"Not much else to do." Except worry and hold her hand. She still couldn't believe he'd stayed by her side all those long hours. That must have been so hard on him.

"I've tried to make you into the person I wanted you to be. And I'm sorry for that, too."

Nobody made her into anything. "Parker—"

He shot up a hand. "Let me say this." And it didn't seem to be easy for him from the look on his face. "I've realized that I don't care if you don't want to be an investigator any more. I mean, I don't mind if you'd rather do something else. Teach or work on the road crew or sing at the Gecko Club with Coco or just stay at home."

What was he talking about? "I can't even carry a tune."

"That's not the point. Whatever it is you want, I still love you. I love you for you. Not for some role I want you to play."

She looked down at her hands, touched the diamond-and-sapphire ring on her finger. How did she ever end up with such a thoughtful, caring man?

Then she drew in a breath and gave him a hard look. "I've got something to say, too."

"What is it?" He turned a little pale.

She gazed out the window at the gorgeous scenery as she spoke. "When I was out I had a crazy dream. Or a vision. Or maybe an out of body experience. I don't know what it was. I think I saw my brother. I don't know who he was, but he showed me my life and I saw—that not all of it was bad."

"I hope not, at least the past few months."

"No, bits of all of it. My father, my neighbor, Amy. I had moments of joy all throughout my life. I think he was telling me to think about those things and not the bad parts. I mean—" What did she mean? "I mean I don't think I'm going to have any more nightmares."

He smiled. "That would be wonderful."

"This person told me I had a destiny to fulfill. And a gift I had to use. And that's when I woke up."

"Oh?"

She rolled forward and poked a finger into his hard, muscled gut. "So if you take that away from me, buster, you're playing with cosmic forces."

He laughed in sheer disbelief. "You mean you want to go away with me on assignment as I planned?"

"Yeah, I do."

"Are you sure?"

She pursed her lips, teasingly. "Well, I think I've got a few months of physical therapy ahead of me, but as soon as I'm fit again, a herd of wild jackasses couldn't keep me away." It was the best offer she'd ever heard in her life.

"My darling, I can't wait." His heart soaring, Parker reached down, drew her to her feet and kissed her as hard as he dared. She was making his dreams come true.

Miranda grinned through his kiss and the sudden tears in her eyes. With the majestic mountains beyond, she felt like she was flying. And with his lips on hers, she longed to be well again and home making love to him.

She kissed him back with all she had. She didn't think her heart could hold any more happiness. She had the best job in the world.

More than that, she had her daughter back. She had a home and friends who cared about her. And best of all, she had Wade Russell Parker the Third.

A man who loved her. A man she could trust as much as she now trusted herself. A man she could go through life with. And now she knew for sure it wouldn't be just a good life.

It would be a great one. She couldn't wait to get started, either.

THE END

ABOUT THE AUTHOR

Writing fiction for over fifteen years, Linsey Lanier has authored more than two dozen novels and short stories, including the popular Miranda's Rights Mystery series. She writes romantic suspense, mysteries, and thrillers with a dash of sass.

She is a member of Romance Writers of America, the Kiss of Death chapter, Private Eye Writers of America, and International Thriller Writers. Her books have been nominated in several RWA-sponsored contests.

In her spare time, Linsey enjoys watching crime shows with her husband of over two decades and trying to figure out "who-dun-it." But her favorite activity is writing and creating entertaining new stories for her readers.

She's always working on a new book, currently books in the new Miranda and Parker Mystery series (a continuation of the Miranda's Rights Mystery series).

For alerts on her latest releases join Linsey's mailing list at linseylanier.com.

For more of Linsey's books, visit her website at **www.linseylanier.com**

Edited by
Donna Rich

Editing for You

Gilly Wright
www.gillywright.com

Made in the USA
San Bernardino, CA
17 September 2019